"Damn. That's the last

"That's the last wat

the Spa and have her se

I pulled my cell phone out of my pocket and speed-dialed a number.

He answered on the first ring. "I was hoping you'd call," he said. A thrill raced through me as I heard his voice. I got up from the table and walked a few steps away. "Did the restaurant close early? Am I gonna get lucky tonight?"

I sucked in a breath. Getting lucky with Jack would be better than catching a thousand leprechauns, superior to an infinite number of rabbits' feet. Not that it had happened yet. "Maybe," I teased. "I need you to do me a favor."

"Is it *that* kind of favor? The kind where I do something for you, then you do something for me?"

"Sounds like a win-win to me." I grinned stupidly. "Listen, I have a friend here who needs a ride out to Liza's. Are you busy?"

"I'll be there in fifteen minutes. Where are you?"

"I'm out in back of Spiro and Inky's new place. See you then."

When I returned to the table, Melanie was gone. I squinted in the darkness and made out a humanoid shape over by the small toolshed where the lawnmower and gardening equipment were kept. "Melanie," I said. "Don't go over there in those shoes. You're liable to step on a nail . . ."

I heard a gasp and saw the shadow of her arm fly to her mouth. I ran over, nearly gagging as a smell intensified. An odd braided rope—was it made of plastic wrap?—lay on the ground. And crumpled between a pile of two-by-fours and some sheets of insulation lay a body.

Berkley Prime Crime titles by Susannah Hardy

FETA ATTRACTION
OLIVE AND LET DIE

Olive
and Let Die

Susannah Hardy

BERKLEY PRIME CRIME, NEW YORK

An imprint of Penguin Random House LLC
375 Hudson Street, New York, New York 10014

OLIVE AND LET DIE

A Berkley Prime Crime Book / published by arrangement with the author

ISBN: 978-0-425-27166-7

PUBLISHING HISTORY
Berkley Prime Crime mass-market edition / November 2015

PRINTED IN THE UNITED STATES OF AMERICA

10 9 8 7 6 5 4 3 2 1

Cover illustration by Bill Bruning.
Cover design by Diana Kolsky.
Interior text design by Kelly Lipovich.

To Mom and Dad,
for always believing in me

ACKNOWLEDGMENTS

To my mom, sisters, and aunts, thanks for being my biggest cheerleaders.

To my editor, Michelle Vega, and the rest of the amazing team at Berkley Prime Crime, and to my agent, John Talbot, thanks for helping me bring Georgie and the rest of the Bonaparte Bay gang to life.

To my friends and colleagues at the Connecticut Chapter of Romance Writers of America and Sisters in Crime New England, thanks for being the best support system, professional and personal, a writer could ask for.

And, as always, to Mike and Will. For everything.

Hope of ill gain is the beginning of loss.

—EPICURUS, ANCIENT GREEK PHILOSOPHER,
341 B.C.–271 B.C.

◈ ONE ◈

It's not every day a celebrity walks into your restaurant. Oh, there've been a few over the years, mostly old-time entertainers whose careers have been reduced to telling jokes or singing in the lounges of the quiet resorts on either end of downtown Bonaparte Bay, New York. Mickey Rooney. Dick Van Dyke. Once I saw Gordon Lightfoot walking down Theresa Street, but he didn't stop in.

So when Rhonda Allen, my best server, burst into the kitchen that September evening as I was just sitting down to a plate of souvlaki wrapped in a soft warm pita—my five-minute dinner break—I knew somebody interesting had come in.

Actually, my life had gotten a lot more interesting lately. A few weeks earlier I had solved a couple of mysteries—helped bring a murderer to justice, and found some priceless items hidden right upstairs where I lived with my soon-to-be-ex-mother-in-law, Sophie. My friendly divorce would be final in a few weeks, and I had a developing relationship with a gorgeous Coast Guard officer. There were some details to be worked out, but life was looking pretty good for Georgie Nikolopatos.

"Come on, Georgie!" Rhonda grabbed my arm and pulled me along. "You're not going to believe who's in the top dining room!"

"Okay," I said, laughing. "Who is it? Daniel Craig? Johnny Depp?" I felt a little panicky thrill. What if it really were Daniel Craig or Johnny Depp? I straightened my skirt and ran my fingers through my hair, doing my best to fluff it and wishing I'd made time to go to the salon to have my roots touched up.

"You'll see!" I followed Rhonda past my office and toward the open pocket doors leading into the largest of the dining rooms. There were a satisfying number of customers, not so many that we were crazy busy, but enough that we'd make a nice profit tonight. No disgruntled faces. In fact, there was a low, excited buzz, and eyes seemed to be turning periodically toward the front window overlooking the main drag of Bonaparte Bay.

A woman with teased-out platinum hair and a scarlet tank top ablaze with sequins sat in profile to me. Her matching red linen jacket was draped casually over the back of her chair. She extended a hand, ropy with blue veins and sporting an enormous diamond cocktail ring and a set of lethal-looking bloodred nails, toward her dining companion, a youngish woman with dark hair and glasses. The younger woman was typing furiously into her phone, as though she were taking dictation.

There was something familiar about the other woman, who was clearly in charge. I couldn't quite place her.

Rhonda tugged at my sleeve. "You know who that is, right?" The air practically vibrated with Rhonda's excitement.

I glanced over again, doing my best not to stare while still getting a better look at my guest. Nope, recognition still eluded me. "Okay, you'd better tell me."

"I can't believe it! It's Melanie Ashley!" she stage-whispered.

Melanie Ashley. Of course. The grande dame royal witch of daytime television's most popular soap opera, *The Desperate and the Defiant.* She'd been on the show for twenty years and had been married and divorced a dozen times, half of those to the same man. At least the writers had finally stopped giving her pregnancy story lines, since she had to be pushing sixty.

"Go get Sophie, will you? She wouldn't want to miss this." Sophie was a huge fan of the show, which she watched during her afternoon break while she pretended to be sleeping.

I busied myself by greeting the diners at table eight, then moved counterclockwise around the room, making stops along the way. I wondered how quickly I could get the lone reporter from the *Bonaparte Bay Blurb* over here for a photo op and some free advertising. Sophie appeared in the doorway, rolling her lips together. She had just applied a new layer of "Passionate Coral" lipstick, a color (according to her) she'd been wearing since the early nineteen sixties. I never had figured out where she bought the stuff. She barreled over to the table, heedless of me, and I hurried to catch up with her.

"Why you divorce that beautiful man? Again?" Sophie demanded, her Greek accent thick and her little fists balled up onto her scrawny hips. Heads whipped around to watch. Melanie turned toward Sophie, and barely had to look up to meet her eyes.

Damage control time. "It's lovely to have you here at the Bonaparte House," I interrupted. "This is the owner, Sophie Nikolopatos, and I'm her daughter-in-law, Georgie." Melanie stared at me, her glossy red lips slightly parted to reveal brilliant white teeth, and I felt a strange flicker of . . . something. Recognition? Well, of course I recognized her, I thought, surreptitiously studying the artificial tightness of Melanie's expertly made-up face and looking for suture lines. I'd seen her on television and in the tabloids often enough. "We'd like to offer you and your guest a complimentary bottle of wine, or a dessert, if you'd prefer."

"No, we don't like," Sophie fumed. "That beautiful man. How could you leave him for that, that, Toy-Boy?"

I took Sophie's arm. "Sophie, it's just a television show. Ms. Ashley is an actor. You know that, right?"

"I know she's one of those, those, tiger women!"

"You mean 'cougar.'" I smiled apologetically at Melanie, who continued to stare at me. It was getting a bit uncomfortable, actually, and I still had that nagging feeling. Her assistant glanced up occasionally from her smartphone but seemed to decide the situation did not warrant her interference.

Melanie shook her head slightly, as though to break some spell, and turned to Sophie. She apparently understood that no amount of explanation would change Sophie's mind. She leaned toward my mother-in-law and whispered, "I'm just trying to make Vincent jealous. I'm not planning to go through with the divorce this time." Her voice, low and with a throaty rasp, sent another tendril of recognition twining up my spine. I sucked in a breath.

Sophie's eyes narrowed. She pursed up her orangey lips

and seemed to think for a moment. "Give her a drink," she ordered me, then turned on the heel of her white walking shoes and left the dining room.

I'd never done this to a customer in my life, but I pulled out an empty chair at Melanie's table and sat down. Hard. I searched Melanie's face. She'd had a lot of work done, between face-lifts, brow lifts, and Botox and collagen injections. Her hair was different. Her nose was narrower. She'd had her boobs enhanced. Her voice was different, perhaps from years of smoking or because of a voice coach. But up close, I knew this woman. The last time I'd seen her, I was eighteen years old, had just graduated high school, and was about to start my first job waitressing here at the Bonaparte House. She kissed me on the cheek, got on the back of a Harley behind a Hell's Angel, and roared off toward Route 81.

A whole range of emotions surged through me in rapid succession: joy, relief, and disbelief, before I finally settled on something that felt just right. Anger.

"What the hell are you doing here, Shirley?" I hissed. I couldn't bring myself to call her "Mom."

✦ TWO ✦

"No need to get nasty, Georgie."

Really? I had eighteen years of pent-up resentment and I definitely felt the need to be nasty.

"Couldn't you have given me some warning before you just showed up here? Maybe an e-mail? A phone call?"

"And don't call me Shirley," she said, her voice low, as she cut her eyes to the other patrons in the restaurant. She smiled and wiggled her fingers at one table.

Great. Now she was a comedian as well as an actor.

"Fine, *Melanie*. Why are you here?"

Melanie turned to her assistant, who was watching our exchange with interest. "Be a good girl and run over to the drugstore. I need a Kit-Kat."

"But you haven't even had dinner yet," the young woman pointed out.

"Last time I checked, Caitlyn," she said frostily, "I sign your paychecks. Or at least my accountant signs your paychecks. I want a Kit-Kat *now*." Caitlyn dropped her phone into her over-sized bag and walked away, leaving her salad untouched.

Was that display of power intended for me? I was unimpressed.

"You have a nice little place here," Melanie said. "Do you own it?" She looked at her fingernails and frowned. I followed her eyes to a small chip in the polish on her ring finger.

I gritted my teeth. She'd hit a nerve, almost certainly intentionally. If she'd had the resources to find me, not that that would have been difficult, she would have easily learned that I only managed this place. The historic Bonaparte House was owned by my mother-in-law, Sophie. Now that my soon-to-be-ex-husband, Spiro, had moved out to be with his true love, the guy who ran the tattoo shop down the street, I was in a tenuous situation. Sophie loved me, and I loved her back, but this arrangement couldn't go on forever. Especially now that Jack Conway had entered my life. I was doing my best to convince Sophie to sell me the building and the business, but so far she hadn't budged.

"Well, gosh, no I don't. I work and live here with the woman who took me in after I was abandoned by my mother."

Melanie winced, just a little, then shot back. "Don't you have a husband? A daughter?"

I was done. "You know what?" I whispered. "My life stopped being your business twenty years ago. Just tell me why you're here so I can get on with it."

At that moment Caitlyn came back and set half a dozen candy bars on the table, then plunked herself down in her chair. Melanie should have sent her on a longer unnecessary errand than just across the street. Caitlyn started in on her salad, which was now soggy from having sat for too long in the dressing. She forked up a limp piece of lettuce and frowned. I signaled for Rhonda to come over. "Bring a couple of fresh salads, please, and tell Dolly to hold up these dinners for a few minutes." She nodded and whisked away the plates.

"Well?" I glared at Melanie.

She made an attempt to raise an eyebrow at me, but she appeared to be too Botoxed to be able to accomplish that maneuver anymore. She gave an almost imperceptible nod to Caitlyn, who had pulled out her phone and was again typing furiously into it, oblivious. *Later*, she mouthed. Her mouth didn't seem to work quite right either.

Fine. I mouthed back. "Where are you staying?" I asked aloud.

"We're staying at the Spa. On Valentine Island."

My friend Liza ran an exclusive spa on an island just a short boat ride from the mainland, catering to the very rich and very famous. Sometimes in the early spring, when we had not yet opened for the season, or in the late fall, when we closed for the winter, Liza would treat me to a world-class pampering session. Right about now I longed for a hot stone massage and a soak in one of her special relaxation tubs. I could almost smell the fragrant herbs sprinkled on the warm water. Valentine Island, take me away.

"And how long will you be here?" I tried to keep my tone neutral.

"I'm booked at the Spa for a week, perhaps two." Two fresh salads appeared, and she forked up some greens,

wrapping her unnaturally plump lips around the utensil carefully so as not to smudge her lipstick. "The boat is coming
at eight o'clock. I'm going to send Caitlyn on ahead to make
sure the rooms are satisfactory." The assistant nodded. "I
believe I'll look around the shops until the next boat comes
at nine o'clock," she said, looking pointedly at me.

I nodded to show I understood, then got up. "Enjoy your
dinners. They should be out shortly. By the way, there's a
jewelry shop just down the street you might want to check
out." I don't know why I played along with her little game. It
wasn't like I owed her anything. But she owed me, at the very
least, an explanation, and I didn't want to alienate her before
I had a chance to confront her. After I had my answers, well,
she was fair game.

A woman from table six made a beeline for Melanie. She
held out a pen and a piece of cloth—one of my table
napkins—and asked Melanie for her autograph.

It was a short walk out of the dining room and down the
hall to my office. I closed the heavy wooden door, none too
gently, and unlocked the deep bottom drawer of my desk. I
pulled out a plastic cup and a bottle of expensive Merlot pur-
loined from the wine cellar, and poured myself a couple of
swallows. I rummaged around in the drawer and came up
with a bar of dark chocolate, peeled back the foil, and broke
off a big square, which melted deliciously on my tongue. A
few deep breaths, and my mood improved somewhat.

I'd actually dreamed of this day, the day my mother
would come back into my life. I had several different ver-
sions of the meeting. In one, I'd lay into her, never let her

get a word in edgewise, blast her for everything I was worth, say everything I'd been saving up for all these years, maybe even slap her! Then I'd walk away, leaving her standing there openmouthed. In another, we'd sit down and calmly discuss what had happened, we'd cry, she'd apologize profusely, she'd reveal that she had a terminal wasting disease, I would magnanimously forgive her, and we'd go on to have a mature and loving relationship for the two weeks or so she had left to live. But never in a million years had I pictured this scenario. My mother was a television star? I only occasionally watched the show, but I was no stranger to it. She looked very different, and she sounded very different from when I'd known her. From when she'd been my mother.

Melanie, or Shirley as she'd been then, hadn't actually been a horrible mother as I was growing up. I had no father, or at least I didn't know his name, but I was hardly the only kid at Roswell P. Flower Elementary School who didn't have one. Mom was tough but mostly fair. When I reached my teens, I realized that she was detaching. She was home less and less, and as long as I didn't get into trouble at school, she pretty much left me to my own devices. She didn't care much about grades, never had, but I managed to do well enough without or in spite of her lack of encouragement. Once I graduated and had secured the waitressing job and an apartment over Fat Max's Bar with four other girls, it was only a couple of weeks until she said good-bye, riding off with some guy she barely knew to California. She never sent money, sent a postcard once. She'd sold the house, left me her junker car, and was gone.

I drank down the last of the wine, considered pouring more, but corked the bottle and put it away, since I was technically still on duty. I ate another square of chocolate, looked at the remainder longingly, but rewrapped it and dropped it back in the drawer. What could she possibly want now? I'd made one attempt to find her when my daughter, Callista, was born. But it wasn't as easy to find people then, before the World Wide Web became mainstream in everyone's lives, and I hadn't wanted to spend the money on a private investigator. Had I ever heard about Melanie Ashley having a family? She would have been only thirty-six when she left, and she must have gotten her gig on *The Desperate and the Defiant* shortly after that. Did I have a half sibling or two out there somewhere that she hadn't bothered to tell me about? Bitter? Yes, I guess I was.

A knock sounded at my door. "Come in," I called.

Dolly, our cook and general right hand, opened the door. "Sophie sent me to find out if the tramp left yet?"

The tramp. Yeah, that about summed it up on a number of levels. "She should be finishing up soon. Want me to get her autograph for you?" Not that I wanted anything more to do with Ms. Melanie/Shirley than I had to, but Dolly wouldn't be caught dead up in the dining rooms.

"Naw," she said. "I don't care about them soaps. Now, if it was one of them WWE wrestlers or maybe Dale Junior, that'd be different." Her eyes went a little dreamy.

I glanced at my watch: seven forty. Caitlyn would be leaving for the boat soon. "Tell Sophie I've got a headache, will you? See if she can close up tonight."

"She ain't gonna be happy," Dolly said.

"I know, but I need to go lie down."

Dolly looked at me skeptically. "If you'd switch to real booze instead of that red wine you drink when you're upset, you wouldn't get headaches, you know. But I'll tell her." She paused. "You want me to sneak upstairs and turn on your television and lock your door?"

"Would you?"

"No problem." She waggled an eyebrow. "Have fun with that Captain Jack."

My heart gave a little flutter. I sincerely wished I *was* going to meet Jack somewhere. Dolly closed the door and I grabbed my purse. I took off my apron and tossed it onto the filing cabinet, then out the window into the back parking lot I went.

I reached Roger Shawcross's Jewelry Shoppe and ducked inside. No Melanie yet, but my watch said it was just eight o'clock now. I fingered some lovely hand-hammered silver earrings and chose a pair, plunking them down on the counter. "What brings you here on a work night, Georgie?" Roger asked, placing them into a pretty green box.

"Uh, I needed to pick up a gift for Dolly. It's her birthday," I lied.

"Again? Isn't that the second one this summer?"

I laughed. "Oh, you know Dolly. She actually gets younger every birthday. It's a pretty good system." I pulled out my wallet and laid down some bills for the earrings. Most of us local businesspeople try to pay cash with each other as a professional courtesy.

"Want me to wrap that for you?" I looked around. Still no Melanie.

"Sure, that would save me some time."

Roger headed into the back room, presumably for wrapping supplies. The door chimed and Melanie blew in.

"It's about time," I said.

"You should be thanking me," she retorted. "I just signed seventeen autographs and promised to come back to your restaurant tomorrow night if people wanted to bring copies of my autobiography."

I seemed to recall something about her autobiography coming out earlier this summer. "I don't suppose the fact that you have a daughter is in there anywhere?"

She flushed. "No, I don't suppose it is. You have to understand. These things are ghostwritten. It's mostly all fiction. God knows I wish I actually *had* had the one-night stand with Jon Bon Jovi."

"I don't have to understand anything." Roger returned and handed me the gift-wrapped box. He stared at Melanie, as if trying to place her. "Roger, this is Melanie Ashley. The famous television star? She's looking for something really unique. Something *expensive*. I know she'd like to buy it directly from you. And pay cash." I smiled pleasantly at my mother.

Roger thought for a moment. "I know! How long will you be in town? I'll make you something one of a kind if you'll be here for a couple of days. Silver or gold?"

"Oh, gold, definitely," I said. "Make it eighteen carat."

Melanie gave me a subtle jab in the ribs. "Yes, make it a bracelet, something absolutely unique. I or my assistant will be in to pick it up."

"Super!" I said. "Come on, Melanie, let's go for that tour

of downtown I promised you." I looped my arm through hers and steered her toward the door.

"What about Dolly's gift?" Roger said.

"Have somebody deliver it to her in the kitchen, would you?" Dolly would enjoy the surprise, even if she had no idea what it was for.

Dusk was settling over Bonaparte Bay as we exited the store. I walked Melanie quickly down Theresa Street and up the walk to what had been the Sailor's Rest, a restaurant that was closed for remodeling. "Follow me," I ordered, and Melanie complied as I led us around to the back, where I knew there was a small outdoor table and chairs. I sensed that she was falling behind me and turned to see her appear several inches shorter, her ridiculously high heels having sunk into the grass. "Oh, come on," I snapped.

"I'm older than you are, and better dressed, remember?" she shot back, disengaging herself from the turf.

"Yeah, and I'll bet you've got a personal trainer keeping you fit, so don't give me that."

We sat down on opposite sides of the table, Melanie facing the restaurant. There were several Dumpsters out here full of construction debris, as well as some piles of building materials under the covered porch. The new owners of this place were my husband, Spiro, and his partner, Inky LaFontaine. They were transforming it into a nineteen-fifties-style diner. How they planned to do that to a late Victorian house was a mystery yet to be revealed. But they were hoping to have the place open in time for Columbus Day, and then close it up until spring.

A cool breeze blew up off the St. Lawrence River. On

the one hand, I was grateful because it kept the mosquitoes down. On the other, it stirred up a funky odor, which I couldn't quite place. But I wished I'd brought a fleece. Melanie tugged the sleeves of her jacket down and folded her arms across her ample chest.

"All right," I said. "Why are you here?"

She opened her purse and stuck in her hand, coming out with a silver compact. She opened the compact and studied herself in the mirror. "Would you believe it if I told you that I missed you? That I wanted to get to know the woman you've become? Get to know my granddaughter?"

"After twenty years?" I snorted. "Spare me."

She smoothed an errant lock of hair back into place. "I know I've made mistakes. I'm trying to make up for them now."

"You left me. I was just a kid."

She sighed. "You were born when I was only eighteen, just a kid myself. I did the best I could for you while you were growing up. When I knew you could handle it, I left to try to make something better for myself. For you."

"For me?" Of all the self-serving statements I'd ever heard, that took the cake. "You know at the end of that summer, when the town shut down, I had nowhere to go? Thank God Sophie took pity on me and let me stay here while I took some college classes. On scholarship."

"And if I hadn't left," she said gently, "you'd never have married Spiro . . ."

"Yeah, thanks for that. I had a great marriage. He's gay, you know."

"And you never would have had your daughter."

The air rushed out of my lungs and I felt suddenly deflated. She was right, of course, not that I was going to admit it. Every moment of that sham marriage had been worth it, when I thought of how my Callista had turned out.

"She's not here. She's in Greece visiting Sophie's relatives and working on an archaeological project at the Parthenon."

"I know. I had Caitlyn do a little research before I came."

What else had been researched? I wondered if she knew about the Bonaparte table and the jewels I'd found a few weeks ago. Was she looking to get a piece of that pie? I gave an inward chuckle. The jewels were probably going to have to be returned to the Spanish government. Whether there would be a finder's fee remained to be seen. And the table, though worth close to half a million dollars according to Christie's, technically belonged to Sophie. The chances of my seeing a penny of that money were slim to none. "So why all the secrecy? Caitlyn doesn't know about me?"

"She does. But I wanted to see you first before it goes public."

Something about this just wasn't ringing true. Oh, I had no doubt she wanted to find me and Cal. What mother wouldn't, even if she was the one responsible for the separation? But there was something more to this visit. I was sure of it. I was also quite sure she wasn't going to tell me until she was good and ready.

"Are you happy, working at the restaurant?" She dropped the compact back into her purse and picked up a twig that had fallen on the table, poking it in and out of the holes in the metal mesh table.

I considered. "Yes, I guess I am. I love the history of the old place, I love the people I work with, and I love the job." A little twinge of discontent surfaced. It was no longer enough for me to just manage the Bonaparte House. I wanted to own it, make it mine.

"Do you have money of your own?" She picked at the stick until a piece peeled off.

"Not that it's any of your business, but I have some saved up. I draw a regular salary, and I don't have a lot of expenses. I'm not a big spender."

Melanie looked me up and down, at least the half that was visible over the table top. "You don't spend much on clothes, that's apparent." She wrinkled her nose. "What is that smell? It's disgusting."

"Uh, Melanie, you ever work in a restaurant? We serve *food*, and sometimes the food spills? Clothes have to be practical. It's hard work." I swatted at a fly. There seemed to be a lot of them buzzing around.

"How much do you need? I could help you out. That old lady can't be planning to work there forever."

I bristled. "That 'old lady' is only a few years older than you are, M-O-M." She looked around to make sure we were still alone. Then her words registered. Melanie had offered to help me buy the Bonaparte House. I was sorely tempted.

"I visited a lawyer recently," she said. "I've made Callista my beneficiary. I didn't think you, my only child, would want my money, but I knew you wouldn't turn it down for your daughter." I breathed a small sigh of relief. Not that I hadn't sometimes wished I had a sister to hang out with or confide in, but it was a relief to know that I wouldn't be receiving any more surprises. "Well, thank you. I'm touched." And I found I really was. A little. I looked at my watch. "Looks like you missed your ride."

"Damn. That's the last one, isn't it?"

"That's the last water taxi ride." I offered to call Liza at the Spa and have her send a boat. "Wait, I have a better idea." I pulled my cell phone out of my pocket and speed-dialed a number.

He answered on the first ring. "I was hoping you'd call," he said. A thrill raced through me when I heard his voice. I got up from the table and walked a few steps away. "Did the restaurant close early? Am I gonna get lucky tonight?"

I sucked in a breath. Getting lucky with Jack would be better than catching a thousand leprechauns, superior to an infinite number of rabbits' feet. Not that it had happened yet. "Maybe," I teased. "I need you to do me a favor."

"Is it *that* kind of favor? The kind where I do something for you, then you do something for me?"

"Sounds like a win-win to me." I grinned stupidly. "Listen, I have a friend here who needs a ride out to Liza's. Are you busy?"

"I'll be there in fifteen minutes. Where are you?"

"I'm out in back of Spiro and Inky's new place. See you then."

When I returned to the table, Melanie was gone. I squinted in the darkness and made out a humanoid shape over by the small toolshed where the lawnmower and gardening equipment were kept. "Melanie," I said. "Don't go over there in those shoes. You're liable to step on a nail . . ."

I heard a gasp and saw the shadow of her arm fly to her mouth. I ran over, nearly gagging as the smell intensified. An odd braided rope—was it made of plastic wrap?—lay on the ground. And crumpled between a pile of two-by-fours and some sheets of insulation lay a body.

❖ THREE ❖

Based on the incredible stench and the number of flies buzzing around, I knew there was no hope for this poor person. I pulled out my cell phone and dialed 911. I had an unsettling rush of déjà vu as Cindy answered, just as she had the last time I'd discovered a body.

"Nine-one-one, what is your emergency?" she trilled.

"Cindy, it's Georgie. Send the police over to the old Sailor's Rest. I'm out back."

"What have you got, another body?" She giggled.

"Yes."

Silence.

"Cindy? I need you to send Chief Moriarty over, okay? It's too late for an ambulance."

"Maybe you should put the cops and the coroner on your speed dial and call directly next time," she said.

I hung up. I hadn't ever really liked her.

Melanie was still standing over the body, breathing through the front of her jacket, which she'd pulled up over her mouth and nose.

"Melanie, come away from there. The police will be here soon."

She looked up at me, her eyes sad and scared at the same time. "I know who this is."

What? She hadn't lived in this town in twenty years. How could she possibly know?

She had produced a small penlight, which she shined on the face. "It's my cousin Doreen. I'd know her anywhere. In any condition." She shuddered.

My mother had a cousin? Which meant I had a cousin? Or used to have one anyway. I felt a wave of sadness wash over me and my eyes threatened tears. My grandparents had died when I was small, not that I'd ever met them, and as far as I knew, we had no other family. If Sophie hadn't taken me in and given me a home and eventually a husband, I would have been completely alone.

Melanie still had the light trained on the woman. I forced myself to look at the face. Bloated purplish flesh, dry, frizzy dark hair fanned out on the grass. It was impossible to tell how old she might be, but she was wearing a nylon windbreaker, capri-length jeans, and flip-flops with some sparkly jewels on the straps. Her toenails were professionally pedicured in a hot pink shade and looked freshly done.

"Hand me that light, Melanie." She complied, and I did a quick search around the body. I wasn't sure what I was looking for, and I didn't find it. A sudden thought struck me. "Melanie, let's go out front until the police get here. We might be in danger. What if she was murdered? Why else would her body be here?"

She had the sense to take off her heels as we ran across the soft lawn out to the sidewalk and the relative safety of the small crowd of bar-hoppers congregated under the street-lights. I was relieved to see the flashing blue lights of one of the two cruisers owned by Bonaparte Bay. The driver double-parked and I heard the door click closed. Tim Arquette, second in command of Bonaparte Bay's finest, walked over toward us, in no particular hurry.

"What's up, Georgie?" His jaw was working as he rolled a piece of gum around in his mouth. A whiff of artificial watermelon wafted over. At least it smelled better than the corpse.

"There's a body out back."

Tim froze. "I thought Cindy was kidding!" He put his hand on the butt of his gun. He pulled out his Mag flashlight with the other hand and switched it on. "Show me," he ordered.

"You first." I didn't want to lead the parade. I walked a step behind Tim, who was sweeping the yard with his light. "Over there, by the tool shed. She's on the ground."

Tim reached the body, scanned it, and pulled out his radio. "Call in Rick and the sheriff," he told the dispatcher. "We're going to need the crime scene techs and the medical examiner from Watertown. Over."

He turned to me and Melanie. "Now, ladies, suppose you tell me what you're doing in back of a closed-up restaurant at this time of night. Georgie, who's your friend?"

"She's not my friend." The words were automatic, and I

hardly had time to regret them before a sharp elbow jabbed into my ribs. She really, really needed to stop doing that.

"I'm Melanie Ashley," she purred. Tim ran the flashlight up from her feet to her cleavage, where he let it rest. "Georgie is just showing me around town."

Tim seemed mesmerized by her boobs, then finally looked up to her face. Recognition dawned. "My God!" he exclaimed. "You're Belinda Mallory! We watch your show at the station. You're even more beautiful in person."

Melanie smoothed her hair, then fingered the neckline of her tank top. "How nice of you to say so."

"Uh, Tim?" I felt compelled to bust up this little love fest. "There's a dead woman here."

"She's not going anywhere." He continued to stare at Melanie, who was smiling at him.

"There are marks around her neck. I've seen enough *CSI* to know that's strangulation, not a natural death. What if the perp is still here?" Goose bumps rose on my arms and I shivered.

"Naw, she's been here at least a day, based on that smell. The perp is long gone. So, Melanie, what brings you to town?" He blew a big pink bubble, then sucked it back in, licking his lips.

"How's your wife?" I asked.

At that moment a warm hand touched mine and I wheeled around. Strong arms wrapped around me. "Are you all right?"

I buried my face against a hard chest, returned the hug, and pulled back to look up. Jack Conway's familiar face was chiseled against the night sky. He planted a small kiss on my forehead. "I saw the cruiser out front and I was worried."

He was worried about me. For so many years I'd been strong, in charge, and taking care of things for so many people. And now someone was taking care of me. His eyes searched my face.

"I'm okay." He smoothed my hair, looked into my eyes, then gave me a real kiss, soft and warm, on the lips. A delicious tingle raced through my body. I kissed him back.

"Ahem." Melanie coughed.

I pulled back, the moment broken. Temporarily, I hoped. "This is Jack Conway. My . . . friend."

She looked him up and down. "Where do you get a friend like that? I wouldn't mind one."

I bristled. Jack laughed. "I'll keep my eyes peeled for one for you. I'm taken," he said, and I felt instantly better. I was new to being kind-of-in-love, and it was taking some getting used to. In a good way. "And you are?"

She held out her hand. "Melanie Ashley."

"Nice to meet you, Melanie." No flicker of recognition. Melanie seemed a bit miffed.

Tim shone his light on the body with one hand and plugged his nose with the other. "You're right, Georgie," he called. "She's got ligature marks on her neck."

Jack raced over. "Can I help? I've got first aid training." He pulled up short. "Oh. Do we know who it is?"

"It's Doreen Webber. I knew her years ago," Melanie said. Her agitation level was creeping up, based on the increasingly edgy quality of her voice.

"Webber," Tim said. "There were some Webbers over in Clayton. Is she from that family?"

"They're all dead now, as far as I know," Melanie said. "If she was married and changed her name, I can't say."

Tim eyed Melanie. "How exactly do you know the victim, Miss Ashley?"

The backyard suddenly lit up, bright as the sun. I blinked, then shaded my eyes with my hand. My soon-to-be-ex-husband, Spiro, stood on the back porch, his hand on the light switch. His partner, Inky LaFontaine, stood nearby, surveying the situation, before they both approached, their strides matching.

"What the hell is going on?" Inky demanded, the tendons in his neck making the snake tattoo that wound its way up and onto his shaved head undulate realistically. I don't have any tattoos, and never intend to get one, but that was some beautiful, creative artwork, I had to admit. Despite the temperature, he was wearing a tight white tank top and dark wash jeans, both of which showed off his impressive physique. His black boots gleamed in the artificial light as did the chain looping off his black leather belt.

Spiro looked from me to Jack, where his eyes lingered a bit too long. *Pity*, they seemed to say. Fortunately for me, Jack did not play for the other team. "Shouldn't you be at work? The restaurant isn't closed yet. The neon is still on."

I bristled. "Your mother's been closing the restaurant for years. She knows how it's done. I decided to go for a walk. I have a headache."

He cut his eyes to Jack. "I'd like to have that kind of headache."

"Uh, I'm right here, kids," Jack said. He hugged me.

"You've got a problem, guys," I said. Actually, Bonaparte Bay had a problem. A second murder in just a few weeks? A knot formed in my stomach. Sure, we had our share of crime, especially since we were situated right on the Canadian border. But smuggling drugs across the river was a far cry from murder. Our little town was no longer insulated from the harsh realities of the world. "There's been another death."

Inky looked from me to Spiro and then they both turned toward Officer Arquette. "Looks like Fred is going to have to add another stop on the Thousand Islands Ghost Tour," Spiro said matter-of-factly.

Leave it to Spiro to come up with a way to make money off someone's death. Still, in theory I couldn't really blame him. The tourist season is very short so far north and we business owners need to make money any legal way we can. But the Bonaparte House would not be naming a drink or a sandwich after poor Doreen anytime soon, if I had anything to do with it. Which I did.

Melanie stood there, shivering. Her bravado had disappeared, and she didn't look well. I scrutinized her face. This harsh light did nothing for her complexion, highlighting every flaw and surgical alteration, and she appeared to be nauseous. She might have been acting, but it seemed real enough. I made a decision. "Melanie, you can't go to the Spa tonight. You'll be sick on the boat ride. Let's go check you in at the Camelot Inn and you can leave in the morning."

She nodded weakly. "Is there a bar at the Camelot?" she whispered. "I'm going to need a martini. Maybe two or three."

"Jack, do you have your car? I don't want to go get mine

at the Bonaparte House." The last thing I needed was for Sophie to start asking questions. There'd be plenty of time for explanations tomorrow.

"Your carriage awaits, milady. Or should I say, miladies."

"I'll just check in with Tim and tell him we'll be available for statements in the morning," I said. Déjà vu all over again.

❖ FOUR ❖

Twenty minutes later we had Melanie checked in at the hotel and were waiting for her in the bar while she freshened up. Jack ordered a local Riverbrew Beer, and I ordered a blackberry Margarita. Jack held my hand, rubbing my palm lightly with his thumb. "Maybe we should get a room too," he suggested.

"Mmmm, tempting. But I have to get back to the house. Sophie doesn't like to stay alone at night. She's still not quite convinced we don't have a ghost over there."

Our drinks arrived and I took a long pull. It was cold and fruity and quite delicious. My stomach growled, and I called the server back and ordered a plate of cheesy nachos.

"Are you sure you're all right?" The concern was evident in Jack's eyes, and I melted a little closer to him. "That's two bodies this summer."

"I'm better now," I said, and meant it.

Melanie sat down at the table, a blast of Chanel No. 5 settling over us like fragrant fog on a hot summer night. She seemed better and had touched up her makeup, presumably in case she was recognized. The crowd was thin here tonight, and we were tucked into a back corner, so there wasn't much chance of that.

"Do you want me to bring you a nightshirt to sleep in?" I asked, even though I didn't want to. Being solicitous was ingrained in me from years in the restaurant business.

"A . . . nightshirt? No, I always sleep in the raw." She looked pointedly at Jack. "And I keep a fresh pair of undies in my purse."

Ew, ew, ew. That was not the kind of thing a person wanted to hear from her mother, no matter how long estranged.

Jack jumped in smoothly, seemingly oblivious to the innuendo. "So. How do you two know each other?"

Melanie's face was making all sorts of inelastic movements.

"I don't keep secrets from Jack, especially when I don't know why a secret is necessary in the first place." I turned to him. "Melanie is my mother. My *biological* mother," I corrected.

She looked hurt, but I didn't care.

"My lips are sealed," Jack said. If he was surprised, the expression on his lean, tanned face didn't betray him. He relaxed back into the seat and a lock of sun-bleached blond hair fell over one blue eye. "What brings you to town?"

"Yes, Melanie. What does bring you to town? Inquiring minds want to know." I dug into the nachos with gusto, pulling up a crisp tortilla chip and scooping up the warm, stringy cheese. I wondered if I could make nachos Greek-style and made a mental note to play with the recipe tomorrow.

Melanie lifted her vodka martini and took a sip. She wiped her lips delicately and set the napkin down, a smear of scarlet lipstick staining the paper like blood on new-fallen snow. Finally, her eyes met mine.

"I've made mistakes, Georgie." Well, that was an understatement, and she'd said the same thing earlier tonight. As though she'd rehearsed it. Jack squeezed my hand under the table.

"I'm listening."

"And I hope it's not too late for us to have . . . some kind of relationship." She fished around in her glass and pulled out the stick full of olives, sucking one off.

I almost wanted to believe her. Almost. "Why now?"

She hesitated. "You're a grown woman. There are things I should have told you sooner. Things about . . . our family."

Our family? Intellectually I knew at some time, somewhere, I had blood relations, but it had been so long, and no one had ever tried to contact me, I just assumed everyone was dead.

"My parents were very traditional," Melanie said. "When I found out I was pregnant, unmarried, they told me not to come home again." I felt a little twinge of sadness, both for the girl my mother had been, a girl who desperately needed the support of her parents, and for the girl I had been, growing up without a family network. I thought about my daughter, Cal, wondered what I would do if she came home and told me she was pregnant. But I didn't have to wonder. I knew. I'd support her in whatever way she wanted or needed.

Not that I was anxious to be a grandmother anytime soon, mind you. A fierce protectiveness welled up inside me.

Another thought struck, and I wondered if or when Melanie was going to bring it up. There was one pretty big meatball between us—she'd never told me the identity of my father. I'd asked a few times when I was a kid, but she would never say, and eventually I gave up.

"They're dead." I said.

Her blue eyes swam with unshed tears. "Yes. They died within a year of each other and left the farm to Doreen. She was living there."

"Did Doreen have anyone we should notify? A husband or kids maybe?"

"As far as I know, she never married or had any children. We're all that's left, Georgie. You, me, and Callista." She drained her martini and signaled the server for another.

Poor Doreen. As small as my family unit was, I was still better off than she. Jack shifted a little closer to me.

Flash. A bright white light went off somewhere in my peripheral vision. I turned toward it. "Well, crap. This day just gets better and better." A second light flashed and I raised my hand instinctively to cover my face, but it was too late and I knew it. Melanie seemed to recover herself and smiled, showing a really spectacular set of dazzling capped teeth as a third flash went off.

Melanie's second martini arrived at the table at the same time as Spencer Kane, the one and only reporter/photographer employed by the village's newspaper, the *Bonaparte Bay Blurb.*

Spencer pulled up an unused chair from a nearby table and

sat himself down. He set his bottle of Genesee Beer on the table and pulled a handheld digital recorder out of a pocket in his frayed and faded khaki shorts. "You've been holding out on me, Georgie," he admonished, smiling a crooked grin. "Where should I start? Let's see." He rubbed his stubbled chin dramatically. "One, you've found another body. Two, you're sitting here having drinksies with a famous actress and you didn't call me." He shook his head. "And three, it's late and you're in a hotel bar, not at home with your mother-in-law." He looked from Jack to me and then raised his eyebrows. "Let me just send a quick e-mail to Joyce. She'll love this!"

Jack reached across the table, lightning fast, and snatched the cell phone out of Spencer's hand. "Hey!" Spencer squeaked out.

Jack deftly deleted the pictures and took the battery out of the phone. "These ladies have had a difficult time tonight and you're not going to exploit that. And I've read Joyce's gossip column. You're definitely not giving her any material." His voice was edgy and commanding, probably honed by his years as an officer in the Coast Guard. Spencer didn't argue, just sat there with his mouth open like a muskellunge fresh out of the St. Lawrence River.

Jack handed the phone battery to a passing server. "Give this back to Spencer here after we leave, will you? He tossed a five on her tray and she smiled at him, dimpling. "Melanie, Georgie, I think it's time we all called it a night."

Melanie looked from Jack to me and nodded, clearly impressed. She tossed back the rest of her drink and stood up, placing both hands on the table and leaning forward. Her considerable cleavage was about six inches from

Spencer's face, and he seemed mesmerized. She put the pad of one finger under his chin and lifted. Her long, glossy-red fingernail dug into the soft flesh just a little, but he didn't seem to notice as his eyes met hers.

"Listen to me . . . Spencer, is it?" Her voice was low but forceful, with an unmistakable hint of take-me-to-bed. "We don't want our pictures taken tonight, understand? But I'll be staying at the Valentine Island Spa for a few days, and if you give me your number, I'll have my assistant call you when we're back on the mainland. We can do as many photos as you want and I'll give you an exclusive interview. But let's leave Georgie out of it. Okay?" It came out as a question but she clearly was not looking for a response. Spencer nodded dumbly and handed her a business card.

Jack and I took that as our cue to leave and stood up as well. The three of us headed toward the front desk. We passed a mirror with an ornate gold frame on one wall. Something flashed on the silver surface and I looked back. Spencer was holding out his cell phone and wearing a smug smile. "I always keep an extra battery in my pocket. Wouldn't want to miss any photo ops!"

Jack made to go back to Spencer. I was tempted to let him, just to see what would happen, but I put my hand on his arm. "Forget it," I said. "He didn't get our faces." I felt a little pang of fear as I pictured my round backside on the front cover of Thursday's *Blurb*. "Let's just get out of here."

We walked Melanie to her door. "Are you sure I can't get you anything? They probably have toothbrushes at the front desk." What was I doing? I didn't want to be nice to her. She still had a lot of explaining to do, and she'd given me no reason to trust her. In fact, her whole reappearance smelled like a spoiled fish in yesterday's catch.

Melanie turned the key in the lock. "Well, tomorrow won't be the first time I've woken up in a hotel room with nothing but the clothes I was wearing the night before." She cut her eyes at Jack.

"I've got tomorrow off from the station," he said. "How about if Georgie and I pick you up in the morning and we'll get you over to the Spa?" He looked at me for confirmation, his eyes twinkling. Oh yes, the sooner we got Melanie out of Bonaparte Bay and trapped—I mean settled—on the island, the better. My best friend Liza would keep her occupied with facials, hot stone massages, herbal detoxification elixirs, meditation sessions, and yoga routines until she'd be so relaxed maybe she'd finally spit out the reason she'd come back.

"We'll be here at nine o'clock. Liza can give you breakfast when you get to the Spa."

The corners of her mouth turned down ever so slightly. "Make it ten."

"Make it nine. I've got things to do tomorrow. Just because you've decided to show up now doesn't mean I can drop everything to be at your beck and call. I have my own life, and I'll continue to live it." I took a deep breath. That felt good.

Melanie rolled her eyes, but her tight eyelids barely moved. "Oh, all right," she huffed and shut the door. I heard the sound of the chain being slid into position, then the faint metallic click of the lock.

Jack took my arm and steered me toward the exit. "Do you really have things to do tomorrow? Because I was hoping we could spend at least part of the day together." He gave my arm a light rub, and a tingle ran through me as we walked toward his Jeep. He held the door open for me and I climbed in.

"Not really. Now that we're past Labor Day, the restaurant's only open Friday through Sunday, so tomorrow I'm off. Sophie and Marina are going shopping in Watertown, assuming they can get Dolly to drive. I thought I'd get a haircut maybe."

"Come with me tomorrow then," he said. "There's someone I'd like you to meet."

A little stab of panic hit my gut. "It's not . . . your mother, is it?" I'd had about all the mothering I could take at any given time. And I definitely wasn't ready for that.

Jack laughed and gave me a little hug.

"You'll meet my mom and dad and my sisters and their families someday. No, I'm meeting an older woman at her home and I think she might feel more comfortable if there were another woman present. It's been a long time since I've seen her."

"Sounds . . . intriguing." Jack had the top off the Jeep and I leaned back as we rolled through the streets of Bonaparte Bay, which were mostly empty this time of night and this time of year. I looked up into the sky, remembering how I used to try to count the stars when I was little. I never got very far, as I recall, before my eyes went a little buggy and I settled for finding the Big and Little Dippers and Orion's belt. Tonight they were like rhinestones on deep blue velvet, and I sighed, contented.

Jack killed his lights and pulled into the employee parking lot behind the Bonaparte House. A movement over by the Dumpster caught my eye, and a familiar redhead was illuminated by the floodlight. I waved to Brenda Jones, Bonaparte Bay's Dumpster Diva, and she raised her hand in greeting. She added a couple more long-necked bottles, which glowed amber in the evening light, to her sack, then cinched it up and pushed her grocery store carriage, probably from the new Dollarsmasher out on Route 12, across the gravel of the parking lot. Brenda made the rounds of the restaurants and the docks every night, twice a night during the busy summer season in July and August. I always left the Bonaparte House returnables out for her. She had a nice little business, and it was good for everybody: She made money, and she kept the village clean.

Jack came around to my door and opened it, offering me a hand to step down from the high vehicle. As I reached the ground, he put his arms around me and drew me in for a kiss that curled my toes. "Sophie could be watching," I said, my lips close to his.

"I don't care," he said.

At that moment, neither did I. But I was too old to be sneaking around like a teenager and afraid my mother—or in this case, my soon-to-be-ex-mother-in-law—would catch me. I'll come clean with her soon, I promised myself. But who was I kidding? She probably already knew. I kissed him again and said good night.

❖ FIVE ❖

The next morning I stayed in bed, reading a steamy romance novel by Raphaela Ridgeway. I wished I'd remembered to close my bedroom window last night, because an uncomfortably brisk wind was blowing across my bare arms. I considered covering up with the quilt and reading under the covers with the clip-on book light I kept in the nightstand. Unfortunately, sleeping in any later was not an option today.

The distinctive rumble of Dolly's ancient Crown Victoria sounded in the parking lot. I jumped out of bed and ran to the window, pulling back the curtain just a tiny bit so I could see out. Sophie and her cousin Marina, each wearing the same windbreaker in a different color, Sophie's fuchsia, Marina's lime green, climbed into Sophie's cavernous car. Dolly parked her own car, then got behind the wheel of the pristine white Lincoln. Sophie rolled down the window and waved up at me, even though I knew she couldn't see me. The woman had some kind of sixth sense, I tell you. Always had.

The breath I hadn't realized I'd been holding came out in a little whoosh. A hot shower and some breakfast would wake me up.

I emerged from the bathroom in a cloud of scented steam, toweling my hair. I dressed quickly, threw on a pair of beaded earrings bought at the last Bay craft fair, and gave my lips a swipe with the rose-tinted natural lip balm Liza made over at the Valentine Island Spa. My phone chirped, indicating a message. Jack's handsome face appeared on the screen when I opened the text. On my way, it said.

Twenty minutes later we arrived at the Camelot and I knocked on the door of Room 8. When there was no answer, I knocked again and put my lips to the crack between the door and the jamb. "Melanie? It's us, Georgie and Jack."

A sound like furniture being moved came from behind the door, then the metallic clink of the chain being slid back and the deadbolt being turned. I resisted the urge to roll my eyes, immediately feeling guilty. She had every right to take security precautions, was probably wise to do so. I wondered if I'd remembered to rearm the security system back at the Bonaparte House.

Melanie opened the door. Deep purplish half-moons sat in the hollows beneath her eyes. Her hair stuck up in platinum blond tufts—clearly uncombed. Lines etched her face, and it appeared she hadn't slept, but at least she was dressed, thank God. She rummaged around inside her huge Fendi bag and pulled out a baseball cap, which she jammed on her head. I had a sudden image of Mary Poppins and wondered if next she'd pull out a coatrack. At least it wasn't underwear. A pair of oversized Jackie-O-style sunglasses completed her ensemble. "Get me out of here before I scream," she said. She picked up the bag, and I couldn't help noticing that her hand trembled as she reached for it. "I need a shampoo and a bath with products that don't make me itch. Clean clothes. And some coffee."

Wow. Melanie was in a state. I felt sorry for Caitlyn, who I suspected was going to bear the brunt of Melanie's morning crabbiness when they were finally reunited. She lowered her chin, pulled her glasses down to the tip of her nose, and looked up at Jack. "I need Starbucks, and you're just the man to get it for me."

Jack chuckled. "It's a long way to a Starbucks from Bonaparte Bay." He opened the door and held it open for us to exit.

"The Express-o Bean makes great coffee," I said, a bit defensively. So far our little village had managed to keep out the national chains, which suited me—and every other business owner I knew—just fine.

It didn't take long before we were sitting in Jack's boat, a thirty-eight-foot Bayliner with a cuddy cabin and the most adorable little kitchen below decks. Jack put his coffee—black with one sugar—into the cup holder on the console and throttled up the engine. The vibrations traveled from the soles of my feet right up through to the top of my head. I unwrapped the sandwich I'd bought at the Bean, replaced the leaf of spinach and the sundried tomato that had fallen off the egg, and took a bite. Heaven. A lone figure stood on the dock as we pulled away. Spencer put his camera to his eye and started snapping away.

Melanie pulled the baseball cap lower and adjusted her glasses. "That man is a serious pain in my butt." Mine too, but I was pretty much resigned to the pictures by this point. Fortunately, the *Blurb* had a circulation of about twelve. But I certainly wished that every photograph did not show me from behind or depict me cramming something into my mouth.

The morning sun glittered off the surface of the St. Lawrence, making me long for my own sunglasses. The breeze was cool, no surprise for a late September morning on the Canadian border, and I pulled the zipper of my North Face fleece all the way up. I leaned back on the bench seat and got comfortable. I'd lived on the river my entire life, but it had only been since Jack entered my world a couple of months ago that I'd come to truly appreciate the beauty of this area. I sipped at my very good coffee and watched the islands and the Victorian mansions whiz by.

Our destination was the Spa on Valentine Island. Owned by my good friend Liza Grant, whose family had built the place a hundred and thirty years ago, Valentine Island epitomized the golden age of the Thousand Islands. Prior to the Civil War, her distant relation, General Ulysses S. Grant, had been stationed at Sackets Harbor, a U.S. Naval base strategically located where Lake Ontario and the St. Lawrence conjoin. After the war and during his presidency, the general had visited the Thousand Islands again as a guest of George Pullman of Pullman train car fame. The area grew in popularity among the wealthy, and hundreds of grand residences had been built on the many islands and along the shore. Not quite as grand as the Newport, Rhode Island, mansions of the uber-wealthy such as the Vanderbilts and Astors, some serious Victorian bucks had nonetheless been invested in these houses and the local economy. We were still riding that wave today with our restaurants and gift shops and tours.

Melanie had been staring off the starboard side of the boat the entire ride, and had not uttered a word. I didn't really know her, so I couldn't say if she was preoccupied or just not a morning person. Perhaps a bit of both. "Melanie," I said. No response. "Melanie." A bit louder this time. Absent at roll call. Why had I expected anything different?

Jack looked from her to me and his face broke out into an adorable smile. The sun reflecting off the surface of the water had nothing on those pearly whites. "Aw, let her sleep. Let's just enjoy the ride." One hand left the wheel of the boat and his fingers threaded through mine, warm and strong. Our palms pressed together as a gentle buzz of energy ran up my arm. All those years I'd been married to Spiro, I'd never felt a contentment like this. Jack was right. I would put Melanie out of my mind for the moment. We'd be dumping her at Liza's soon, and then I could get down to the business of enjoying my day off.

My chest constricted with a pang of guilt. What about Doreen? When I got back to shore, I would make some inquiries. If Melanie and I really were Doreen's only next of kin, I'd have to get started on funeral arrangements. Which Melanie could pay for. I hadn't known poor Doreen in life, but I would do right by her in death. I squeezed Jack's hand a little tighter.

A few minutes later we pulled up at the Valentine Island dock. Jack cut the motor and jumped nimbly over onto the wooden structure. I tossed him a line, and he tied the bow of the boat to a metal cleat with a few deft movements. I tossed him the stern line and he repeated the process. This boat wasn't going anywhere until we said it was time to leave—a lesson I had learned the hard way once when I allowed Liza's boat to float away, untied, and it ended up a couple of towns away.

Melanie roused herself from the stupor she'd been in and looked up. My eyes followed hers up the rough-cut stone steps until they landed on Liza's home and business. A fairy-tale castle complete with crenellated turrets and sky-high walls made of local limestone lay a couple of hundred yards up a slight hill. There was no need for a moat or drawbridge, the entire island being, of course, surrounded by water. Chrysanthemums in shades of rust, gold, lavender, and crimson lined the stone walkway. Combined with the reds and golds of the leaves on the maples and oaks that dotted the landscape, the assault of color was intoxicating.

A figure came toward us, his feet making a series of gentle thuds echoing on the dock. A little taller than average, but shorter than Jack, the man carried himself with the easy physicality of a lifelong athlete. His jet-black hair was wavy and worn just a little too long to be presentable, as though he'd canceled his hair appointment in lieu of one too many pickup lacrosse games. He smiled and reached for Melanie's small bag.

His eyes were like a couple of dollops of dark chocolate ganache, and they had a Stallone-y dreaminess. "Liza's tied up with a problem in the kitchen, so she asked me to come down and greet you. I'm Channing."

I'd never needed an escort to visit Liza before. But then I

realized this little midmorning snack of studmuffin was for Melanie's benefit. Liza knew how to treat her spa guests well.

Melanie looked him up and down and apparently liked what she saw. "Get me to the dining room stat, McYummy. I need a wheatgrass smoothie with a sea algae chaser *now*." She placed her hand at the crook of his elbow and gave a little rub as they started up the path. I gave an eye roll. Jack laughed.

"Come on, Georgie," he said, offering me his arm. "Let's get Melanie settled, then we can get on with our day."

I looped my arm through his and we followed.

Caitlyn met us at the huge double oak doors. She was in full assistant mode, cell phone in hand, black-framed hipster glasses planted firmly on her tiny freckled nose. "You missed your hot river-stone massage this morning. I've rescheduled it for later this afternoon. If we can get you ready in the next"—she glanced at the screen of her cell phone, which I thought might be permanently fused to her hand—"fifteen minutes, we can get you back on track with the glacial microsand exfoliation and water lily full-body wrap."

Melanie disengaged herself from Channing, letting her fingers trail along one brown, muscled forearm as she did so. He didn't seem to mind. Was probably used to it, in fact. I'd never seen him before and I wondered what he did here. Liza ran a full-service spa, but I didn't think it extended to providing gigolos for her guests. But anything was possible.

Melanie turned to Caitlyn. "I'm going to the dining room first. Did any messages come in for me?"

Caitlyn shook her head, her shiny brown bob swinging. "Just the usual fan mail. And hate mail. No phone calls."

Melanie frowned. Channing offered her her bag and she took it.

"Maybe I'll see you at the pool," he said to Melanie. She brightened. Understandable.

He turned to me and Jack. "You're Georgie, right? Liza said I should tell you that she's tied up, so she can't come and say hello, but she'll call you later."

I nodded. Although she would never divulge the identities of her rich and famous guests, wealth being much more important than fame, it turned out, the Spa was about as exclusive as they came. Imagine a whole castle full of Melanies, and you'd have a pretty good idea of what Liza probably dealt with on a daily basis. "That's fine. Melanie, Caitlyn? I'll talk to you later."

Melanie nodded at me, and the trio was swallowed up by the giant oak doors.

"So where are you taking me?" My words were loud enough to be heard over the whine of the twin engines, but not so loud I sounded like I was yelling. I hoped.

"We're almost there. Relax. You've had a tough couple of days."

I couldn't argue with that. Finding another body and being reunited with my long-lost mother definitely qualified as *tough*.

Just past Wellesley Island we pulled up at a dock attached to an ornate stone boathouse on the shore. The boathouse was bigger than the house I'd grown up in, so I couldn't wait to see the mansion that was associated with it. We repeated the tying-off process, and Jack offered me a hand.

We followed a gravel path up to a splendid Victorian. Its many gables and dormers were painted in a dove gray accented with bright white and periwinkle blue embellishments. Baskets of hot pink geraniums trailing dark green ivy hung at regular intervals from the covered porch, which wrapped around the house, giving views of the river on three sides. Antique white wicker furniture was placed in casual groupings. I loved the Bonaparte House, which was probably at least fifty years older than this place and much less ornate, but I had to admit it would be a delight to sit on this porch with a glass of wine on a summer evening and read a good novel or to talk quietly with someone I loved.

Love. I glanced up at Jack. I was pretty sure I was in love with him, my judgment being less than stellar in that area historically, but I was no teenager anymore. There was a big difference between being in love, and loving somebody, and we'd only been a couple for, well, a couple of months. I'd jumped in feet first, and it felt good to let go and not worry about the outcome. But a nagging feeling had me wondering if things had progressed too quickly. Too fast to last. Too good to be true.

I shook my head. I would worry about all this later. Right now my curiosity was getting the better of me. "Are you going to tell me who we're visiting?"

Jack grinned. "There's really no mystery," he said as he pressed the button for the doorbell. A set of chimes rang inside the house. "Gladys is a friend of mine, and I thought you'd like to meet her."

I mentally ran through my personal list of Gladyses and came up short. Clearly I didn't know as many people as I thought.

A set of slow footsteps sounded behind the door. It swung inward, letting out a blast of cool air, which felt lovely. The day was warming up. A tall, thin elderly woman appeared in the doorway, her white curls waving gently in the breeze. The sleeves of her pink track suit were pushed up to reveal bony wrists and a couple of simple gold bangles. Her cheeks were flushed and her breath seemed faster than normal.

In one of her hands, she held a stout stick with a rock lashed to one end.

◈ SIX ◈

"Put down the war club, Glad," Jack said. "I promise we're not hostile."

"Jack Conway, is that you finally?" The woman presented her powdery cheek to Jack and he dutifully kissed it. "And this must be Georgie. From the restaurant, right? Lovely to meet you, dear. I've been meaning to pop in and try some of the food I keep hearing about, but Dom used to get all bent out of shape if he found out I ate someplace other than the Sailor's Rest." Her face fell. "Not that I won't miss the old bastard."

So she'd known Big Dom. Not surprising really. Dom had been murdered in August, a victim of my former almost-boyfriend and his greedy schemes. I'd like to think I had something to do with solving the case, but I'd really just fumbled my way through the entire situation. "Were you a relative?" I asked.

"No, no. But he was a distant relative of my late husband,

a cousin on his mother's side. Which, I suppose, is why he felt free to ask me for money when he got himself into a crack. And why I felt free to turn him down. Of course, I didn't know he'd end up dead. But whether I'd given him money or not, the outcome would have been the same. He just couldn't keep himself out of trouble." She swung the club about absentmindedly, then seemed to come back to the moment. "But where are my manners? Please come in."

She stepped aside and Jack and I entered a moderately sized foyer. A dark oak staircase lined with intricately carved spindles lay to our left, a wooden cherub perched atop the newel post. The walls were rimmed with lovely wainscoting along the bottom, and a heavily patterned wallpaper—which I suspected might be original to the house, or at least a very good reproduction—along the top.

"Let's go on out to the kitchen and get something to nibble on." Gladys led the way down the hallway, past several rooms on either side, into a bright, spacious kitchen. A round oak table with claw feet sat in the middle of the space, ringed by matching chairs. "Would you like coffee or tea?"

Both Jack and I asked for coffee. "May I help you?" I said. "I'm not used to being waited on, I'm afraid."

Gladys laughed. "I can certainly give you something to do. Why don't you slice up that banana bread? There's cream cheese to go with it."

Ah, now I was in my element. I crossed to the sink and washed my hands, then set to work slicing the moist, fragrant bread with a serrated knife I found in a knife block on the counter. I scooped some cream cheese, which had been sitting out to soften, into a little crystal dish, then arranged all

the components on a gorgeous antique platter. Gladys provided the coffeepot, and Jack helped her bring over the cups,
teaspoons, cream, and sugar.

"We could go into the front parlor," Gladys suggested.
"That's where I usually entertain."

I looked around me at this cheerful room with its white
beadboard cupboards and dark green quartz countertops.
"I'm fine here," I said. I was never as comfortable as when
I was in a kitchen, no matter whose kitchen it was.

"Me too, Glad. As long as you're feeding me, I'm happy,"
Jack said.

"Then sit down, handsome." She grinned, turned to me,
and gave a little wink. I grinned back.

"After we have this snack, maybe we could take a tour
of the house?" Jack said as he chewed. "I'd love to see the
rest of the house again, and I know Georgie would. She lives
in a historic place too." His eyes were fixed on the war club,
which Gladys had placed on the counter.

Gladys gave him a playful swat on the arm. "Of course
I'll give you two a tour. And we'll spend a nice long time in
the collection room." She smiled at me. "I suppose he didn't
tell you why he really wanted to come and visit an old lady?"

Other than the fact that she was charming and apparently
a fine baker? The bread was delicious, perfumed with the
deepest banana flavor I'd ever tasted. I almost didn't want
to spoil it with a swig of coffee, but I did. "I don't really care
why we're here, as long as you give me a copy of this recipe,"
I said, swallowing. There was a secret ingredient in there, I
was almost sure of it. And it would nag at me until I found
out what it was.

"I'll write it down for you before you leave," Gladys promised.

Jack was cheerfully slathering cream cheese on his third helping. He seemed to be able to eat whatever he wanted with no consequences. "So how do you two know each other?" I asked.

"My parents were friends with Gladys and Herman—we called him Monty," Jack said. "My siblings and I spent a lot of time here when we were kids." *That's right*, I thought. Jack was in the process of getting a permanent transfer to the Bonaparte Bay Coast Guard Station from the Oswego Station, and it made sense that he was reacquainting himself with the people he'd known as a kid. "Gladys's late husband was a great collector of First Peoples artifacts. He took me with him on a few of his expeditions out into the countryside. I dug up some arrowheads when I was a kid and was bitten by the bug."

A memory glimmered somewhere in the back of my mind. The word "SCOOM"—"Seneca, Cayuga, Onondaga, Oneida, Mohawk." Every junior high school kid in New York State did a unit on the federated Iroquois nations who lived here and provided the foundation for the fledgling American government in the eighteenth century. Of course—I could still hear the voice of my seventh grade social studies teacher—most of the tribes had sided with the British during the Revolution and were not treated very well by the victorious patriots. We learned how to build a longhouse—a skill I hoped I'd never have to actually put to the test—and I found I could still remember some of the steps involved. I didn't know a lot about the archaeological history of the North Country, though.

"I'd love to see the collection too," I said.

"Then let's go have a look, shall we?" Gladys got up and, regretfully, covered the banana bread with a piece of plastic wrap. I brought the coffee cups to the sink and offered to wash up. "No, Georgie. I'll do the dishes later. Sometimes it's the highlight of my day." At my look of horror, she laughed. "Kidding! If I'm bored, I troll for pictures of hot men on the Internet. I especially like the ones in uniform." She batted her eyes at Jack.

"You're a devil in disguise, Gladys," Jack said. "If I weren't so smitten with Georgie here, I might take a walk on the wild side with you."

Smitten? He was smitten with me? A warm tingle spread throughout my body, immediately accompanied by a twinge of panic. I wasn't very good at relationships—yet.

We followed Gladys out of the kitchen and back down the hallway. "Powder room," she said with a sweep of her arm that made her gold bracelets jingle. "Here are the parlors." We entered a beautiful room furnished in an eclectic mix of antique and more modern furniture. One wall of the room contained a wide opening into a second parlor. As we passed through the opening, I realized it must contain pocket doors. We had similar ones back at the Bonaparte House.

Exiting through the front room, we crossed the hallway to the library. I was immediately jealous. The room was lined with books floor to ceiling, with a couple of comfortable-looking chairs upholstered in faded pink velvet. I longed to park my behind in one of them and reach up for a book, any book.

"This is where Herman spent most of his time," Gladys

said. "I haven't changed much in the twenty years he's been gone. Would you believe these chairs used to be red until the sun got to them?"

"It's a lovely room," I said.

Jack nodded. He was staring at a painting on the wall, framed in gilt. My eyes followed his. The painting was moderately sized, done in thick oils, and it depicted dogs . . . dressed like people and playing cards and smoking cigars. The painting seemed oddly familiar, as though I'd seen something similar once.

Gladys rolled her eyes. "Oh, that thing. You like it, Jack? Personally, I think it's ridiculous. But Herman loved it, so I kept it."

It was kind of silly. But there was something compelling about it too.

Jack peered at the signature. "Kash Koolidge, a local artist. I remember this, of course. It's hard to forget. I wonder if it's an original or a reproduction?"

"I have no idea," Gladys said. "And I have no clue where Herman picked it up. Now this"—she indicated a bronze sculpture on a pedestal in a corner of the room—"this I know is an original. At least the insurance company says it is, based on the premiums they charge me."

There was no mistaking what that sculpture was—a Remington. It depicted a horse and rider in exquisite detail, the metal giving off a dull sheen. I was no horsey girl, and I wouldn't necessarily want art like that in my house, but I could appreciate the artistry that had gone into it. I wondered what it was worth. I'd visited the Frederic Remington Museum in Ogdensburg when my daughter was little and her class had gone on a field trip, so I knew that there were more than one of each of the Remington bronzes—they simply cast them in the same molds, then broke the molds after a certain number.

"And back here are the arrowheads and spear points." She indicated a glass case that spanned most of the length of the back wall.

Jack leaned over the case and gave a low whistle. "Wow! You weren't kidding, Glad. I don't remember the collection being this big."

Rows of arrowheads, spear points, and a few shards of pottery were arranged in neat rows, and each object was labeled with a number. There were some other items I couldn't identify but I assumed they were stone tools or weapons of some kind. There was a largish empty spot, and I had to wonder if that was where the war club Gladys had used to greet us at the door was located.

"What are the numbers for?" I asked.

"Herman was extremely meticulous about cataloging where and when he found these artifacts. Back in the sixties and seventies, when he was traipsing around the North Country doing most of his digging, of course, that wasn't common for amateurs. And in those days there weren't all these regulations about calling in the state archaeologist and trying to send whatever was found back to the tribe it belonged to. Repatriation, I think it's called. At least for human remains."

"Georgie, did you know that the North Country is full of earthen mounds made thousands of years ago? There are some particularly baffling ones over at Perch Lake. The archaeologists have not come to any solid conclusions about who made them—or what purpose they served. My sister Trish works for the state archaeologist now."

I hadn't known that. I knew something about the Bonapartes, of course, since they were connected with my own house. But this history apparently went back much, much further, long before this area was explored by the Europeans.

"So, Jack, I was hoping you could carry down the boxes from Herman's office upstairs. They're full of his notes and measurements on each of these items, plus photographs. You remember where the office is?"

Jack smiled. "Of course. I loved this house when I was a kid. I'll be right back." He left the room and went up the stairs just outside the library door, two at a time.

"Well, dear. Why don't you and I go out to the kitchen and I'll get you that recipe?"

She didn't have to ask me twice. A couple of minutes later I was parked back at the oak table with a shoe box crammed full of paper in front of me. Gladys handed me a pen and an index card decorated with sunflowers. She pulled a pair of bright red cheaters on a chain from underneath her light sweatshirt and placed them on her nose, then began to thumb through a second box. "Ah, I found it. Here, I'll let you copy it down."

I read quickly through the recipe and smiled. There it was, the secret ingredient I'd been wondering about. Yet it was so simple, I wanted to smack my forehead for not thinking of using it myself. Instead of milk, which most recipes called for, this one substituted banana-flavored Greek yogurt. That's what made the rich, moist texture and deep flavor. I made a quick copy and stuck the card in my back pocket.

"Thanks, Gladys. I don't suppose you have any other recipes you'd like to send my way?"

Gladys looked pleased. "I love to cook. I throw potlucks and dinner parties for my neighbors at the condo complex in Florida all winter long. Keeps me in practice."

"I'll bet you've got lots of friends and admirers," I said. The woman was charming, attractive, and could cook, which probably made her a hot commodity in the senior community. Rather like my mother-in-law, Sophie, although I might sometimes debate the extent of her charm. She was more like a bulldog than a French poodle.

"Oh, well, I do all right," Gladys said modestly. "I have an idea. I'll be going back to Florida next week. These old bones don't like the cold and snow anymore, and you know how quickly the snow comes here. Why don't you take these recipes with you and you can copy what you want over the winter? There are some old ones from my mother and grandmother in there too. You can just return the boxes next spring when you're done."

"Really?" I was salivating. And an idea was starting to form. Now that Cal was gone, and I wouldn't be spending my winters in Greece with Sophie and Spiro anymore, I was going to need something to keep me busy when the snow came. Maybe I'd write a cookbook—a Thousand Islands cookbook. A thrill of excitement ran through me.

"Well, if you're sure you trust me with them, I'd love to take you up on the offer."

She patted my hand. "I can tell they'll be in good hands. Jack is an excellent judge of character, and if he likes you, that's good enough for me."

I could feel my cheeks heat up. Were we that obvious?

Gladys smiled at me, her eyes shining. "Take care of that boy. Herman and I never had children of our own, and so we took a special interest in Jack and his sisters. Which is why I wouldn't trust Herman's artifact collection to anyone else."

"Are you giving it to Jack?" I said in surprise. He was renting an apartment over the Laundromat right now. Since it wasn't right on the water, he was getting a nice deal on it. I guessed he'd find room for the stuff somewhere.

"Not exactly. Jack's sister Trish works for the New York State Archaeology Department. Since I have no living relatives, and since I don't need the money, I decided it was time to make arrangements for the collection to go to where it can stay together and do the most educational good. Trish couldn't make it here from Albany before I leave for Florida next week, so Jack agreed to package up and deliver the items to her."

Jack returned. "I've loaded all the paperwork into the boat—good thing it's all in covered plastic boxes. I suppose it would have been simpler to just bring a car, though it would be a tight fit in my Jeep."

Gladys nodded. "Boat, Jeep, it's all the same to me. So when can you come back and pack up the actual collection for Trish?"

"I've bought containers, but it looks like I'll need to run to Watertown and pick up a few more based on the size of the collection. How about tomorrow afternoon?" Jack said.

"That'll be fine. Why don't you come for lunch, and bring Georgie too? We've had a nice chat and I'd like to get to know her better." Gladys smiled.

"I'd like that too, Gladys. I've got some . . . friends in

town, so I'll have to see what their plans are." My thoughts drifted back to Melanie and Caitlyn.

"Feel free to bring them along. I'll be leaving next week and I've got a refrigerator full of food to use up. Just call ahead of time and let me know how many plates to set."

She was adorable. I wasn't sure if I wanted to expose her to Melanie just yet.

❖ SEVEN ❖

Jack and I had a late, leisurely lunch of thick, juicy burgers and crispy French fries at the Black Bear Café in the next town upriver from the Bay. We motored back to the Bay and he delivered me and my boxes of recipes to the door of the Bonaparte House. Its two-hundred-year-old solid stone walls weren't quite as fancy as Gladys's grand Victorian, but it was beautiful to me. Jack gave me a quick kiss, again not bothering to check if anyone was watching, and said he'd call me tomorrow to see if I wanted to go retrieve the rest of the arrowheads with him.

I unlocked the back door—Dolly, Marina, and Sophie apparently hadn't returned from their shopping trip yet—and went through the kitchen and down the short hallway to my office. I set the recipe boxes on the small table inside the door, hung up my jacket, and booted up my laptop. Although it was tempting to rip into those recipes immediately, there was work to be done first.

What are you doing back in my life, Melanie? And why now?

A search box opened and I plugged in "Melanie Ashley." I scrolled through the results. A whole gallery of photos popped up. She'd been linked romantically at one time with a much younger former Disney star, so there were numerous pictures of the two of them draped all over each other. He was cute, with dark hair and electric green eyes. Couldn't blame her for that. I found a picture of Melanie all glammed up alongside Caitlyn, who faded into the background with her mousy looks. Here she was at the Daytime Emmy Awards, wearing a gold lamé gown that was cut so low it might have been stolen from J-Lo's closet. The caption read, *Skunked Again.* The Emmy still eluded her, as far as I knew.

I backed out of the pictures and perused the gossip about her. Messy breakup with the grown-up Disney kid. Speculation about an affair with Jon Bon Jovi—she'd told me that wasn't true, which Mrs. Bon Jovi would be relieved to hear. No mention of any children or her family life. I guess that was a blessing.

My gut clenched as I read the next entry, dated two weeks ago. *Soap Star on the Verge of Bankruptcy.* Melanie had put her Bel Air mansion up for sale. I hit Print, then opened my bottom drawer. If this didn't call for dark chocolate, nothing did.

I leaned back in my chair, letting the candy melt on my tongue as the reality sank in. If the gossip sheets were to be believed, Melanie was in financial trouble. There'd been some national news coverage of the discovery of the jewels here at the Bonaparte House a couple of months ago, which she could easily have heard about. And there was also the matter of the late-eighteenth-century table that had belonged to Joseph Bonaparte—a table that was being authenticated and was expected to bring in a half-million dollars at auction.

I sighed with some relief as I remembered what my mother didn't know. The proceeds from these treasures were never going to trickle down to me. The jewels were tied up in litigation with the Spanish government. A finder's fee might be awarded at some point, but that was probably years down the road. And the table belonged to Sophie, fair and square. So my mother-in-law, already well off, was going to be a very rich woman indeed. She'd already told me that she planned to leave a percentage of her wealth to Spiro, with the bulk going into trust for Callista until my daughter turned thirty.

Me? Well, I didn't have expensive tastes and I saved most of the salary I earned from my work managing the Bonaparte House. Not that that was exorbitant, but I'd be okay even if Sophie sold the restaurant out from under me. Sad, but okay. That thought called for another square of chocolate.

And what about Doreen? I wasn't exactly sure when Melanie had gotten into town, but it had to have been just about the time Doreen was killed. I felt sick to my stomach. Would Melanie stoop to murder? If it was true that Doreen had no family other than Melanie and me, Melanie would, ironically, stand to inherit her own parents' farm, even after they'd cut her out of the will. And yet the farm couldn't be worth that much. Farmland was cheap and abundant in the North Country. Drive down any country road in Jefferson or St. Lawrence County and you'd see at least one or two abandoned farms, the buildings standing bravely against the frigid winters until eventually they caved in.

I shook my head. She might need money, but I had to believe my mother was not a murderer.

Doreen. I had to make arrangements for her.

I dialed the BBPD.

"Bonaparte Bay Police Department. How may I direct your call?" Cindy. Of course.

"Cindy, this is Georgie. Can I talk to Rick or Tim?"

"Why, did you find another body?" She snickered.

"Did you miss your sensitivity training workshop, Cindy? Death isn't funny. Put the chief on, will you? I've got a casserole in the oven and it only has a few minutes to go." Only a bit of a fib. More like a prediction. As soon as I got off the phone, I was going to put together a pastitsio for dinner.

She harrumphed but I heard a click on the line. "Moriarty, here. What can I do for you, Georgie?"

"Rick, I've just found out that I might be related to Doreen Webber, the dead woman. Have you found any family?"

"I've had people out at her house looking through her personal effects. We found a copy of a will that lists a—there was a sound of shuffling papers—Shirley Bartlett aka Melanie Ashley as her heir and executrix. Isn't that the actress from *The Desperate and the Defiant*? I heard she was in town."

So it was true. "Yes, Melanie is in town, staying over at the Spa. I . . . know her, so I'll contact her to get the ball rolling on the arrangements." I tapped at the wood of my desk with a fingernail. "Has there been an autopsy?"

"Preliminary results are in—I don't see any harm in telling you, since you found the body and it was a clear case of strangulation. We recovered a length of what appears to be restaurant plastic wrap braided into a rope, which you also saw."

I wondered if the CSI team from the State Police or Sheriff's Department had found anything, but Rick was unlikely to tell me more than he already had and I didn't want to press my luck by seeming too nosy.

"Rick, I'm not sure what the protocol is here, but would you tell the coroner or whoever's in charge that when the body is released they should contact Clive Miller at the Miller Funeral Home?"

"Sure thing," and he hung up.

I made a quick call to Clive, with whom I'd gone to high school, to let him know to expect Doreen. I told him to contact me when the body arrived and I'd come in to arrange the services. Then I headed to the kitchen. Nothing but doing some cooking for people I loved was going to help me sort through this muddle and make me feel better.

I washed up and donned an apron, then filled a big stainless steel stock pot with water and set it on the burner, which I turned all the way up. I added a generous sprinkle of salt, and gave the saline mixture a stir. While I waited for the water to boil, I chopped an onion and cooked it with some ground beef, drained it, then added plain tomato sauce, cinnamon, and nutmeg and set it to simmer while I whipped up a flavorful béchamel, loaded with cheese. In Greece I would have used a traditional cheese like mizithra, but since that was not available anywhere close to Bonaparte Bay, I substituted fresh-grated parmesan.

When the bucatini was still slightly underdone, I drained it and dumped half into a baking dish, then layered it with the meat sauce, the rest of the pasta, and then topped everything with the cheesy béchamel. The whole heavy pan went into the oven.

I whipped up a salad of romaine lettuce, cucumbers, and tomatoes, dished up some plump, briny olives, and pulled some homemade bread dough out of the freezer to bake just before serving. When they returned, I'd invite Dolly and Marina to stay for dinner. There would be plenty of delicious Greek comfort food—Spiro and Inky could come too, if they didn't have other plans. I felt a need to have my family—my real family, which was not necessarily my biological family—surrounding me.

I set the timer on the oven, put my apron on its hook by the back door, and returned to my office to see if I could find any more information on my mother. I'd barely sat down when the buzzer for the kitchen door rang. Probably Sophie, with her arms full of packages. She loved to shop—although, she also managed to keep her bedroom pretty much clutter-free, a skill I'd never mastered and probably never would.

"Coming," I called out and hustled to the back door to help. I threw open the door, then felt as though I'd been gut-punched. It wasn't my mother-in-law standing in the doorway. It was my favorite cop—Lieutenant Edmond Hawthorne.

◈ EIGHT ◈

"Well, well, well. We meet again." He was six-foot-three of imposing bulk wrapped in a gray New York State Trooper's uniform that showed off his physique to paramilitary perfection. He took off his hat and his mirrored aviator sunglasses, revealing close-cropped dark hair and a pair of midnight blue eyes fringed in enviable long lashes. He hung his hat on a hook by the door.

My heart raced. Last time I'd seen Lieutenant Hawthorne, I'd been sitting in the back of his cruiser, being lectured about not taking investigations into my own hands—and not sure if I was being taken to the county lockup. He'd ultimately dropped me off at the restaurant, though, and there hadn't been any legal repercussions for me. But every time I saw him, I felt a little off balance, as though I'd done something wrong and was about to get caught.

"Come in," I gulped. "Can I get you something to drink?"

I didn't really feel like being hospitable, but I could never seem to help it.

He stared down at me. "Something smells good," he finally said.

What did he want, an invitation? Not hardly. "Dinner for the family. Restaurant's closed till the weekend. What can I do for you, Lieutenant?" I hoped I sounded confident because I certainly didn't feel that way.

"I'll get right to the point," he said. "Why is it that there've been two murders in the Bay in just a few months—and you've found the body both times." It wasn't a question.

I hadn't done anything wrong, yet I felt guilty as sin. "Trust me when I say I wish that weren't true."

He continued to stare. I tried not to squirm. "So," he said. "The murder victim is your cousin." He consulted a small notebook that he pulled from a trouser pocket. "Doreen Webber. Age sixty. Lunch lady at the Bonaparte Bay High School."

Lunch lady. I hadn't known that. I wondered how much the lieutenant already knew. I owed Melanie nothing, but I wasn't quite ready to give her up to the po-po either. "I didn't find that out until yesterday. I never knew her."

His chiseled jaw was firm, but a tiny muscle twitched just in front of his left ear. "Are you sure about that? This is a small town."

What a jerk. I smiled sweetly. "Size doesn't matter, Lieutenant."

The corner of his mouth moved up, almost imperceptibly. "What do you know about Melanie Ashley?"

I debated. Did I tell him about our relationship? He'd find

out eventually. Might already know. I really needed to talk to Melanie so we could get our stories straight.

"She came in to the restaurant for dinner last night." Not a lie.

"And was that the first time you'd met her?"

"Yes." Also not a lie. Technically, last time I'd seen her, she wasn't Melanie Ashley.

He gave me a hard look. "I'm going to need you to come down to the barracks tomorrow and give me a statement."

"Sure. No problem." Would he never leave? "I'll come by in the morning, if that's all right. I have an appointment at noon."

He tapped a long finger on the dimple in his chin. "Would that appointment have anything to do with Jack Conway?"

I bristled. "I don't see how that's relevant, Lieutenant."

"It isn't," he said. "But you might want to be careful who you associate with, is all I'm saying."

I took a deep breath. What was that about? Jack was as honorable as they came. I had serious doubts about this state trooper, though. A little worm of doubt wiggled into the friable earth of my mind. Lieutenant Hawthorne wasn't the only person who'd said something like this to me. I felt defensive. I wasn't wrong about Jack. I knew it.

"If we're through, I'm expecting my mother-in-law back any moment. She'll be upset if she sees you here. I'll be by in the morning."

He pulled his Ray-Bans out of his pocket and put them on, then took his hat off the hook by the door and placed it on his head, adjusting it till it sat at the perfect angle. The delicious fragrance of the pastitsio wafted our way, and the lieutenant looked toward the ovens. His normally stony expression seemed a bit wistful.

"You do that, Georgie," he said, and was gone.

"Good morning! How's my ex-wife?" I found myself wrapped in a bear hug that squeezed a puff of Drakkar Noir–scented air up between us.

Wonderful. Spiro, Inky, Dolly, and Marina had joined me for dinner last night. We opened a couple of bottles of retsina, not my favorite wine with its faint pine-tree flavor but I drank it anyway, and played a few hands of Pitch at a nickel a point. Sophie scooped her big pile of coins into her hand, then into her pocket. We should have just given her the money in the first place, without even bothering to play cards. She always won. She said good night to us and headed upstairs with her winnings. Spiro and Inky dropped Marina off at her home, then left for their digs over the new restaurant. I went to bed early too. I'd slept fitfully, and I was dreading going to give my statement to the police, so my attitude was none too peppy this morning. I took a sip of my coffee.

"I'm not your ex-wife yet, Spiro." It wouldn't be long now, though. We'd be free of each other—legally anyway—by Christmas. I didn't know how I was going to feel about it when it did happen. Sad, because twenty years of marriage was down the toilet? Happy, because I could finally live my life the way I wanted, a life that might include Jack? Afraid? What if Sophie threw me out? Or maybe I'd just be relieved, now that I was no longer living a lie. We'd have to wait and see.

"Oh, poor Georgie," Spiro's partner, Ignatius "Inky"

LaFontaine, said, dropping a kiss on top of my head. "Spiro, you should try to be more sensitive. Georgie's finding dead bodies again."

Spiro helped himself to coffee and dropped into a chair near the waitress station. I brought over my cup and sat down, followed by Inky.

"You're not expecting breakfast, are you?" I couldn't think why they'd be here this early in the morning unless it was in the hopes that I would cook for them.

"No, no," Spiro said. "We went out to the Family Diner this morning. I don't know why Marina doesn't open during the week. There's nowhere else to get grilled cinnamon rolls."

"You know why." I resisted the urge to shake my head. "Same reason we only open on weekends this time of year. The tourists have gone home."

Inky patted my hand. "We know. He's tired. We've been working to get Spinky's up and running and it's meant a lot of long days."

I just about blew coffee out my nose. Spinky's? And yet, it was kind of catchy. The cute name, plus the casual burgers and sandwiches they'd told me they planned to serve, would fill a restaurant void in the Bay. I wondered if they'd keep the big old wooden ship's anchor that sat outside the front door and had been there all through the time Big Dom DiTomasso had owned the place. Before he died.

"Good morning, Sophie," I said as my mother-in-law approached. "Can I get you anything?" She looked from Spiro to Inky then back to Spiro, before taking the fourth seat at the table.

She wore a pale green sweater, the color of a luna moth,

embellished with sparkling crystals all across the shoulders. I detected Dolly's influence in this fashion choice. The color brought out little flecks of green in her eyes, and the effect was quite flattering. Her short hair, which she dyed a deep purplish burgundy, looked a little flat in the back. My guess was that she was off to the Hair Lair for a fresh set and bouff.

"Later," she said. She stared at Spiro, and he began to squirm almost imperceptibly. "Why you here so early?"

"Can't a man come to visit his own mother without getting the third degree?" he said.

Inky's expression was carefully neutral.

Sophie's eyes narrowed. "You never get up so early. Maybe this guy"—she nodded to Inky—"is good influence on you?"

Spiro seemed to relax. Inky smiled. Sophie had accepted their relationship quite gracefully once it was presented to her as a fait accompli. I think it was a relief to her to finally have everything out in the open. Now if I could just come clean with her about Jack, we'd all be one big, painfully honest family.

"So . . . how's everybody here?" Spiro asked. Once he'd moved in with Inky, he'd only been back to get his clothes.

"We're fine," I said. He was up to something, I just knew it.

"Where's Dolly? I'd like to say hi."

Hmmm. Curiouser and curiouser. "I imagine she'll be in later. She'll want to get a start on prep for the weekend."

Inky was studying a fingernail.

I glanced from one to the other. Of course. I should have guessed sooner.

"So," I said, fixing my gaze on Spiro and forcing the issue. "How's the staffing coming along at Spinky's?"

"Spinky's? Dumb name." Sophie aligned the silverware so

that it was perfectly oriented parallel and perpendicular to the edges of the table. Despite the fact, of course, that we'd have to reset this table anyway, now that we'd all been sitting at it.

"Well, you know how it is," Spiro said. "Most of the experienced people in town want their winters off."

And one experienced person who wouldn't be averse to a year-round job might also happen to be one of the best cooks in the Bay. And might also happen to be *my* cook right here at the Bonaparte House—one Dolly Riley.

The same thought must have gone through Sophie's head because she let loose on Spiro in Greek. They began to argue, and knowing them, it would take some time for them to hash it out. "Come on, Inky," I said. "Let's go make another pot."

He followed me out to the kitchen. "Sorry," he said. "I told him it was a bad idea to try to steal your cook away from you."

"I appreciate that." I fiddled with the coffeemaker and got it going. The cooler yielded part of a pie made of wild blackcaps—in other parts of the country these little dark gems are called black raspberries. They're common here, but labor intensive and somewhat hazardous to pick because of their sharp thorns. And of course the pickers have to compete with the bears and the turkeys. This pie represented almost the last of the berries I had frozen this summer.

Pie for breakfast? Why not? I offered Inky a slice, but he declined (thank goodness). So I squirted on some whipped cream and took a bite. Tart, sweet, and with a flavor like no other, the tiny seeds crunched between my teeth. The crust, despite having been refrigerated, was still flaky, crisp yet tender. And made by Dolly. Nope, I wouldn't give her up. If she needed a raise to stay, I'd give it to her gladly. Besides, I considered her a friend.

"But we do need a cook. And, well, a full wait and kitchen staff. No bartender yet—the liquor license hasn't been transferred. So if you know of anybody looking for a job, let me know."

I would get on that immediately. The sooner I found Spinky's some employees, the sooner I could rest easier about Dolly. "Let me make some calls for you."

"You're a doll," Inky said. "You sure you don't want to come in for a tattoo? I'll do it for free."

"Uh, no. I could never decide on a design I could wear for the rest of my life." I was destined to remain a tat-virgin and that was okay by me.

Inky looked thoughtful. "You know who might have made a good short-order cook? Doreen. Too bad she's dead."

I was taken aback. "Did you know her?" Why hadn't he mentioned this before? Doreen's body was found out behind his restaurant and had been there for at least a day, according to Chief Moriarty. No, no way was Inky a murderer. I refused to believe it. And yet . . .

"She had a tat done a week or so ago. I remember we laughed because she'd come from work at the school cafeteria and she'd forgotten to take off her hairnet."

I frowned. "Why didn't you mention you knew her when the paramedics carried her body out of your backyard?"

"I didn't get a good look at her as she went past, and it was dark." True. "I heard it was her later."

My curiosity got the better of me. "Did you two talk

about anything while she was getting inked?" My thoughts shot back to Lieutenant Hawthorne. I was in for another lecture if he found out about this. The argument between Spiro and Sophie was still going strong in the other room.

"Let's see." Inky's brows drew up in concentration. "She came in, said it was her first tat and she wasn't sure what she wanted. She wasn't wearing her lunch lady uniform, but it was about two o'clock on a weekday so I figured she'd come straight from school. She smelled like turkey and gravy, and I got a little hungry."

Not surprising. Inky was always hungry. He clearly had a lightning-fast metabolism and/or worked out a lot— probably both—because his lean frame didn't seem to carry an ounce of extra fat. *Jealousy doesn't become you, Georgiana Gertrude*, I admonished myself, and took another bite of my pie. "Go on," I prompted. "What else happened?"

"Well, she looked through my design books. There was no one else in the shop, so I sat down with her to flip through the pages. The scent of turkey was strong—like an entity floating around the room! Finally, she let out a huge laugh. She had one of those dry, wheezy kinds of laughs like she'd smoked for years then given it up. 'That's the one,' she said, and pointed to a picture." He paused for dramatic effect.

I took the cue. "And? What did she pick?" I found myself caught up in the story.

He leaned back against the counter. "A stylized dollar sign." He smiled and a dimple appeared in his lean left cheek and the snake that was inked up onto his shaved scalp twitched with the movement. "Which she wanted me to put right around her belly button. Then she changed her mind and put it on her arm so more people would see it." Inky reached over with a tanned hand and broke a piece of crust off my pie and popped it into his mouth. "Wow, this is good. Spiro wasn't kidding."

"I'll find you a cook," I said absently. My mind was racing. Why would a sixty-year-old cafeteria worker suddenly decide to get her first tattoo? And why a dollar sign? That seemed an odd choice. Of course, I had no idea what Doreen's financial situation had been, but she couldn't have made much more than minimum wage at the school. She lived outside of town at the family farm (I winced. That was my family farm too, even though I'd never been there), so her taxes were probably low, but it would cost an arm and a leg in the winter to heat an old farmhouse. "Did she end up getting the tat? Did she say anything else?"

Inky continued to eye my breakfast, then shoved his hands in the pockets of his jeans, presumably to keep from picking anything more off my plate. I walked to the cooler, pulled out the last piece of pie, and handed it to him with a fork, regretfully. He forked up some berries, then looked at me. "Where's the whipped cream? She said she was going to come into a pile of money in a few months, then retire. She was celebrating early."

Interesting. My thoughts turned again to the jewels and the priceless table I'd found upstairs. Had Doreen thought she was somehow entitled to some of that money through her heretofore unknown relationship with me? Had she been planning to blackmail me perhaps? I tried not to snort. My life so far had hardly been interesting enough to engender blackmail. Sure, my husband preferred men, but that was out in the open. I'd thought long ago about having an affair, but that had been short-lived. I couldn't reconcile being the mother of a junior high school kid and being involved in a secret affair simultaneously, so I'd ended it almost as quickly as it had begun, choosing to be able to look my daughter in the eye at the dinner table over potential sex with somebody I didn't love. I'd liked the guy, and he'd liked me, but the fireworks were noticeably absent.

"Did she say where the money was coming from?" Another thought struck me. Maybe it wasn't me she'd been planning to blackmail. Maybe it was Melanie. In fact, maybe she'd already made her demands on Melanie and that was why my long-lost mother had decided to reappear in Bonaparte Bay. To try to stop her. What if Melanie had agreed to meet Doreen, and it had gotten physical? What if Melanie snapped and strangled Doreen in an effort to silence her, then showed up here at the Bonaparte House as if nothing had happened? A cold lump formed and twisted in the pit of my stomach.

"Georgie?" Inky's voice brought me out of my thoughts. "You okay, honey? You look like you've seen a ghost."

I shook my head to clear it. "Uh, yeah. Just remembering finding Doreen, that's all."

"Such nastiness. And she wasted all that money on a tat that she barely got to enjoy." He finished off the pie and set the plate in the big stainless steel sink. "You know what else is a piece of nastiness? We got a shipment of stuff in from the restaurant supply house in Watertown, you know, dishes, silverware, utensils? Well when Spiro and I went to put everything away, the roll of plastic wrap had been opened and almost half of it was gone."

I sucked in a breath. Doreen had been strangled with a rope made from braided plastic wrap. I studied Inky's face. He wouldn't have seen the murder weapon that night because it was too dark. He didn't seem to have made the connection between his missing wrap and Doreen's death, which was obvious, so it was clear he had not heard what the murder weapon was.

"And not only that," he continued. "But the key we keep under the back mat was missing too."

◈ NINE ◈

A crash sounded from the dining room. Inky vaulted around the counter and raced in the direction of the noise. I followed, not quite as nimbly. When we arrived, Sophie's face was nearly as red as her hair, and her hands were fisted on her bony hips. Spiro lay sprawled on the floor, a chair lying next to him on its side. He got up, sputtering. I looked from Sophie to her son. I had a new respect for her. There had been times when I had also wanted to knock the seat out from under him.

"Oh, quit looking at me like that, Georgie," Spiro sputtered. "She didn't do this. I was tipped too far back in the chair and I lost my balance." He got to his feet and righted the chair. "Come on, Inky. Let's go. We've got work to do." He turned to his mother and planted a kiss on her cheek. "I'll see you later, Mana. *Signomi.* Sorry."

Sophie nodded. "Bye." Just like that, their argument was over.

Inky took Spiro by the arm and they started for the kitchen.

"Inky?" He turned back toward me. "Uh, that roll of plastic wrap? You can't use that now, but don't throw it away. In fact, don't touch it . . . in case it's contaminated with something." Spiro, my germaphobe almost-ex, shuddered. There was no way he would touch it now. "I'll come over and pick it up in a few minutes."

Inky's eyes held a question, but he nodded. "Door's open anytime." They left.

Sophie smiled, triumphant. "We gonna keep Dolly," she said.

I smiled back. "I never had any doubt." Sophie had won. She always did.

"What do you have planned today?" I hoped she didn't want me to entertain her. Not that I minded spending time with her, but I had to give my statement to the police, then I was scheduled to go back to Gladys's to help with boxing up the artifacts. Oh, and I needed to talk to my bio-mom.

Sophie stared at me. I held my ground, managing not to squirm. She let me off the hook. "Marina is starting to pack up her house today. I'm gonna help. Then we got our bus trip."

The Turning Stone Casino would never be the same. "When does she go back to Greece?"

"Next week. She's got a hot date over there—Dimitrios Papadopoulos. He been waiting for her to come back."

"I have some errands to run today. I probably won't be back until dinnertime or later."

She stared at me again, most likely waiting for me to tell her what those errands were. When I didn't oblige, she said, "I'll eat with Marina. We gotta clean out her fridge."

"Do you need a ride?" Sophie could drive, but preferred not to. And Bonaparte Bay was always safer if she didn't get behind the wheel of her enormous Lincoln.

"No, I'll have Spiro drive me, or maybe that Inky guy. You go on." She headed toward the spiral staircase that led to our living quarters upstairs, then turned back. "Stay out of trouble."

I smiled. "I'll try."

I dialed Melanie's number. The phone rang, then made a little beep and rang again.

"Caitlyn Black." The voice had a slight edge to it, as though she were keyed up. I guess I'd be keyed up if I had to put up with a diva like Melanie. If Melanie really were in financial trouble, I hoped Caitlyn was still getting paid because she deserved every penny she made.

"Hi, Caitlyn, it's Georgie. Is Melanie there? I've had an invitation to lunch at one of the big houses and you two are invited to join us."

There was a pause at the other end of the line. "She's having her American ginseng infusion bath right now, then she's scheduled for a massage. Let me check with her." Music began to play, the schmaltzy orchestral theme song from *The Desperate and the Defiant*, when she put me on hold. She came back on the line a moment later.

"Melanie says she doesn't feel like it. Just between us, she's been in a bit of a state since we got here. She's upset about her cousin."

I'm sure she is, I thought. But was she upset because Doreen was dead? Or because Doreen was dead and Melanie had somehow caused her death? No, until I had some kind of proof, I had to believe my mother was not a cold-blooded killer. Could I get more information out of Caitlyn? Only one way to find out.

"So," I began. "We haven't really had a chance to talk. What brings you two to Bonaparte Bay after Melanie's long absence?"

There was silence on the other end of the line. Caitlyn was all business when she responded. "I go where Melanie goes. She doesn't always confide in me. And I don't expect her to."

Well, drat. Melanie had found herself a discreet assistant. I was disappointed at not learning more, but I had to admire Caitlyn's professionalism.

"If you change your mind about going to lunch, call me. It's at one of the big Victorians and the house is spectacular. I'm sure Melanie would like to see it."

"Hold on, she's yelling for me." The soap opera orchestra played again, then Caitlyn came back on the line. "She wants to know whose house it is. Whether it's somebody famous."

Why wasn't I surprised? "No, nobody famous. A kind woman named Gladys Montgomery."

Caitlyn didn't bother to put me on hold this time as she repeated the name to Melanie. I heard a faint splashing noise, then an emphatic "No."

"She says no."

"I heard her. All right. Why don't you schedule her to

come over to the mainland tomorrow? She needs to go check on that bracelet she's having made and we need to plan Doreen's funeral." *And I need to talk to her*, I thought.

"I'll see what I can do," she said, and clicked off.

The call had barely ended when the back doorbell rang. I shoved the phone into the pocket of my jeans and opened the door, just in time to see a brown uniform walking back to a matching brown delivery truck. A package lay at my feet. The return address revealed that it was a shipment from the independent bookstore in Vermont that I liked so much, but rarely got to. I checked the mailbox and the day's post had been delivered, so I picked that up too and went inside to deposit everything on my desk. I thumbed through the mail. An envelope made of thick creamy paper was at the bottom of the stack. The return address, *MacNamara and MacNamara*, was embossed in pretentious black cursive letters.

If my divorce lawyer spent a little less on stationery, he wouldn't have to charge me a couple hundred bucks an hour. I had to sell a lot of baklava to afford James Benjamin Mac-Namara Jr. I'd have to sell twice as many to afford his father.

I tore open the envelope. *Dear Ms. Nikolopatos. Please make an appointment to come to our offices and sign paperwork pertaining to your legal matters. Sincerely, James Benjamin MacNamara Jr.*

Really? A tree had to give its life when JB Jr.'s assistant, Lydia Ames, could have just picked up the phone and called me? Or maybe this paper was made of cotton, not wood. Whatever. The law firm billed in six-minute increments, so this was costing me at least twenty desserts.

I tossed everything on my desk, then picked up my purse and headed out the door.

First stop, Spinky's.

The back door was unlocked as I entered the kitchen. Construction debris littered the black-and-white-tiled floor, and boxes were stacked high around the perimeter of the room. Noises like furniture being moved came from the front of the house, so I assumed Spiro and Inky had workers in rearranging the booths they'd just had reupholstered in cherry red vinyl. I was tempted to go in and take a look to see how they'd come out, but I was running behind as it was.

I scanned the room. There was the big industrial-sized roll of plastic wrap, sitting in its box on the prep counter. The lid was open. The roll inside looked to be about half full, maybe a little more. My initial thought had been to bag this up, without touching it directly, and take it with me to my meeting with the state troopers. Now, I realized that wasn't a good idea. Kind of stupid, really. I didn't want to contaminate any evidence, or smudge any fingerprints that might be on it. But I didn't want anyone here touching it either. I wondered if it had already been moved.

I pulled a piece of paper out of my purse and scribbled a quick note: *Don't touch.* Then I draped the clean trashbag I'd brought with me over the box, and left the note on top. I wondered if the police had investigated inside or only the outside crime scene.

An hour later I'd given my statement. The detective—not Lieutenant Hawthorne—was nonplussed about the plastic wrap, but I saw him jotting something down in a small spiral-bound notebook. I told him where they could find Melanie, and that she'd be in town tomorrow night.

I dropped my car at the Bonaparte House, then sat on a bench on the dock to wait for Jack while I reviewed my mental to-do list. I had just ended a call with Clive at the funeral home, arranging a meeting tomorrow to discuss the details, when Jack pulled up.

His movie-star good looks gave me a little thrill. "Hello there, gorgeous," he said, offering me a hand. "Let's head out to Gladys's place. I need to get this project done today so I can deliver everything to Trish this weekend."

"And I need to get back to the Bonaparte House this afternoon so I can start the prep work for the weekend. Moussaka waits for no one."

He smiled. "But would you wait for me?"

What did that mean? "Wait for what?"

His face was inscrutable and there was a firm set to his jaw. "Oh, wait for me to kiss you once we get out of town and out on the water."

Somehow, I didn't think that was what he really meant.

Twenty minutes later, and after some kissing that lived up to its promise, we had pulled up at Gladys's dock. We unloaded the extra plastic boxes Jack had bought and Gladys directed us to put them in the library.

"I can't tell you how much I appreciate this, you two," Gladys said. She brushed a bit of flour off her apron, which was light blue with a pattern of red hearts. "Lunch will be ready in about an hour, so go ahead and get started and I'll call you for a break." She set a silver tray containing a crystal pitcher and glasses on the table. "Help yourself to lemonade while you work. I made it fresh this morning." My mouth puckered. Real lemonade was such a treat. And it was oddly touching that Gladys had brought out the good crystal just for us. Although at her age, why not use the good stuff all the time?

Jack dropped a light kiss on the top of her head and managed not to mess up any of her white curls, which looked freshly set. A light scent of White Shoulders wafted toward me. Still a lovely perfume—old-fashioned and feminine. I never wore it myself, but I appreciated it on other people.

"Off you go," Jack said. "Leave this to us." Gladys retreated to the kitchen and my stomach growled as I wondered what manner of scrumptiousness she was preparing.

In the library, Jack opened the boxes and inserted the plastic dividers. I poured us two tall glasses of lemonade, making sure each glass had a slice of lemon and lots of ice, then set to work cutting bubble wrap and cotton batting into assorted-size pieces. When I had a pile, we donned gloves so the oil from our skin wouldn't alter the artifacts. Jack handed me an arrowhead, which I carefully wrapped and handed back to him. He placed the hand-numbered card from the display case, yellowed with age, into one of the compartments of the box, then took the wrapped piece from me and placed it atop the card.

We work well together, I thought as we developed a rhythm and made good time filling up the first box. Jack snapped on the lid and we moved on. I couldn't ever remember sharing a project with Spiro in the twenty years we were married, so the sensation was new. And I liked it.

It didn't take long for us to empty the first two display

cases. I stood up and stretched, then rolled my head side to side to stretch out my neck muscles.

"That wasn't so bad, was it? One more case to go, then we're done."

Before I could answer, Gladys appeared in the doorway. She'd removed her apron to reveal a pair of nicely tailored charcoal trousers and a sweater twin set in a lovely shade of orchid that made her bright blue eyes stand out even more. On her feet she wore pristine white tennis shoes, the same brand that Sophie wore if I wasn't mistaken. The effect was charming. Style and comfort. "Lunch is on the table."

I peeled off my gloves and set them on one of the side tables. "I'd like to wash up before we eat. Could you show me to the powder room?"

"Of course, dear! I should have thought. Those artifacts must be dusty. Nothing's been out of the case for years, other than the fake warclub. That's not going to Trish, by the way. That was just Herman's idea of a joke. Jack, you can use the bathroom upstairs, or just wash up in the kitchen sink."

I followed her down the richly paneled hall. She indicated a dark oak door. "In there," she said. "I'll start dishing up and you can join us when you're ready."

"You have a lovely home here, Gladys." Despite the dark Victorian splendor, the house managed an air of coziness.

"Thank you, dear." An enigmatic smile appeared on her face. "Take your time."

The powder room was fairly small and contained the usual accoutrements. A large window, framed in gleaming natural woodwork, took up more than half of the wall nearest the toilet. I turned on the tap and let the water run until it was warm, squirted some lavender soap into my palm, and scrubbed my hands. I dried them on the towel hanging on the wall.

Movement outside drew my attention to the window. I pulled apart two slats of the wooden venetian blinds and peeked out. My eyes scanned an expanse of green lawn to a chain-link fence that was partially covered in dark purple morning glories, still hanging on this late in the season since we hadn't had a frost yet. The fence appeared to contain an in-ground swimming pool.

Standing in front of the fence were two figures, who appeared to be deep in conversation. I squinted as a ray of midday sun illuminated them. The woman had her back to me. The man was tall, dark-haired, and dressed in shorts and a polo shirt. He looked vaguely familiar and I racked my brain trying to remember where I'd seen him. Liza's. At the Spa. What was his name?

Channing. What the hell was he doing here?

The woman turned her head. A pair of black-framed glasses appeared in profile. I sucked in a breath, then reached for the wall to steady myself.

It was Caitlyn Black.

◈ TEN ◈

What the heck were these two doing here? What could they possibly have to talk about? When I looked through the space in the blinds again, Caitlyn was gone and Channing was inside the pool enclosure, where his movements were obscured by the fence and the flowers.

If Caitlyn was here, did that mean Melanie was lurking around somewhere? I pulled my cell phone out of my pocket and fired off a quick text to Liza at the Spa.

Where is Melanie?

A moment later my phone chimed, indicating a reply.

I just saw her in the facial room getting an herbal steam treatment. Do you need to talk to her?

No. Just checking in. I'll catch up with her later.

What's going on?

I wondered that myself.

Nothing. Thanks.

Come over to the Spa sometime. I miss you.

Aw. We hadn't seen each other in a couple of weeks, and I missed her too.

Me too. I'll see you soon.

So Melanie was at the Spa, but Caitlyn was here, as was Channing. They'd been standing close together—a romantic tryst? Nothing against Caitlyn, but that guy was *Gentlemen's Quarterly* material and she didn't seem his type. Had they somehow followed us here? I couldn't think of a single plausible reason to explain what I'd just seen.

And where had Caitlyn gone?

I ran outside. Caitlyn was nowhere in sight. There was no sign of a car other than a full-size red pickup truck, which I assumed was Channing's. Nothing to see here, folks, so I made my way to the kitchen, where Jack and Gladys were at the table, laughing.

A heavenly aroma wafted up and filled my nostrils. A white bowl was full of steaming dark red tomato soup. Next to it on a matching plate was a buttery grilled cheese sandwich, and in the middle of the table sat a plate of peeled apples that had been dusted in cinnamon sugar. All thoughts of Caitlyn left my mind as I spooned up some of the soup. It was thick, chunky with bits of caramelized onion and full of fresh garlic, with, I thought, a base of rich chicken stock and a hint of cream. The sandwich had been conveniently cut into quarters, the thick yellow cheese oozing out the sides. I dipped a corner of one piece into the soup and wondered if I'd died and gone to heaven. I looked up to find Jack and Gladys watching me with amused expressions.

"Pretty good, huh?" Jack said. Gladys seemed pleased.

I was only a little embarrassed at being caught enjoying the food-porn in front of me. "Best tomato soup ever," I said, turning to Gladys. "Will the directions for this be in the recipe box you gave me?"

"Of course."

Mental fist-pump. Would she let me serve this at the Bonaparte House if I gave her credit on the menu? Then I remembered what I'd witnessed out the bathroom window.

"Gladys, I saw someone out at your pool just now. A man." I decided to leave Caitlyn out of it for now.

She looked thoughtful. "Oh, that must be Channing." She took a sip of her water and dabbed daintily at her lips with the cloth napkin she pulled from her lap. "He's here to close up the pool."

Pool. Liza also had an outdoor pool at the Spa, so that would explain his presence in both places. I'd gotten the impression at Liza's that he was some sort of eye-candy handyman, which still made sense. People in the Bay had to be generalists rather than specialists to make a living.

"I could have done that for you, you know," Jack admonished Gladys. "You don't have to pay somebody to do that kind of thing when I'm around."

Gladys smiled and patted his hand. "That's sweet of you, Jack, really. But I've got plenty of money and I like to keep local people employed if I can. I've been using him and his father before him for years."

So Channing had a legitimate reason for being in the backyard. But that didn't explain Caitlyn's presence. How had she gotten here? Liza had a couple of boats that she used to ferry guests back and forth to the mainland. Caitlyn and Melanie must have a rented car somewhere.

We made quick work of our soup and sandwiches. I reached for a slice of apple, then let the spiced sugar melt on my tongue. September and October are apple season, and New York State produces some of the best around. I bit into the flesh. It was crisp and juicy at the same time, an heirloom Esopus Spitzenburg, I thought.

"So," Gladys interrupted our crunching. "Jack, I've had an idea. Feel free to say no."

Jack raised an eyebrow, then smiled. "You know I can't refuse you anything, Glad."

She patted his arm. "Did your permanent transfer come through with the Coast Guard? Where are you living?"

"The transfer's in the works, though I'm close to my twenty years and I need to decide whether to reenlist. I've been living in an apartment over the Suds-a-Rama. Why? Do you want to come and be my live-in cook?"

"No, no, but don't tempt me. I've got my casino trip coming up, and I'm due back in Florida. But I was thinking. I usually shut up this house for the winter. Maybe you'd like to move in here? It's got to be more comfortable than your apartment. And the fellow I usually have check on the house once a week while I'm gone is going in for back surgery and he'll be laid up all winter. So you'd be doing me a favor."

Jack looked thoughtful. "That is a very tempting offer. Are you sure? I didn't get in touch with you to freeload."

Take the house! I silently cheered. Selfishly, I wanted him near me. And this place was beautiful.

"You're not freeloading if I suggest it. And if you want to earn your keep, you can paint the upstairs bedrooms. I'll leave a list of projects I'd like done, how's that?"

"Oh, so *you're* taking advantage of *me*." He laughed. "Gladys Montgomery, you've got yourself a deal."

A self-satisfied smile appeared on her face. She reminded me of Sophie, who always got what she wanted too. "Now go get back to work, you two. I'll take care of the dishes."

We worked methodically, finishing up the wrapping and packing. The display cases sat empty, looking forlorn. I thought about Mr. Montgomery and hoped he was happy that his life's work was going to a museum where the collection could be studied and cared for properly.

Now that the work was done but for carrying out the boxes, I had a moment to examine some of the framed photographs on the wall above the cases. Most were eight-by-tens and five-by-sevens, all black-and-white and framed in a mishmash of styles. Monty, at least I assume it was Monty, had been a handsome fellow, with fair hair and sleeves rolled up to reveal muscular forearms. In one of the pictures he had one of those arms thrown around the shoulders of a lovely woman with dark hair. I looked closer. It had to be Gladys. I smiled. They looked so happy.

Jack took a stack of boxes and carried them out.

Gladys came from behind and stood next to me. "He was a good man," she said.

"He must have been," I agreed.

"Of course, our families didn't want us to marry."

I looked at her with surprise. "Why not?"

"Well, I came from a large family. We were poor, but we got by. Monty came from money and they didn't think I was good enough for him. His mother was a Bloodworth."

"A Bloodworth?" The name meant nothing to me.

"One of the old families in these parts. Not that Monty ever saw any of their money. He, and his father before him, were self-made men."

I glanced around. My eyes came to rest on the Remington bronze—not exactly priceless, but worth a good chunk of change. The house and land were probably worth close to a million dollars by now.

Jack came back in for another load. "My ears are burning. Are you two talking about me again?"

"Wouldn't you like to know?" Gladys said sweetly.

Jack dropped a kiss on Gladys's head. "I'm glad I'm taking you up on the offer to move in here for the winter. It's quite a bit nicer than my digs over the Suds-a-Rama. And quieter too."

She seemed delighted. "Wonderful! Thanks to you, I won't have to go to the trouble of shutting up the house. Move your things in anytime."

Jack turned to me. "Are you ready, Georgie? We should get going."

I gave Gladys a hug. She was such a sweet woman. "Thank you for lunch, Gladys."

She waved her hand. "You're very welcome. It was a small price to pay for your lovely company and your help with Monty's collection. It's a relief to have that taken care of."

"And thank you again for the recipes. I can't wait to start looking through them."

We piled into the boat and motored back to Bonaparte Bay. When we were just passing the Edgewood Resort, my cell phone buzzed in my pocket. I pulled it out and looked at the screen. Spiro. What could my almost-ex want? I remembered I'd promised to find him a cook. Well, if that was what he was calling about, I had nothing to say. I'd call him back later.

At the dock we unloaded the boxes into Jack's car. Brenda was making her afternoon returnable can and bottle rounds. Her hair was a strawberry blond today—she never seemed to be able to settle on a hair color, but it was always a shade of red. The pickings had been slim for her, apparently, because she only had a couple of small bags filled up. Not surprising. This time of year the only tourists we got came on the weekend.

She waved me over.

Jack smiled. "This is my cue to leave. Brenda wants to talk with you. Consider yourself kissed."

"Consider yourself kissed too." I felt a little stab. This was ridiculous. I was a grown woman and I was hiding—and not doing such a hot job of it—my relationship with a perfectly suitable guy.

He folded down the backseat of his Jeep Wrangler and finished loading the boxes, which barely fit in the small compartment, and left.

I made my way over to Brenda. "How's it going?" I asked.

"Can't complain," she said. "Business will pick up this weekend."

"What can I do for you?"

She rearranged some cans that had fallen over, then looked up at me. "Just so you know, your mother-in-law asked me to keep an eye on you again."

I rolled my eyes. This wasn't the first time Sophie had asked Brenda to spy on me. I couldn't even work up any anger about it—too much else was going on. "Did she pay you enough?"

Brenda smiled. Her teeth were a bit crooked, but her smile lit up her face. "Not enough for me not to tell you about it."

I wondered if she wanted something in return. We'd sort of bonded during my last adventure. Underneath the bad hair and the uneducated veneer, there was a savvy businesswoman that I'd grown to admire. She was far more intelligent than anybody, including me up until a few weeks ago, gave her credit for. Something occurred to me. Caitlyn and Melanie.

"You know we've got a celebrity in town?"

She shrugged, but her eyes were calculating. "Sure. That Melanie Ashley from the soaps."

"Have you seen her?"

Brenda looked thoughtful, then reached into her cart and rearranged some of her hoard. "Not her. But that girl she's traveling with. She's been back and forth from the Spa. She's driving a black Beemer with tinted windows and she comes and goes from the public parking lot. Always playing with her phone." Brenda shook open a fresh trash bag. "Unfriendly."

"Thanks."

"Anytime."

I walked back to the Bonaparte House, mulling over everything Brenda had told me. An hour later, after processing some paperwork for the restaurant and running some more Internet searches on Melanie, I was still mulling, more determined than ever to find out exactly what my mother and her assistant were doing in Bonaparte Bay. I pulled out my cell to call her, just as it started to buzz. Jack. "Hi. Did you miss me?" I wasn't practiced at flirting, but I gave it the old college try.

"Of course," he said. "But that's not why I called." There was a pause. "My apartment's been broken into."

I gulped. A memory of my own home being broken into flashed through my mind and I remembered the sick feeling of violation it had engendered. "Was anything taken?"

"Well, I haven't moved everything from my storage unit from my place in Oswego, so there's not a lot here. Just clothes, bedding, and some beer in the fridge." He paused. "I went out to run some errands, and when I returned, I must have spooked whoever it was. I heard someone on the fire escape as I came in. He was gone by the time I got to the door and out onto the stairs."

My heart leapt into my throat. I willed myself to calm down. Petty thefts happened all the time in the Bay, though less frequently when the tourists weren't around. "Are you okay?"

"I'm fine. But I can't say the same for Monty's files. They're scattered all over my living room floor."

◆ ELEVEN ◆

I frowned. "Monty's files? What would anyone want with a bunch of old paperwork about arrowheads?"

"Exactly," Jack said. "I'd barely gotten the boxes unloaded from my Jeep, so I have to think the guy was watching me, waiting until I left. The collection is fairly large, but it's not terribly valuable monetarily. To a scholar like my sister, yes. But the items themselves are relatively common."

"Does it look like any of the files were taken?"

"I can't tell. I don't think so. But the only way to know for sure is to go through them and put them back together. Trish will kill me if any of the documentation is missing."

"Did you call the police?"

"Just before I called you. They don't seem concerned, just asked me to come down and fill out a report later. It's probably a waste of time. I think whoever it was got mad there was nothing in the apartment worth stealing and just decided to be destructive."

That made sense. I reviewed what I had to do that afternoon. "I need to get Melanie over here, then go see Clive at the funeral home about Doreen. I could come over tonight and help you sort out the papers."

Jack laughed. "You shameless minx. I've never heard it called that before."

I was glad he couldn't see the flush that crept up my neck and face. "Oh, stop. You know what I mean."

"I do. But I couldn't help myself. How does tomorrow look? Some of the guys from the Bay Coast Guard Station asked me out for a beer, and I thought it would be a good way to get to know them."

It was still a novelty to me that Jack had asked for a transfer. I sorta, kinda hoped it was because of me, but I did my best not to read too much into it. Still, if he was making friends here, there was a better chance he'd want to stay.

"Sounds good. Tomorrow Dolly and I will have to get the food prepped for the weekend service at the restaurant, but we can do that in the morning. Then I'll have the afternoon free."

"See you then. I'll try not to be hungover." He laughed and rang off.

I checked the display on my screen. Good. Enough battery left to call Melanie. She picked up herself without letting the call roll over to the wandering Caitlyn.

"Hello." Her voice held the barest nervous edge.

"It's Georgie. You're coming over to the mainland this afternoon, right? We have a meeting with the funeral home, and we should go to the bank and let them know about Doreen. I assume she had her account here in town."

Silence, then a long exhale. "Can't you just take care of it? I don't know anyone in town anymore."

Maybe you shouldn't have stayed away for two decades, I thought. You might know people. Like your own grand- daughter.

"No, Melanie, I cannot just take care of it. You are named as Doreen's executrix in the will, so you're the only one who can act officially." A thought struck me and I wondered why it hadn't occurred to me before. "Why exactly would Doreen leave everything to you anyway? According to the police, she knew your new name. Seems odd, considering even I didn't know it."

There was another dramatic pause. "Fine. I'll explain it when I see you. Let me see if I can get us a ride over around two o'clock."

"Don't worry. Caitlyn knows how to get a ride." Would she take the bait?

"Of course she does. She's very capable. Not that I like to tell her that very often. She'll get complacent."

That got me nowhere. I'd just have to wait and confront her later.

"Fine. Two o'clock. Meet me here at the restaurant." I hung up.

I had an hour to kill, and it was a beautiful fall day, so I decided to take a walk. The Bay's shops were mostly closed up as I passed them, but by the weekend they'd be bustling with tourists as long as the weather held. My friend Midge Binford waved to me from the door of the T-Shirt Empo- rium, so I stopped in.

"Hey, Georgie. Seems like ages since I've seen you." She shook out a long-sleeve T-shirt and refolded it so that "Bonaparte Bay—Heart of the Thousand Islands" was visible, then stacked it neatly onto a pile of similar items. "What's new?"

I couldn't even begin to answer that. "Oh, not too much. Getting ready to close up for the season, same as you. I was just going up to the Bean for a quick latte. Want to join me?"

She looked around the shop. "Why not? This stuff will be here when I get back. Let's go."

The Bay's coffee shop was located a block or two up Theresa Street. Its bright green door picked up the green of the letters overhead: "Express-o Bean." I ordered a vanilla latte with extra foam and a sprinkle of cinnamon. Midge opted for a cappuccino. We took our drinks outside and sat at a metal-mesh bistro table.

"How'd your season go?" I asked between slurps. "We did all right at the Bonaparte House."

Midge tucked an errant strand of glossy brown hair behind her ear, showcasing a rose gold hoop earring that glowed pink in the autumn sunshine. I'd seen a similar pair in Roger's Jewelry Shoppe. "Oh, can't complain. The economy seems to be picking up and the Canadian dollar is close to par, so there've been lots of people from across the border."

I nodded. Most businesses in town took Canadian money at par, meaning that one Canadian dollar equaled one American dollar, regardless of the current exchange rate. Some years we made money on the deal, others we lost. It was just part of doing business along the international border. "What's new with you, Midge? Is Jennifer settled in at Cornell?"

"Oh, yes. She couldn't wait to get back to school. Thank

goodness for scholarships, though. Otherwise I'd never be able to afford to send her there." She frowned. "It's not like I get any help from her father."

Midge had been divorced for years from her alcoholic ex-husband. I knew it had been tough for her until she got the shop up and running. As strange as my own family situation was, at least I'd never had to worry about money or our physical safety, and Spiro was a loving father to our daughter. Things could have been a whole lot worse.

"Cal's in Greece." I missed her, no sense in denying it. "I'm not sure when she's coming back."

Midge patted my hand. "Well, you'll just have to take a trip over there, then. Once we close up after Columbus Day, I'm taking a road trip to see Kevin out in Seattle."

"Seattle? Is that where he ended up?" Midge's son was some kind of computer genius, so I was sure he'd landed a very good job out of college. "That's a long drive by yourself," I said.

She blushed ferociously as though she'd just walked naked into a biker bar. "Uh, I'm not going by myself."

Interesting! "Are you seeing someone?" I asked, racking my brain to recall if I'd heard any rumors. Nope.

Midge shifted in her seat, then leaned forward. "Well, we're not exactly advertising it, but I've been spending some time with Roger and, well, I like him."

A broad smile plastered itself on my lips. "Of course. I'm so happy for you! Roger's a sweetheart." The fact that he owned a jewelry store was a nice little perk, not that I'd say that to Midge. She deserved to be happy, and I was thrilled for her.

"So," she said. "Let's change the subject. Have you heard anything more about the murder? Poor Doreen."

My ears perked up. "Did you know her? I've been sort of put in charge of handling her arrangements—it turns out we're related, though I don't remember ever meeting her. And I'll need to put together some kind of lunch at the restaurant for after the funeral."

Midge looked at me thoughtfully. "Hmmm. I knew her through Paloma—you know, Paloma Martinez that worked for me over the summer? She worked in the cafeteria with Doreen during the school year."

"Would Paloma know who Doreen's friends are, do you think? I wouldn't want to miss anybody I should notify." And if my mother decided not to be entirely forthcoming about her return to the Bay and her sudden inheritance, Paloma might be able to shed a little light on things.

Midge smiled. "I don't see why not. Walk me back to the Emporium and I'll give you her number."

We rose. "Yes, time for me to get going too. I've got to run over to the lawyer's and sign some paperwork before I go to the funeral home." We picked up our empty cups and dropped them in the trash can.

A few minutes later, phone number written on the back of a business card and stuck in my pocket, I made my way in the opposite direction and a couple of blocks away from downtown. The law offices of MacNamara and MacNamara were located in a two-story Queen Anne–style Victorian sided in white clapboards with black shutters framing each tall, narrow window. I climbed up on the porch past planters full of red geraniums and trailing ivy. Clearly they were covering the plants at night to protect them from the cold. Dolly had replaced the Bonaparte House annuals with mums a couple of weeks ago. I opened the big red door and walked into a rather narrow hallway.

The reception area was in a room to my right. Behind the desk sat Lydia Ames, MacNamara the Younger's assistant. She'd eaten at the restaurant last weekend (souvlaki and Greek salad, if I recalled correctly), and I'd comped her a dessert. Since I was pretty sure she did most of the work in this place, for not enough pay, I figured it didn't hurt to keep her on my good side so she'd keep things moving along with my divorce.

Lydia looked up from her computer screen and gave me a big smile. "Hi, Georgie. You here to sign your divorce paperwork? Just have a seat and give me a second to finish up something here and then I'll find your file."

I sat down in one of the visitor's chairs and rummaged around on the table until I found a Hollywood gossip magazine. I thought about wrapping it up inside a *Smithsonian* or a *National Geographic* to disguise the cover, but figured what the hell. So what if I liked gossip? I was hardly the only one. I flipped through absentmindedly. My eyes landed on a familiar head of thick blond hair and a set of scarlet collagen-plumped lips. Melanie. Mom. *Melanie Ashley, star of* The Desperate and the Defiant, *puts Bel Air mansion up for sale*.

Hmmm. I could hardly give *Celebrity Update!* credit for Pulitzer Prize–winning journalism, but still. This was the second mention of Melanie's financial difficulties I'd found. I thought of Doreen, who had told Inky that she was going to be coming into some money. And now Doreen was dead and Melanie was her sole beneficiary. I still didn't like where this was headed.

Lydia motioned me over. As I approached the desk, it occurred to me that there was a legal process that had to be gone through to carry out Doreen's will. Might as well kill two birds with one stone. "Lydia, when someone dies, what do the relatives have to do? Legally, I mean."

She rummaged around in her pencil cup and pulled out a blue pen, then opened a manila file folder. "Is there a will?" When I nodded, she continued. "The will would have to be submitted to the probate court. There's a lot of paperwork to be filled out, including inventories of real estate and personal property. Once that's all prepared and submitted, it takes a few months for everything to go through, then the assets are distributed to the heirs according to the will."

I decided to level with her, sort of. "You know Doreen Webber? The woman who was murdered? The executrix of her estate happens to be in town and I'm helping her sort things out. What do we need to do to get the ball rolling?"

Lydia tapped the pen on the mahogany desk. "You know, I'm pretty sure we prepared Doreen's will—and not that long ago either. Call me later and I'll pull the file. Will the executrix want to have the MacNamaras probate the will?"

Might as well. It would be easier than going to one of the law firms in Watertown twenty miles away. "Sure. I'll bring her by. Now, what is it I need to sign?"

She handed me the manila folder. "It's the formal separation agreement. You and Spiro sign it, we submit it to the court, and in a few weeks the divorce can be finalized. Just read it over and make sure the division of property is the same as you understand it."

I sat down and scanned the document. Because I had been taking a salary to manage the restaurant all these years and had lived well within my means, I had a fair amount of savings and a retirement account. Those I'd get to keep. I wasn't getting much else, but the fact was that Spiro didn't technically own anything but his clothes and his Mercedes. Sophie owned the restaurant and all its contents. She also owned the business itself, as well as all the property in Greece. I could have fought for a share of everything upon Sophie's death, but that could take years to sort out. And it seemed wrong. Sophie could do what she liked with her money and possessions. She had told me that her will provided amply for Spiro, but that the bulk of her estate would go into trust for Callista. And that suited me just fine. Still, I felt like I was signing away a piece of myself as I scribbled my signature on the line Lydia indicated. The end of one era and the beginning of another.

"That's that," Lydia said sympathetically.

"Thanks for all your help." I picked up my purse and prepared to leave.

At that moment, the inner door opened. An arm wearing a dark sleeve held open the door while an older woman passed in front of him.

"Gladys?" I blurted out.

She looked startled, then her face broke out into a broad smile. "Georgie! What a coincidence. I'm just here to take care of a few items before I leave for Florida."

"We have to stop meeting like this," I joked.

"Well, I'll be off. Benjamin, thank you. I know the trust is in good hands."

James Benjamin MacNamara Jr. helped Gladys put on her light jacket. He was clean-cut and good-looking in a preppy way. Only a year or so out of law school, he might have made a good catch for Callista. But there was something about him that rubbed me the wrong way—just a little. Not that I could put my finger on it.

He gave me a boyish grin. "Did Lydia give you the paperwork, Ms. Nikolopatos—or will you be going back to your maiden name?"

"Uh, yes. All signed." There was another decision that needed to be made. It had been a long time since I'd been Georgiana Bartlett. Would it bother Cal if I took back my name? I'd have to broach the subject with her.

"Good, good." His voice held a slightly smarmy edge, as though he thought he was just a little bit better than I was. Well, he wasn't above coming into my restaurant and sucking down ouzo-tinis with his flavor-of-the-week girlfriends. Yet more reason to keep him away from my daughter.

◆ TWELVE ◆

I hustled back to the Bonaparte House. Melanie was sitting at the employee picnic table out back, drumming the long gel nails of one hand on the wood. The other hand was inside her Fendi purse and she kept glancing around as though she were looking for someone. And she didn't look happy at being kept waiting. *Ha!* I thought. *Try being kept waiting for twenty years when your mother abandons you.*

"Hey, Melanie. I suppose you want to drive to the funeral home? I can't see you walking three blocks in those heels."

"Yes, I do want to drive," she huffed. "Why can't you do this? I was just starting to relax at your friend's spa." "Starting" being the operative word here. She didn't seem to have gotten very far. She removed her hand from her bag and picked it up by only one strap, spilling some of the contents. A can of pepper spray fell out. She hurriedly grabbed at it and shoved it back in the bag.

"Uh, do you have a permit for that?" Did she need one?

"Isn't this the boondocks? Is a permit really necessary here for anything?" She zipped up the bag and teetered toward my car.

"This is New York State, not the Wild West."

"Then it's a good thing I bought this legally. Now get in the car and let's get this over with," she snapped.

Ooh, someone was cranky. And armed. Potentially not a good combination. I frowned. No, Doreen had been strangled, and I was pretty sure pepper spray wouldn't kill you, just hurt a lot. Somehow, that didn't make me feel any better.

We drove the few blocks to the funeral home. "So, Mel, where's Caitlyn?"

"Caitlyn? We're not joined at the hip, you know. I left her back on the island. I had a few tasks I needed her to finish."

"Did you actually see her before you left?" I could feel Melanie's eyes boring into the side of my face as I drove.

"What kind of question is that? Of course I saw her. She must have been outside in the sun because her face was red. I keep reminding her she needs to wear sunscreen every time she goes outside if she wants to have a good complexion like mine. Why?" she demanded.

"Oh, no reason." Liza didn't just lend out boats to her guests, so unless Caitlyn was an Olympic-caliber swimmer, somebody on that island ferried her back and forth. The likely suspect, of course, was Channing, the pool guy I'd seen her talking to at Gladys's house. But Channing was still working on Gladys's pool when Jack and I had left and Caitlyn was nowhere to be seen. It was possible she'd gotten herself back to the Spa in time to see Melanie before she left for her meeting with me, but it would have been tight. It was also possible she'd rented herself a small boat.

A few minutes later we were seated in Clive's office, tastefully and simply decorated in shades of pale green and white. A creamy-colored sculpture of a pair of praying hands sat on the credenza behind him, next to a bouquet of flowers in autumn colors.

Melanie just sat there, so I began. "Clive, this is Melanie Ashley. She and I are apparently Doreen's only next of kin. Do you have the body from the coroner yet?" A sick lump formed in the pit of my stomach. I hoped she hadn't suffered.

"Yes, she's here." Clive offered Melanie a piece of paper with a gold seal that glinted as it came toward her. She just sat there with her lips set in a hard line, so I took the paper.

Clive shrugged. "Death certificate. You'll need that to handle her affairs, pay her bills, collect on any life insurance policy she may have had, etc."

I glanced at Melanie to see if she had any reaction to the mention of an insurance policy, but it didn't appear to faze her. Well, she was an actress.

"So what do we need to do, Clive? I've never gone through this process before."

He nodded sympathetically. "The first thing is to schedule the calling hours and the funeral. I assume you'll want those on separate days? People usually have the calling hours one night and the funeral and committal the next. Unless it's winter and the ground is frozen, of course, then the committal would be in the spring. But we don't have to worry about that. Are there family coming in from out of town that need to be accommodated?"

I shook my head. "What about an obituary? We should put something in the *Bay Blurb* and the *Watertown Daily Times*, right?"

"Yes," Clive said. "We usually write that up here and send it in to the papers. I'll get some information from you before you leave."

Good luck, I thought. I knew nothing about poor Doreen. Melanie was just going to have to step up to the plate here.

We decided to hold the calling hours tomorrow evening, with the funeral the next morning. I'd have to call Dolly in early to prep the luncheon, and a couple of local servers to man the buffet line, but I was pretty sure none of them would mind the extra hours and I would pay them well for the short notice. Sophie would probably pitch in. My baklava was passable, but hers was perfection.

Within the hour we'd chosen a casket—who knew those were so expensive?—given Clive enough information to write the obituary, and determined that there was room for Doreen to be buried in her parents' plot at the Bayview Cemetery. Melanie handed Clive a credit card for the deposit. He jotted down the numbers and expiration date, presumably to run it later. I hoped the transaction would go through, considering the potential state of Melanie's financial affairs. Well, I was sure Clive would let me know if there was a problem, and I'd cover it if I had to.

I checked my watch as we headed to the car. It was too late to go to the bank now. It had been a long and busy day, and I was beginning to get tired. But there was still a lot of work to be done.

Someone was in the car parked behind mine. He got out and came toward us, camera in hand.

Oh, heck. Spencer Kane.

"Quick, Melanie. Get in the car if you don't want your picture taken."

She went wolverine on him. "I told you I'd give you an interview when I'm ready. Well, I'm not ready. Go away," she said through the half-opened window.

He grinned. "Pictures are worth more than an interview, you know. And I've already gotten some."

Her eyes narrowed as far as they could go. Which was not that far considering the eye lifts. "Maybe you'd like to take a picture of me and my lawyer. Because he's going to be very familiar to you if you don't leave me alone. Trust me when I say I'm not in the mood."

"Aw, Mel—or should I say Shirley? Don't be that way. You're breaking my fragile heart." He flipped open his notebook and poised a mechanical pencil over it. "So what brings you back into town just when your cousin gets killed? There's a story there."

"No. Comment." Her teeth were clamped tight. "Back up, reporter. We're leaving." She rolled up the window and turned to me. "Drive."

Spencer backed away from the car, but not before giving me a serious look that didn't quite match the lighthearted tone he'd taken with Melanie.

Hmmm. I pulled out.

"Melanie." She didn't respond and appeared to be deep in thought. I reached out and gave her a gentle poke. "Melanie."

"What?" she snapped.

"We need to find out who Doreen's friends were so we can tell them about the arrangements. And don't you think we should go to her house so we can figure out what to do about her stuff?" A sick feeling washed over me. "Oh, no! What if she's got a pet that needs to be taken care of?" I hadn't even thought about that and I'd never forgive myself if an animal died because of my inattention.

The corners of Melanie's lips turned down slightly. "I don't think she had any animals, unless it was barn cats to keep the mice down, and they can take care of themselves." She pulled down the vanity mirror on the visor and applied a fresh coat of bright red color to her lips. "And besides, haven't the police been out there already? They would have let one of us know if there were pets or livestock."

Right. The police wouldn't allow animals to be neglected. But how would Melanie know Doreen didn't have pets after so many years of being in California? Unless she'd been in touch with Doreen recently. But why?

"What about clothes? We need to get Clive an outfit for her to be buried in. So we'll need to go to her house for that."

Melanie dropped her lipstick back into her purse. "She was a lunch lady, for heaven's sake. And not a very fashionable one. As I recall," she added quickly. "I'll send Caitlyn to the mall in Watertown in the morning to get her something new. We should get our money's worth on that rental car anyway."

"Where did Doreen live?" I have to admit I was curious about the home where my mother had grown up. The little house I'd shared with Melanie—Shirley, at that time—on

School Street was now owned by the family of one of my servers and was being used as a vacation rental. Not that it would command a high rental price, since it wasn't located on the water, but there seemed to be cars parked there when I occasionally drove past, so they must have been doing all right.

"The farm is out on the Blue Lake Road in Rossie. And fine. If I have to choose an activity—and mind you I'd much rather be at your friend's spa at the Bikram yoga class right now—let's go talk to Doreen's friend."

The Blue Lake Road was out by the Rainbow Acres Farm, where we got our produce and fresh dairy. Now that I thought about it, I should talk to the detective in charge of the investigation. Doreen had been murdered, so it stood to reason that her home would be investigated for clues. They might not have finished yet, so Paloma it was.

Melanie and I entered the Bonaparte House through the kitchen. I sat her down at one of the counters with a glass of ice water with a slice of lemon, then pulled out my cell and dialed the number Midge had given me.

"Paloma?" I said when she picked up. "This is Georgie, from the Bonaparte House restaurant. Could you come over for a few minutes? I'll make you dinner and we can talk. It's about Doreen."

There was a silence, then the sound of a nose being gently blown. I held the phone away from my ear slightly. "Sorry," Paloma said. "She was my friend. But why would you want to talk to me about her?"

"It turns out I'm a relative, though I just found out about that." I cut my eyes to Melanie, who was sipping her water through the straw. "And I'm making the funeral arrangements.

I was hoping you could help me come up with a list of people I should notify?"

"Oh. I'd like to help if I can. What time should I come?"

"If you're free, now would be perfect."

"I just live around the corner. I'll be there in ten minutes."

I pulled out the makings for a Greek salad—romaine lettuce, Kalamata olives, crisp cucumbers, and end-of-the-season ripe tomatoes. I dressed it with a splash of vinegar, a few swirls of olive oil, then crumbled a generous portion of fresh salty feta over the whole thing, finishing it off with a few grinds of black pepper. I heated up the last few pieces of the pastitsio, found a loaf of crusty bread and a bottle of New York State red wine, and loaded everything up on a serving tray.

A knock sounded at the kitchen door. The door opened partway and a head poked in. "I figured I should come to the back, since the restaurant isn't open," the woman said. "I'm Paloma."

"Come on in," I said. "Dinner's ready. Follow me."

I hefted the serving tray up onto my shoulder and headed for the bottom dining room, Melanie and Paloma following me dutifully. Not that I could blame them. Dinner smelled delicious, if I did say so myself, and my stomach was growling. It had been hours since I'd eaten at Gladys's.

"Melanie, could you grab that tray stand so I'll have a place to set this down?" She looked around and shrugged.

"Here, I've got it," Paloma said. She brought the stand over from its place by the wall and opened it up efficiently, then smiled at me, one food server to another. I liked Paloma already.

I served up the dinner family style, salad and entrée on the same plate, and set the dishes before my guests. Melanie helped herself to the wine, then deigned to pour each of us a glass. I sat down and dug in.

"I'm really sorry about Doreen," Paloma said. "She was a good friend to me. I'm going to miss her." She forked up some salad.

"Thanks. I wish I could say I knew her, but the family's been . . . spread apart and I wasn't aware of our relationship till now." I shot my mother a frosty look, which she ignored. "It'll be in the paper tomorrow, but maybe you could give me a list of people to call? It would be a shame if anyone got left out."

Paloma nodded. "If you'll give me the details, I can let people know. I'm sure you have enough to deal with right now."

That was an understatement. "Thanks. We're so grateful. Right, Melanie?" I gave her leg a tap with my foot under the table. Not too hard. Honest.

Melanie flashed a lot of teeth in our direction, a smile that probably would have played well in front of the cameras but was lost on the two of us. "Yes. Very grateful." She pulled her napkin from her lap and dabbed at her lips. "So, Paloma, you worked with Doreen at the school."

Melanie, making chitchat. Interesting.

"Yes. She came off as abrasive, but once she warmed up to you, she was friendly enough."

Melanie gave the napkin another twist. It looked tight enough to tie off a boat. *Or strangle someone.* The thought rose unbidden to my mind, and I did my best to squelch it. But I couldn't take my eyes off that twisted piece of fabric she was working either.

"I wish I'd known her. And what an awful way to die," I said.

Paloma's big brown eyes welled up. "I can't believe someone would kill her. I mean, don't get me wrong. She could be pretty cranky, and when she got riled up, she cussed like a sailor. But lately she seemed different. Happier." Paloma took a bite of her pastitsio, and a look of pleasure crossed her face. "Wow, this is so good."

"Thanks," I said. Meat and pasta bathed in a velvety cheese béchamel—what wasn't to love? "There's a piece left in the kitchen. I'll wrap it up for you when you leave. Any idea what made Doreen happier?" Melanie had left off twisting the napkin and had moved on to picking her noodles apart with a fork. She kept glancing up at the portrait of Napoleon that hung over the fireplace, as though the Little Corporal had something to do with our conversation.

Paloma ripped off a hunk of bread and soaked up some of the sauce from the casserole. "Well," she said between dips, "as you can probably guess, cafeteria workers don't get paid crap, pardon my French. Doreen was lucky she had that farmhouse left to her, so she had fewer expenses than most of us."

I glanced over at Melanie. She was still staring at her plate, and she was twirling a tube of pasta around and around on it.

"She must have inherited it free and clear, then, no mortgage?"

"Yeah," Paloma said. "Her aunt and uncle cut their own daughter out of the will and left it to Doreen. Anyway, she came in to school one day and said she was getting a windfall. I figured some other relative had died and she was just waiting for the estate to be settled."

With my limited knowledge of the family history, I had no idea who that might be. But what if it wasn't an inheritance? What if she'd been blackmailing someone? And what if that someone was a relative who'd made it big? How far would that relative go to keep Doreen and her big mouth shut?

"Did she say when she was getting the money?" I forked up a chunk of tangy feta from my salad. I never got tired of the stuff.

"Well," Paloma said. "All she said was, 'The time is almost up.' Then she laughed, and showed us a picture of the new tattoo she was going to get—which came out great, by the way—and then she said she was going to retire at the end of the school year."

The time is almost up. Could mean a lot of things. But it fit pretty neatly into the ugly theory that was developing in my mind. Doreen had something on Melanie. I was sure there were plenty of potentially embarrassing incidents in Melanie's life, but would they be bad enough to kill for? Or had Doreen been going to expose Melanie's real identity? Somehow, I doubted Melanie wanted that part of her past hidden enough to succumb to blackmail. Plenty of people created new identities for themselves with no more sinister motive than wanting a fresh start. No, it had to be more than that.

Yet there was one piece of this puzzle that didn't fit. Why would Doreen leave everything to Melanie in her will? Why would someone blackmail her own heir?

By this time Paloma had cleared her plate—the woman had an impressive appetite, which belied her slim figure.

"Baklava and coffee?" I offered.

Paloma's eyes lit up. "That sounds great, if it's not too much trouble."

I rose. "Come on, Melanie. You can help me clear the plates."

She looked at me as if I'd suddenly sprouted a fully fruited olive tree from the top of my head. Her gaze turned to a glare. She threw her napkin down on top of her plate of mangled but uneaten food, then rose. "I don't suppose there's anywhere to get a decent manicure in this town. I'm going to need one after this little waitressing gig."

Paloma waved a set of long gel nails, done in a rich shade of burgundy with adorable little pumpkins painted on each one. "Of course you can get your nails done here. My friend runs Nail Me, the shop over by the tattoo place? Let Suzanne know I sent you—she gives referral discounts."

Melanie picked up her own plate and set it on the tray along with the rest of the dishes I'd cleared, then stormed off toward the kitchen. I lifted the tray to my shoulder and followed, checking my floors as I walked. If she wrecked my beautiful hardwoods with those stupid spiky heels of hers, I was going to be ripped.

In the kitchen she whirled around as I set down the tray. "What are you doing? You're asking for trouble," she fumed. Her face was unmoving, but bright red spots of color stained her cheeks, as if she'd inexpertly applied a particularly virulent shade of blusher.

I did my best to keep my cool and keep my voice down. "Why don't you tell me what's really going on here, Melanie?

Why did you show up after twenty years, just in time to find your only cousin dead? You had a nice story about wanting to get to know me, but forgive me if that's just a little too tough to swallow. You're lucky I haven't called my friend Detective Hawthorne and told him who you really are." It was a bluff. He must already know. It wasn't that well kept a secret.

She blanched. "Are you staying with Jack tonight?"

She was bringing up my love life? I turned on the coffeemaker with a vicious flip of the switch. "Seriously? That's all you've got to say to me? How is that any of your business?" I pulled a tray of baklava out of the cooler and dug out several squares, plating them on autopilot.

"What about Sophie?" she demanded. "Where's she?"

Oh, for Pete's sake. "Sophie is staying at her cousin's to help her pack and then they're going out of town on a seniors' bus trip to Niagara Falls and the casino. Jack's got other plans. Satisfied? We've got company, so I'm not going to press you right now. But after she leaves, you're going to come clean with me."

I filled up a cream pitcher and added it to a fresh tray, along with coffee cups, saucers, and the desserts.

The back door opened, its hinge grating in a noise that made my teeth hurt. Caitlyn bustled in. Oh, goodie. The other person I wanted to see. She shoved her phone into her pocket and looked from Melanie to me and back again. "Uh, I need to talk to Melanie," she finally said.

"Just give us a minute," Melanie said. "Then we'll join you."

I quickly added another cup and serving of baklava to the tray, then headed for the dining room. "You do that," I said over my shoulder.

I served up the dessert and coffee. Paloma's face took on a rapturous look. "Delicious," she declared. I was just swirling some cream into my coffee cup when I heard the familiar grating of the back door hinges again. Now who was here?

Except no one entered the dining room. No sound filtered up from the kitchen. My eyebrows drew together. "Excuse me just a moment, will you? I'll be right back." I raced out to the kitchen. Empty. Damn! They'd given me the slip. I looked out the back door to see a little black car peeling out of the driveway.

Fifteen minutes later, after promising her a job next summer if she didn't want to go back to the T-Shirt Emporium, I'd managed to get rid of Paloma. She said she'd take care of calling everyone about Doreen's services and thanked me profusely for the dinner. Despite my agitation with my mother, I was able to respond politely enough. Paloma had grown on me.

When she'd gone, I punched Melanie's number into my cell. It went straight to voice mail.

My cell rang. Aha! She'd decided to call me back. But when I checked the number, I frowned. It wasn't my mother. It was Spiro. Just the person I didn't have time for right now, but it was better to get this over with; otherwise he'd just keep calling. I answered.

"Why didn't you pick up?" he demanded. My hackles rose.

"What do you want?" I said, none too nicely.

"It's important, okay? Inky's been arrested."

◈ THIRTEEN ◈

I shook my head. Had I heard that right? "Arrested? When? Why?"

Spiro was agitated, and with good reason. "The cops came and took away the roll of plastic wrap and confiscated our computers. Then they questioned both of us, and arrested him! Shoved him in the back of the cop car and took him away."

I felt some sympathy. I'd been in the back of a police car myself not that long ago, and it hadn't been pleasant. "What evidence do they have? Anything other than the plastic wrap?" And why arrest Inky and not Spiro?

"Well, I was in Watertown at the time of death, shopping at the restaurant supply house. I had a dentist appointment early the next morning, so I stayed over at the Holiday Inn. I guess they checked the security cameras and I was able to account for my whereabouts. But Inky was home that day— alone—and he has no alibi. What do I do?"

I'd always been the one to fix things, to take action when something went wrong. Not even our impending divorce seemed to change the dynamics of our relationship. I blew out a breath. No matter what else I had on my plate, I couldn't refuse to help him.

"Does he have a lawyer yet?"

"No, I don't think so."

I glanced out the window. The sun was low on the horizon. Too late to call anybody, so poor Inky was stuck in jail overnight. "First thing in the morning call Jim MacNamara. Ask for him, not the son. You want somebody with experience. If he's not in, ask Lydia to get him an immediate message."

"Okay. He didn't do it, Georgie."

"Yeah, I know." But who did? I was more determined than ever to find out what role the Prodigal Mommy was playing. "Spiro? It's going to be okay. Inky will beat this once the authorities see that he has no possible motive for wanting Doreen dead."

He didn't have a motive, did he? If he did, he'd stumped me.

"Georgie, I know I've never said it to you in all the years we've been married. So I'll say it now before the divorce is final so at least you'll hear it once. Thank you. For everything. And no, my mother did not tell me to say that."

He rang off, leaving me speechless.

I made quick work of loading and running the dishwasher and putting a fresh cloth and table settings on the table we'd used. I called Sophie to make sure she was settled at Marina's for the night, sent a quick e-mail to Cal in Greece just to say hi. Then I dialed my mother. Who didn't answer.

What should I do? I checked my watch. There was just

time for me to catch the last water taxi of the night if I hurried down to the docks. I debated for only a moment, then sent a text to Liza at the Spa.

> Coming over in a few minutes. If you don't have a room, will stay on couch.

She texted back:

> Mi couch es su couch. See you when you get here.

I raced up to my room, threw some underwear and an oversized T-shirt into a bag, and ran out the door.

Liza met me herself at the dock when the taxi pulled up. I tossed the captain a ten-dollar bill and climbed out. "Come on," Liza said. "I haven't seen you in ages and we've got lots to talk about."

As we walked up the incline to the castle, I felt a little surge of relief. It had been a very eventful few days, and it would feel wonderful to relax and unburden myself. And who better to do that with than my best friend, Liza Grant.

Liza and I met years ago, when Cal was in elementary school. She had just come back to town after living in New York City for a few years when she inherited the behemoth known as Castle Valentine from her parents' estate. Like me, she was an only child, and also like me, she was estranged from her parents, so we immediately had our quasi-orphan state in common. We met up over coffee one day at the Bean, and became fast friends.

The castle took enormous amounts of money to run and

maintain, money that Liza did not have or inherit. In fact, her parents, too stubborn to sell the place, rent it out, or close it up, had deferred almost all the maintenance on the limestone mansion, and it was in a state of minor decay when Liza got there. But Liza was not one to waste an opportunity. She came up with the idea of opening the castle up as an exclusive spa, catering to the uber rich. She learned everything she could about spa therapies, found a spa manager willing to work on percentage for a year and to train Liza to run the place herself, cleaned up the grounds and did some landscaping, and refurbished half a dozen rooms in the building.

As her reputation and finances grew, she finished more rooms, and added bathrooms and treatment rooms until she had a world-class luxury facility right off the shore of Bonaparte Bay. With careful financial management, she'd become a tycoon to rival any of the turn-of-the-century millionaires who built the extravagant homes that populated the islands and shores of the St. Lawrence. She was also my friend and had offered to lend me the money to try to buy Sophie and Spiro out of the Bonaparte House. The offer was tempting—oh, so tempting—but her friendship meant more to me than money, and I wasn't willing to put that friendship at risk for anything.

I followed Liza through the maze of paneled hallways lined with old-fashioned gas lamps that had been converted to electricity. We ended up in her private sitting room, and I parked myself in my favorite squishy chair, upholstered in pink velvet. Liza handed me a glass of wine and sat in a matching chair, kicking off her sandals and tucking her long toned legs up underneath her.

"So," she said. "How's Cal? Breaking hearts over in Greece?"

I smiled. My beautiful daughter was probably doing just that. "Well, Sophie's sister is keeping an eye on her, so I don't imagine she's getting into too much trouble, but she loves it there." The thought was bittersweet. I wanted nothing more than for my daughter to be happy. I just wished she could be happy a little closer to me.

"And the dishy Captain Jack?" She picked up a tray of crab puffs and offered me one. I picked it up and popped it into my mouth, enjoying the savory morsel before I answered.

"He is rather dishy." I grinned. "He's out getting to know the guys at the Coast Guard Station tonight."

"Ah, at the Lighthouse Lounge, no doubt."

"Probably." I sipped my wine, letting the rich fruity tang roll around my mouth. Despite my years in the restaurant business, I was not a wine expert and didn't know a note of oaky blackberries from a clean, crisp finish of citrus. Spiro was the one with the talent for choosing wines for the Bonaparte House, and I hoped he would continue to do that for us. But I did know what I liked when I tasted it, and this was delicious.

Fortified by food and drink, I broached the subject I'd come here to . . . broach. "Liza, you've got a couple of people staying here. An actress and her assistant."

A tiny cloud passed over Liza's beautiful face. "You know I have a vow of secrecy about who's staying here and what they're having done, right?" She reached up and adjusted the headband she wore, smoothing down her Titian locks as she did so.

Good old Liza. The soul of discretion. "Well, Jack and I didn't just deliver her here the other day out of the goodness of our hearts."

One of Liza's eyebrows rose, just a hair. "And?"

I paused. "Melanie Ashley is my mother."

Liza's normally serene countenance flickered. I wondered for a moment if she already knew. Liza tended to know pretty much everything that went on in Bonaparte Bay, but she was priest-like in her ability to keep a secret.

"I thought your mother's name was Shirley," she said.

"She's changed it, along with her face, boobs, and voice. But it's true."

Liza tapped her fingernail on her top lip. "What's she doing back here now?"

"Exactly what I'd like to know." I framed my next question carefully, knowing I was stepping over the line. Well, she'd either answer or she wouldn't. "Has she paid you for her stay here?"

My friend looked at me, as if trying to decide how much she could say. "I require up-front payment from every guest for the number of days booked. Then we settle up any extra charges when the guest leaves. No exceptions."

"So her credit card cleared?"

Liza's eyes probed my face. "Yes. Nobody stays here until their payment clears. What's this all about?"

"The tabloids are reporting that Melanie's broke. I just wondered if maybe that's why she chose now to come back to Bonaparte Bay."

Light dawned on Liza's face. "Ah, she's heard about the items you found in the Bonaparte House. And you think she's here to see if she can get her hands on some of the proceeds."

"Well, it's crossed my mind. But she's in for a rude awakening when she finds out none of that money will be mine. Liza, I hate to ask this . . ."

She waved her long, graceful fingers in the air. "But you want me to keep an eye on her. Done."

"Thanks. So what's new with you?"

"Oh, I'm having an affair." Her voice was casual as she ran her fingers up and down the stem of her glass.

"Really? Is it serious? Spill." I thought about my own budding affair with Jack Conway and felt warm inside.

"No, not serious. Unless you call having a lot of divine sex serious."

I laughed. Jack and I had not progressed to the divine sex part of our relationship—more like the divine extended foreplay part—but it was just a matter of time. I was looking forward to the winter, when I'd have the Bonaparte House to myself and we could take our relationship to the next level. "So who's the lucky guy?" I asked.

"Channing Young. It's nothing emotional."

"The pool guy?"

"Yes, though his talents go well beyond skimming and shocking," she said, laughing. Her smile melted into a frown and she cocked her head. A faint noise came from the direction of the next room. "Did you hear that?"

I listened. "Not sure what that was. Maybe the castle is settling?" I was well familiar with old stone houses. There were always plenty of unexplained noises.

She got up and walked quietly to the connecting door, placing a finger to her lips. If I wasn't mistaken, Liza's private office was on the other side of that pocket door.

I tiptoed over to join her.

Liza threw open the door. Caitlyn stood frozen on the other side.

◈ FOURTEEN ◈

The young woman's mouth hung open for a moment, then she shut it. Had she been listening to our conversation?

"Um," she said. "I got lost looking for the kitchen. Melanie wants a mineral water."

Liza took her by the arm and marched her through the door and into the sitting room. "You definitely took a wrong turn. Next time just have Melanie pick up the phone and dial the concierge."

"Oh, well, she told me to go. So I went. That's what I do."

"This way, then." Liza turned to me. "I'll be right back, Georgie. Maybe you could go into my office and make sure the door is locked. I can't imagine why it wasn't." She took Caitlyn and left.

I went through the interior door into Liza's office. A French provincial–style desk with lovely turned legs was situated in the middle of the room, with a desk chair upholstered in a cheerful yellow and blue floral pattern behind it. White china pots of various lush and healthy-looking green plants lined the sills of the huge windows along one wall. It was dark out now, but I could make out the funky outline of a bright full moon through the original wavy glass.

I crossed the room to the door to the hallway. The door was closed, and I turned the thumb lock, giving the handle a jiggle for good measure. I wondered again what Caitlyn had been doing in here. While I could understand getting lost in this place—there were over a hundred rooms—she'd been here for a few days and she must know where the kitchen was by now. There weren't that many explanations. She really was direction-ally challenged. She'd been spying on Liza and me, probably at Melanie's behest. Or she'd been snooping in Liza's office.

But what would she be looking for? The girl certainly got around. First she was at Gladys's house hanging around Channing. Could it be as simple as her having a crush on the town handyman? It made sense. The guy was definitely hot, and he seemed nice. She could have been in Liza's office to see if she could find out any information about him to help her follow him. I liked this idea—just a girl harmlessly stalking a cute guy.

But another idea popped into my head, something quite a bit less benign. Liza had a lot of famous clientele. She almost certainly kept files on her guests, and the files must contain personal information. If Melanie really was having financial problems—and the fact that Liza had been paid didn't rule that out—she could have sent the devoted and efficient Caitlyn to see if she could find something useful. Again, I was back to blackmail.

I scanned the room. Everything looked neat and tidy to me. No errant papers or files on the desk or any other flat surface. I walked around the desk itself and frowned. A drawer was pulled slightly out. I shoved it back into place with my leg then looked at the floor. A glossy dark hair lay across the gleaming floorboards. Hair the same color and length as Caitlyn's.

What had she been looking for? And had she found it? I was tempted to snoop in the drawer myself, but my conscience wouldn't allow it.

I went back into the sitting room to wait for Liza. She came back shortly, with Caitlyn in tow. The young woman was holding a bottle of Evian. Little droplets of water had condensed on the outside of the glass bottle. She transferred the bottle to her other hand and wiped her damp hand on her skinny jeans. "Caitlyn, I need to talk to Melanie. Can you let her know I'm coming upstairs?"

She started, just a little. "Uh, sorry. Melanie just took a sleeping pill—she wanted some extra water to wash it down. I've been gone so long she may already be asleep."

Stop snooping in other people's offices and you'll be on time. I searched her face. Unfortunately, I believed her about the sleeping pill. I'd seen the prescription bottle when I got the glimpse of the pepper spray she carried in her purse.

"Fine, then. I'll see you both in the morning."

Her lip curled up a little. "Yeah. She's sending me to the closest mall to get a new outfit for Doreen to be buried in. It kind of creeps me out. But I do what she tells me."

I had no doubt she did what Melanie instructed. But did this intelligent young woman have an agenda of her own?

She probably had access to all of Melanie's personal information—she'd have to in order to do her job. Was she leveraging that information?

"Yeah. I better go see if she's still awake. We'll be ready early, if I can get her out of bed." She left the room. Liza and I went to the door and watched her walk up the stairs.

Liza turned to me. "I always lock the door to my office, and I know I did it tonight."

"How did she manage it? I'm no expert but I didn't see any signs that the lock had been forced."

"I don't know. There's only one key, and I keep it with me all the time. There's sensitive information in there about my clients. And it's a new, modern lock. I had them installed on both office doors." Her forehead wrinkled. "That girl is up to something."

I debated whether to tell Liza about Caitlyn and Channing, but decided against it. I hadn't seen anything other than the two of them talking, and Liza hadn't said they had an exclusive relationship. "You might want to check the drawer in your desk. It was open. And I agree. Caitlyn *is* up to something. Melanie too. Tomorrow, I'm going to get some answers."

The next morning dawned clear and bright. Liza had installed me in one of the smaller bedrooms, and I'd slept comfortably under the soft white Egyptian cotton sheets. I woke at six o'clock and went out onto the little balcony, wrapped in one of the blankets from the bed. I shivered and shrank back as I leaned into the cold stone of the castle to watch a spectacular sunrise over the St. Lawrence. There was so much to do today. Doreen's calling hours were tonight, and the funeral and luncheon were tomorrow. Dolly was scheduled to come in and help me prep the luncheon. I'd decided on a simple menu: Greek salad, warm pitas, Greek meatballs called keftedes, lemony rice pilaf, and coffee and cookies for dessert. The two of us worked efficiently together and we'd get it done quickly.

I needed to call Spiro and make sure he'd gotten a lawyer for Inky. Hopefully MacNamara Senior could help him post bail. I hated to think of Inky in the county lockup, but there wasn't really anything for me to do. The authorities must have retrieved the box of plastic wrap from the kitchen of Spinky's and put two and two together, coming up with the sum of Inky. But the back door of the restaurant had been open all day, with workers coming in and out. Anyone could have found the key under the mat. Anyone could have taken the wrap and braided it into a rope. Or planted a half-empty box on the counter.

Which brought me back to square one. Who would want Doreen dead? I went inside, deposited the blanket back on the bed, dressed and went downstairs. I sat down in the breakfast room with a cup of Liza's fine coffee and a croissant, which I liberally smeared with butter and homemade strawberry jam. Eventually the Spa guests started to trickle in, nobody famous enough for me to recognize. I saw quite a few mangled faces covered in sutures and bandages. Liza did a good business with people coming here to hide out— er, recuperate—after plastic surgery.

All heads turned as Channing entered the room. He was

beautiful. Dark hair curling over his chiseled jaw, sharply cut sideburns just a little too long, skin bronzed, presumably from hours in the sun, and wearing a T-shirt and faded jeans that molded to the contours of his body like cake batter poured into a Bundt pan.

He grabbed a coffee and a plate piled high with Danish and looked around for a place to sit. Most of the tables were occupied, though I noticed a couple of middle-aged women scooting their chairs aside to make room for him. His eyes landed on me, and he gave me a questioning look. I smiled and indicated the chair. I felt like I'd just won the bonus round at Bingo—I'd get to admire him up close and maybe get some information about Caitlyn at the same time.

"Thanks," he said, setting his breakfast on the table and sitting down with that easy grace I'd noticed before. He was a runner maybe, based on that lean build. The guy ought to be modeling underwear. "You're the one who brought Ms. Ashley and her assistant the other day, aren't you? What brings you back to the island?" He took a huge bite of cheese Danish and I watched him chew, fascinated by the muscle working in his jaw.

I forced myself to look at his face. Not necessarily a less arresting thing to watch than the jaw muscle. "Uh, yes. I'm Georgie. Liza and I are good friends."

His face took on a dreamy quality. "Liza's great, isn't she?"

"She is." My estimation of Channing grew. It was clear he genuinely cared about Liza, which was charming.

"The age difference doesn't matter to me. I like a woman who knows what she wants."

Liza and I were about the same age. Channing appeared

to be about thirty. Ten years didn't seem like that much to me either. This guy was young and beautiful, but when I thought about what I wanted, I only saw Jack.

"Channing, right? You have the handyman business?"

He nodded, finishing up the Danish in one bite and picking up another with strawberry filling. "Yeah. I close and open pools, do some home repairs and painting, carpentry, and I winterize and caretake several cottages while the owners are away for the season. I get to do something different every day, and I'm my own boss."

I was about to ask him about Caitlyn, but before I could do so, Melanie parked herself at the table. She gave Channing the once-over, as though he were a donut dusted in powdered sugar. She turned to me. "I'll have what you're having."

Hysterical. "We were just having a nice, honest conversation. Something not everyone knows how to do, *Melanie*."

She shot me a frosty look and waved at Caitlyn, who appeared with two cups of coffee and a bowl of fruit salad. No carbs in sight.

Caitlyn sat down. "Good morning," she said to me, then Channing. Did I notice a slight hesitation when she addressed Channing? Her eyes were focused not on his face, but somewhere in the middle of his chest. Not that I could blame her. It was a magnificent torso.

"You two know Channing, right?" My hostess training never shut off.

"Not as well as I'd like to," Melanie said. "But yes, we met you when we first arrived on the island."

"How about you, Caitlyn?" I pressed. "You know Channing?"

Her eyes were big and brown behind the thick black frames of her oversized eyeglasses. "Yes, from around the island." She went back to her fruit salad.

I don't know what I thought I was accomplishing here. She was hardly likely to admit she'd been stalking him, however naïve or harmless her intentions. And he might be too much of a gentleman to embarrass her in front of me and Melanie. And if she hadn't been following Channing in the throes of hipster-lust, she'd been following me and Jack that day at Gladys's house. I needed to sit her and Melanie down for a nice long private chat. And soon.

"Liza asked me to give you all a ride over to Bonaparte Bay this morning," Channing said, draining his coffee cup. "Will you have a lot of luggage? If you do, I'll take the bigger boat."

Caitlyn piped up. "We each have one bag with the essentials. We didn't expect to be attending calling hours and a funeral, so we'll be going to Watertown and shopping for suitable clothes this morning." She tapped at her phone. "And we should get going." The girl was efficient, I had to give her that.

"Then I assume you can carry your own bags if they're small? I'll go get the boat ready. Meet me at the dock. It's a beautiful morning for a ride on the St. Lawrence." Channing headed for the door. The head of every woman in the room, including the three at my table, turned to watch that pair of jeans walk out of the room.

"Damn. That is a fine piece of man-flesh," Melanie said.

"Yeah, you made it pretty clear how you feel about him. He's taken, so claws off." I felt protective of Liza all of a sudden.

Caitlyn flinched, ever so slightly. Maybe she knew about Liza and Channing, maybe she didn't. I hated to bust anyone's romantic bubble, but she'd be better off not getting too attached to Channing the Enchanter.

"'Taken' is such a relative term," Melanie said, spearing a juicy hunk of strawberry.

"Finish up, ladies," I said, waving for a server to come and clear the table. "We have a lot to do today."

"Fine," Melanie huffed. "I rarely eat breakfast anyway. I'm not in the habit of getting up with the chickens. Come on, Caitlyn."

She rose obediently, picked up the two small bags, and we made our way to the dock. I sent a quick thank-you text to Liza. Not very personal, but she'd understand.

A few minutes later we were motoring toward town. Melanie had tied a gray scarf over her blond coif and donned her enormous sunglasses. She hunkered down against the breeze that blew off the water. Caitlyn punched something into her omnipresent phone. Channing looked rather masterful at the helm of the boat. Conversation was pretty much impossible without shouting, so I just watched the scenery go by.

And scenery in September in northern New York is spectacular. The islands and the shores on both sides of the international border, which runs right through the middle of the river, were ablaze with reds, yellows, and oranges set against a backdrop of tall evergreens. With the bright blue sky and the clear water, I took a moment to enjoy the beauty around me. Because when we disembarked, I was going to confront Melanie and Caitlyn and things were going to get ugly.

Channing pulled up at the village dock and extended each

of us a hand in turn. Melanie pulled her scarf farther over her face and headed for the mainland, her stylish but impractical high heels clattering on the hard wooden surface. "Hurry up!" she said to Caitlyn, who hustled along behind her carrying the bags.

I thanked Channing as he tied off the boat. "When you see Liza, tell her I said thank you again, will you?"

A blush rose in his sculpted cheeks. Hot and adorable at the same time. Hotdorable. "I've got a few jobs to finish up around town before the weekend. But I might head back to the island tonight."

I smiled. "I'll see you, Channing. If you want lunch, come around to the back door of the Bonaparte House. We're not officially open again until tomorrow night, but I'll be in the kitchen."

"I might just take you up on that," he said.

Melanie could move surprisingly quickly on those heels. She and Caitlyn were just stepping onto the sidewalk. I set off at a quick trot to catch up with them. I wasn't wearing the right bra for running. This body was made for walking. Even that I didn't do enough of.

I caught up with the two of them in the municipal parking lot. Caitlyn lifted the trunk lid and stowed their small bags in the back. "Hold up," I said.

Melanie glanced around. "Keep your voice down, will you? That reporter is over by the Dumpsters and I don't want him taking my picture when I look like this."

I glanced over. Sure enough, the tall, lanky frame of Spencer Kane was standing there, camera on a strap around his neck, staring in our direction and making notes on a small pad. Melanie ducked into the car, slammed the door, and rolled down the window.

"Melanie. We need to talk. Now."

She huffed. "Later, Georgie. We've got to get to Watertown and get our shopping done. Are there any decent stores at that mall? Probably not even a Lord & Taylor."

No, no Lord & Taylor. The North Country was more of a Penney's kind of place.

I relented. "Fine. Go get yourself some clothes, and get something nice for Doreen. I'll call Clive at the funeral home and ask him to check the size on the clothes she was wearing when they brought her in and I'll text it to you. But you—both of you—come to the Bonaparte House this afternoon. You owe me some answers and I'm not waiting any longer."

"That reporter is headed this way," Caitlyn said.

"Drive," Melanie ordered. "I'll see you later, Georgie." She rolled up the tinted window of the rental car and they peeled out of the parking lot, fishtailing slightly on the gravel and leaving me in a cloud of dust.

Spencer snapped a few pictures of the car as he continued to walk toward me. I glanced around. I'd have to walk right past him to get back home unless I wanted to cut cross-lots behind the rest of the Theresa Street businesses. Oh well, it wasn't me he was interested in.

"Georgie," he said.

Might as well get this over with. "Hey, Spencer. What's up?"

"I could ask you the same question, and probably get a more interesting answer. Look, you and I need to talk."

"If this is about Melanie, I've got nothing for you."

He turned his head in the direction they'd gone. "Yes and no. It's about Doreen."

Had he heard about our relationship? It wasn't exactly secret. I'm sure plenty of people had figured out Melanie's real identity by now, once they learned that she and I were in charge of Doreen's arrangements. Everybody knew everybody in Bonaparte Bay and the environs.

"It's important," he said.

"If you know something about Doreen's death, you should go to the police."

He flipped his notebook shut and shoved it in the pocket of his rumpled khakis. "I have a little more research to do, then I will, I promise. But I want to talk to you first. Tomorrow? That will give me enough time to find the last bit of information I need."

Tomorrow was going to be busy, with the funeral and the luncheon afterward. But I was intrigued. What information could he have that he needed to tell me before he went to the police? "All right. If you promise not to take pictures of the mourners, or bother them in any way, come to the funeral lunch at the Bonaparte House. Once the guests leave, we can talk."

He nodded. "Pinky swear." His eyes gazed squarely into mine. "And Georgie? Be careful." He loped off in the direction of the three-story stone building that housed the *Bay Blurb*.

Be careful? There was a murderer loose in the Bay, so everyone had to be careful until he was caught. But I had the feeling he meant me specifically. Was I in danger? If I was, it was kind of crappy of Spencer to leave me hanging until tomorrow. Maybe I'd ask Spiro to come and stay in his old room tonight. Inky too if he was out on bail.

I made my way to the Bonaparte House, entering through the kitchen door. Dolly was already there, prepping the salad ingredients. "Mornin', boss," she said. "I saw your list, so I thought I'd get started."

"Thanks." I grabbed a clean apron from the neatly folded pile under one of the counters, then crossed to the sink. I squirted some antibacterial soap into my hands, then began to scrub. A fresh pair of gloves and I was ready to work.

Dolly handed me a bowl of finely chopped onions. "Snazzy earrings, by the way. But you know I already had my birthday this summer, right?"

The overhead lights sparkled on the silver hoops. Dolly had another birthday, the one listed on her driver's license and birth certificate, coming up in the winter. She usually had two per year. This year there were three.

"I saw them and thought you'd like them. How's things?" I pulled out packages of ground lamb and pork and dumped them into a large stainless mixing bowl. The chopped onions went on top, along with mint and oregano, fresh bread crumbs, milk, and a pinch of nutmeg. I plunged my hands into the mixture and began to blend gently. This could be done in the food processor or the stand mixer, but hands were still the best tools and it meant fewer dishes to wash. I began to scoop and roll the keftedes into golf-ball-sized spheres.

"Eh, can't complain. Harold finally got the RV running, so we're headed for Branson after Columbus Day."

"That'll be fun." Scoop and roll. The rhythm was hypnotic.

I'd made so many Greek meatballs over the years I could form them perfectly in my sleep. "Uh, Dolly? You're happy here, right?" I held my breath, waiting for her response. What would I do if she said no?

She laughed, a rattly sound that bubbled in her throat from years of smoking. She'd recently quit but she'd be feeling the effects for the rest of her life. Hopefully, it wouldn't kill her. "Ha! You worried Spiro is going to steal me away?" She placed the sliced onions, rough-chopped tomatoes, and sliced cucumbers into separate covered containers. Tomorrow we would mix them together with some olive oil, salt and pepper, and crumble feta over the top. She began to grate cucumber and garlic for the tzatziki sauce.

I grinned. "A little, I guess." Scoop and roll.

"Well, I'm not going anywhere," she said firmly. "I've known Spiro since he was a kid, but you're my friend *and* my boss. Besides, who'd drive Sophie around? We gotta keep her off the roads," she added under her breath.

That was a load off my mind. "If he offers you more money, you let me know. I'll do better."

I could almost hear the calculations running in her head, underneath that mountain of lacquered hair. "Yup," was all she said as she loaded the prepped food into the walk-in cooler.

Dolly mixed up the dough for the desserts—simple chocolate chip cookies and classic lemon squares, which would be a perfect light finish to tomorrow's meal. The trays of meatballs went into a hot oven to brown. I checked my watch. Nearly noon. I was supposed to help Jack reorganize Monty's papers. But Melanie and Caitlyn should be back soon—they'd better be, or we'd have to wrap poor Doreen in a blanket to put her on display tonight. I wondered briefly if a viewing and an open casket were what she would have wanted. No way to know.

My cell phone pinged. A text from Jack. My heart leapt a little.

> Making a quick trip to Oswego to get some things out of my storage unit, then I'm heading over to Gladys's to see if I can help her pack. We'll mess with the files tomorrow. XXOOX, Jack.

The L-word hadn't passed between us yet, but we'd progressed to X's and O's, and that made me happy. It was just as well he'd postponed our paperwork date. It would give me more time with Melanie.

Where was she? I dialed her number, but neither she nor Caitlyn picked up. A little bubble of anger formed in my gut. She'd better not try to pull a disappearing act like she'd done yesterday, running off to hide out at the Spa.

There was plenty to keep me busy while I waited. I ascended the spiral staircase in the center of the building, up and around to our living quarters on the second floor. Funny, but my room was just as cluttered as the last time I'd been here, so clearly the cleaning fairies had not made an appearance. I rummaged through my closet for something suitable to wear tonight. What did one wear to the calling hours of a relative one didn't know? The navy blue jersey dress would be perfect. And tomorrow I could wear my black tailored suit. Miraculously, they were still in their dry cleaning bags, so I stripped off the plastic and hung both outfits on the bathroom door. I rummaged around in the closet and found a pair of simple black pumps. My feet gave a throb in anticipation of wearing heels. Shoes needed to be practical and comfortable in the restaurant business, but I could hardly wear my white sneakers with a skirt. I even found a pair of nude hose, so I was in business.

Downstairs, I opened the door to my office, which had been the Bonaparte House's original library. Autumn sunlight streamed in through the tall, narrow windows, which once overlooked formal gardens but now presided over the employee parking lot.

The urge to slack off—to open up the romance novel I'd been reading, to take a nap—was strong within me. But there'd be plenty of time for slacking off once we closed on Columbus Day. I gazed wistfully at Gladys's box of recipes. I could almost—almost—justify looking through it for culinary treasures. In the end, I planned the specials through the end of the season, placed my orders with Rainbow Acres and the supplier in Watertown, processed payroll, and did the scheduling for the next couple of weeks.

Doodles and sketches filled the pad of paper in front of me, as I made notes for the off-season. The customer restrooms hadn't been upgraded in years and they were showing their age. I called the local contractor and scheduled him to come in for an estimate. It would be nice to redecorate my bedroom this winter. Maybe I'd do Cal's room as well.

Melanie and Caitlyn pulled into the employee parking lot in their black rental car at five o'clock. I was livid. Turns out

they'd been back for hours, had dropped off the burial outfit for Doreen at the funeral home (good thing nobody else
had died, so Clive had time to dress her), and then gone
driving around the North Country. Or so they said. Without
bothering to call me. I took them upstairs into Cal's room
and instructed them to change and be ready to leave in
twenty minutes.

They emerged more or less on time, and we all piled into
the rental car for the three-block trip to the funeral home.
Clive greeted us at the door, looking dignified and handsome
in his dark suit, his silvery hair brushed back to reveal a
widow's peak over a pair of pale eyes. He was probably fifty
or so, with grown kids and an ex-wife.

"Come in," he said. "She's in the front room, if you'd like
a few moments with Doreen before people arrive." He ges-
tured to the right, where white letters on a black easel spelled
out "Doreen Webber." "The clothing fit perfectly, by the way."

Melanie made no move to enter the room, so I led the
way. Doreen lay in a coffin made of polished mahogany with
brass handles. The casket flowers were lovely. I had no idea
what colors she liked, so I had ordered pink roses and white
carnations, figuring everyone liked pink. She looked peace-
ful on her white satin pillow, and her slightly frizzy dark
hair had been tamed into an attractive cap. The high neck
of her blouse covered the evidence of her manner of death.

Melanie stood staring at the dead woman, her face immo-
bile. Impossible to tell what she was thinking.

Flower arrangements lined the room. I read the tags.
There was a tasteful one from the Bonaparte Bay School
District. Another featured gerbera daisies, with letters

spelling B-I-N-G-O on white cards stuck into the arrangement. A photo of Doreen and a half-dozen other ladies, including Paloma, at the American Legion was stuck into the basket. I had to smile.

From out front came the sound of a car door shutting. Melanie sighed. "All right. Let's get this over with."

I wondered if Doreen would mind if I slapped her cousin.

Caitlyn sat in a chair off to the side, tapping something into her phone. I amended my prior thought. I wondered if Doreen would mind if I slapped Melanie with Caitlyn's cell phone. Melanie and I stood at the foot of the casket as the first of the mourners entered the room.

Doreen had known a surprising number of people, based on the steady stream of folks who filed past her. If I had to guess, I'd say at least half the population of Bonaparte Bay was here. Whether it was to pay respects to Doreen, or to get a look at either Melanie or our second murder victim this year, I couldn't tell.

Paloma came in, wearing a lovely peach-colored scarf that looked beautiful with her caramel complexion and dark hair. She was accompanied by several other women, some of whom I recognized from around town.

She knelt in front of the casket, murmured a prayer, and crossed herself before greeting us. Her eyes swam with unshed tears. "I'm sorry for your loss," she said.

How ironic, I thought. I hadn't even known the woman, so had I really suffered a loss? I should be comforting Paloma.

"Thanks, Paloma," I said. "You've been a good friend to her and a big help to me." I cut my eyes to Melanie, who stood there rigid and unsmiling. She seemed uncomfortable, shifting her weight from foot to foot. Not surprising, considering the ridiculous shoes she was once again wearing. How many pairs did she travel with anyway?

Paloma reached inside her purse and pulled out a small sheet of paper covered in purple splotches. She showed it to Melanie. "The girls and I were wondering if we could put this inside Doreen's coffin. We had so much fun on Thursday nights at the Legion."

Melanie tipped her head. "What is it?" Her eyes scanned the room. She was subtly agitated, her body still but her fingers tapping on her thigh.

Paloma smiled. "It's a winning Bingo card."

"I think that's a lovely idea," I said. "Go right ahead."

Melanie rolled her eyes. I gave her a subtle jab with my elbow. What was it to her? I was glad Doreen had had friends.

Paloma waved to the group of women who had congregated near the table of cookies, coffee, and water in the back. They advanced en masse to the casket, where they stood in a line, hands folded in front like fig leaves. Paloma held up the Bingo card, which I could now see bore signatures that I assumed were from her posse.

"O-seventy-five," she said.

"O-seventy-five," the others repeated. Somebody rang a little bell.

The ladies filed past us, reaching out to take our hands and give their condolences. One asked if they could all get their picture taken with Melanie later. She shrugged and nodded. Leave it to Melanie to use a funeral as a photo op.

Which made me think again of Spencer Kane. I wondered if he was out front somewhere, waiting for Melanie to emerge so he could take her picture. Melanie was only a minor celebrity, so while pictures of her might be interesting to her fans, I couldn't see that there'd be a lot of money in it for him. Still, even if one of the tabloids paid him only a few hundred dollars, that was probably a couple of weeks' pay at the *Bay Blurb*.

I was about to take a break from coffin duty and get a bottle of water when a hush came over the room. The low murmur of subdued conversation, punctuated occasionally with a too-loud laugh, was gone. The room was still as, well, death. All eyes were focused on one spot.

Inky stood in the doorway, channeling Bruce Springsteen in a narrow dark suit with a crisp white shirt and a bolo tie. His head was freshly shaved and moisturized, skin giving off a subtle glow in the lights. His little soul patch was sharply outlined on his chin.

Spiro came in behind him. Inky nodded to people, but didn't speak, as they made their way to the front of the room.

I gave Inky a hug and nodded to Spiro, who nodded back. "I told him not to come," Spiro said. "But he insisted."

"I didn't do anything wrong," he announced. "What am I going to do? Go into hiding?" His voice echoed around the room.

Hmmm. Much as I believed that Inky was innocent, it seemed a teeny, tiny bit inappropriate that he was attending the calling hours for a woman he was accused of murdering. Oh well. Who was there to be offended? Melanie? Me?

Inky knelt in front of the casket, said his prayer, and crossed himself. He stood and stared at Doreen, frowning. His hand moved toward the body.

"What are you doing?" I said in a fierce whisper.

He ignored me and began to fiddle with Doreen's arm.

This was a disaster. I scanned the room. Yup, every eye was on Inky. Including the steely blue eyes of Lieutenant Hawthorne of the New York State Police, who had taken a seat in the back of the room.

It wasn't like he could hurt her. I knew it was insensitive, but she was already dead and autopsied. If there was any evidence, the authorities should have gotten it by now or it was going to be buried tomorrow.

"There. That's better." Inky stood and straightened his tie so it hung perfectly straight over his sculpted chest. I looked into the casket. He'd pulled up the sleeve of Doreen's blouse to reveal the dollar sign tattoo on her left forearm.

"She just got the tat and she was so happy about it," he explained. "But she never got to enjoy it. She'd want people to see it."

Melanie's stare was fixed on Doreen's arm. Her face went pale and her hand trembled ever so slightly as I took it. Finally, some emotion from the Vulcan Queen of the Soaps. "Time for a break, Melanie. Let's sit down and have a drink."

"I'm going to the men's room," Inky announced. "Do you know how much water I've drunk since I got out on bail? There's not enough water in the St. Lawrence to flush out the toxins I absorbed in the Jefferson County lockup."

Melanie allowed me to seat her in one of the family chairs off to the side. I realized that Caitlyn was gone, and I hadn't seen her for a while. I poured Melanie a cup of cold water and put a cookie on a napkin for her. A little sugar never hurt anyone. And it quite often helped.

Lieutenant Hawthorne made his way toward us. Great. More to deal with? Bring it on. He lowered his bulky muscles down onto the chair on the other side of Melanie.

She looked up at him and visibly relaxed. I expected her to purr and make one of her suggestive comments, but she was oddly silent. Melanie almost seemed . . . relieved.

It finally hit me. Under that cool, glib exterior, she was afraid. Doreen's killer was still out there, true. But what was Melanie afraid of? She'd been gone for twenty years, so it seemed unlikely in the extreme that she'd be in danger from anyone around here. Or had she killed Doreen—for money—and was afraid of being caught? But if that were true, her look of relief at the cop's arrival didn't fit. I reminded myself that, mother or no, I didn't know her anymore and I'd be wise to keep my guard up.

Inky had reappeared and was chatting with Paloma and the Bingo Goddesses. One woman pulled down the neck of her top and pointed to her left breast. Inky turned his head from side to side, examining it, then nodded. She must want a tattoo there. Because if she wanted him to do more than tattoo her, she'd picked the wrong team in the kickball match.

Lieutenant Hawthorne angled his chair so Inky and Spiro were in his line of vision. I decided on the direct approach.

"Did you know Doreen?"

"Did you?" he retorted.

"What? No. Your investigator already asked me that. We might have been distant cousins, but I didn't know about her and I'd never laid eyes on her until we found her."

"Then why do you ask?" He pulled out a roll of cherry candies and offered me one. I shook my head.

"Because you're here. Why aren't you out looking for the murderer?" Annoyance made me bold.

He cut his eyes to Inky. "Who says I'm not?" His habit of answering a question with another question was infuriating.

His steel blue eyes met mine as I said, "Inky didn't do it." Man, I hoped I was right about that.

He rolled the candy around in his mouth and swallowed, making his clean-shaven Adam's apple bob up and down. A pleasant little whiff of cherry filled my nostrils. "Maybe, maybe not. The fact that he's out on bond doesn't make him innocent. It only means somebody came up with the money to post his bail."

I wasn't sure where he was going with this. Inky had at least three tattoo parlors that I knew of. My understanding was that the one located by Fort Drum and its ten thousand soldiers and spouses made a fortune. He had plenty of money and he was bankrolling Spinky's. Spiro couldn't have come up with the money himself. Since his little escapade a couple of months ago, Sophie kept him on a tight allowance.

"What possible motive could Inky have for killing Doreen? It makes no sense."

"You're right. It doesn't make sense." He ran his hand down his long-muscled thigh, smoothing out the crease in his pressed blue-gray trousers. "Which is why I'm here."

Motive. By all accounts, Doreen had a smart mouth and a prickly personality, but she apparently had a loyal group of friends in spite of it. Might she have simply angered someone to the point that she or he snapped? But she thought she was coming into some money. What was it Paloma had said? *The time is almost up.* That could mean any number of things, including the thought I kept coming back to. She was blackmailing someone for whatever reason, and the deadline she'd given her victim was approaching. Had her victim taken preemptive measures and strangled her? But why leave the body at Spinky's? It was just a little too convenient that that box of plastic wrap was sitting on the kitchen counter, where any number of people had access to it.

Before I could voice this to Lieutenant Hawthorne, Clive appeared in front of us. "Lieutenant? Could you come with me into the hallway? It's important." His normally imperturbable funeral director countenance was faintly flushed and his voice was tense.

The trooper nodded and followed Clive. I debated. Whatever Clive wanted to say to the lieutenant was clearly meant to be private. But if it had something to do with the murder investigation, I wanted to know about it. Inky's freedom was at stake. My mother was involved in this somehow, I was almost sure. Either way, it was my business. Or so I told myself.

I followed them out into the hallway, just in time to hear Clive say "body." Had he found something on Doreen's body? Some kind of new evidence maybe? They went through a door, beyond which I could see the kitchen. I pressed my lips together. In for a penny, in for a pound.

The kitchen's back door was just swinging closed as I reached it. I grabbed it before it shut and left it open a crack, just wide enough for me to see through. I blinked, then looked again. Someone lay on the ground next to a pot of asters in full bloom. But that wasn't the only thing blooming. Thick crimson liquid oozed into a growing pool around the head of the victim.

◈ FIFTEEN ◈

"My God," I whispered. The lieutenant snapped his head up, barked an order for an ambulance into the phone, and headed for me. Too late to shut the door and pretend I hadn't been there, so I stepped out onto the back stoop. "Who is it?" But I knew who it was even before I got too close. Spencer Kane. He wouldn't be reporting—or photographing—anyone for a long time. If ever.

Lieutenant Hawthorne was all business, as usual. "Georgie, do you have some kind of corpse-dar? Go back inside."

"Is he . . . dead?" My guts were twisted up and tears threatened to breach the banks of my eyes. Would the killing never end?

"The ambulance is on its way," Lieutenant Hawthorne said. "But it doesn't look good. Clive, take Georgie back inside. Don't let anybody leave until my backup gets here to take names."

During the next hour the normally subdued funeral home was abuzz with activity. Clive herded all the mourners into another room out of respect for Doreen. I made additional pots of coffee and refilled cookie trays until they were gone. The trooper made short work of taking names, and the funeral home emptied out pretty quickly.

I helped Clive clean up, since his wife was on the same leaf-peeping slash gambling trip Sophie was on, and then turned to Melanie, who was parked in a wingback chair and looking like a zombie. "You two will stay with me at the Bonaparte House tonight."

Caitlyn looked like she was about to protest, but she clammed up when Melanie nodded. "Do you have room for us? I wouldn't want to be any trouble."

I stifled a snort. There'd been nothing but trouble since she'd come back into my life. "There are two extra bedrooms. And this way you'll be in town early for the funeral tomorrow morning."

"I think I feel a migraine coming on," Melanie said. "Caitlyn, did you bring my medication?"

Caitlyn looked slightly affronted. "Of course. That's my job."

Migraine my foot. I gave Melanie a sharp look. "Don't even think about trying to beg off tomorrow. You're going to attend the funeral and the luncheon, and then you are going to give me some answers." I was getting tired of saying that.

After we gave our statements to the police—extremely brief all around, since nobody had seen anything—we piled into my car and headed back to the Bonaparte House. I got

Melanie and Caitlyn settled into Spiro's and Cal's rooms, respectively, each of them claiming they were going directly to bed. I went out the kitchen door.

It was a lovely night. I sat at the employee picnic table and looked up at the stars.

A shuffling noise sounded over by the Dumpster. Brenda came toward me.

"Hey, Brenda. Nothing here for you till the weekend."

"I didn't come for that. I came to see you."

Me? "Sit down. Want a snack or something to drink?"

I was glad when she refused because it seemed like a very long walk back into the kitchen, even though it was only a few yards.

"The girl. She was at the funeral home tonight."

"Caitlyn? Yes, she was there."

Brenda zipped her hoodie up a little higher. "She was in the alley arguing with Spencer tonight."

I rewound the evening in my mind. Caitlyn had disappeared at one point, for quite some time. But arguing with Spencer and bludgeoning him were two different matters.

"Did it get physical?"

"Not that I saw. Like I told the cops, I finished my rounds and came back later. The girl was sitting in your car, fiddling with her phone. While Spencer was bleeding out in the alley."

❖ SIXTEEN ❖

Dolly offered to supervise the cleanup after the luncheon was over the next day. I let her do it. The stresses of the last few days were starting to wear on me, and all I wanted to do was haul my butt up the spiral staircase to my bedroom and take a good long nap. Unfortunately, there were other things that had to be done. Namely, confront my mother and her assistant.

The two of them were sitting at a table near the back. Melanie sipped a mineral water with lemon, and Caitlyn had a cola in front of her. I parked myself next to her. "All right. Everybody's gone. So now you start from the beginning and tell me what's going on. Why are you here?"

"Why do you assume I have an ulterior motive?" Melanie countered, then relented. "Fine. But I don't want to talk here." She glanced around. "It's personal family business."

"Whose family are you talking about? Because my

family lives here in this house." Sort of. Everybody was leaving or had already left now that winter was coming.

"Ouch, Georgie. Why don't you tell me how you really feel?" She sipped at the water. Despite her typically snarky attitude, she was pale and twitchy.

"It can't have escaped your notice that the day you two got into town—or the day you *said* you got into town—was the same day your cousin's body was found. And now the reporter who's been hounding you since you got here is also dead. Does that seem like a coincidence? Because something smells like a broken refrigerator on a hot day."

Caitlyn wouldn't meet my eyes. Melanie blew out a breath. "Fine."

"Fine? What does that mean?"

She put the cap back on the bottle of mineral water, gave it a twist, and put it into her oversized designer handbag. "It means . . . it's time to go out to the farm. We'll take your car. I need Caitlyn to run some errands for me and she needs the rental. I don't want to have to pay for extra miles."

I would gladly pay for gas if it meant getting some answers.

Fifteen minutes later we were on our way out to Route 12. According to Lieutenant Hawthorne, the police were finished with their investigation of Doreen's house and we could go in anytime to close up her affairs. I turned off on the road to the Rainbow Acres Farm Collective, where I bought fresh produce and dairy for the restaurant. Just past the long barns and greenhouses and living quarters was a farmhouse.

"Pull in here," Melanie said. "This is it. The house I grew up in." Her voice was strangely flat, without a hint of nostalgia.

I realized I'd driven past this house many times, but of course hadn't known its significance to my own life. It was a two-story rectangular building covered in clapboards. The roof had the steep pitch typical of older North Country houses, and had been re-covered in bright red corrugated metal material. This type of roofing was becoming more popular in this area, because it could easily withstand the harsh North Country winters and their heavy snowload. Doreen had painted the front door a slightly darker red, and mums were planted along each side of the front steps and in a flower bed a little farther out into the lawn. A garden gnome wearing a New York Giants football jersey stood guard over the flowers. Paint peeled from the white siding material. On her limited income, Doreen had probably had to pick and choose what home maintenance projects she could take on.

Melanie pulled a key out of her purse and stuck it into the lock.

"Where did you get a key?" I demanded.

She regarded me over her giant sunglasses. "Doreen told me where to find it."

"And when was this?" Had Melanie gone to see Doreen before she came to see me? And how long before Doreen's death had Melanie been in town?

"She's my cousin. We've . . . been in touch recently." The front door swung open with a creak.

Wow. Just wow. She'd cut me off twenty years ago but she was still in touch with her cousin? The stab of anger and pain was like a knife to my gut.

"Come on in," she said. "I'll show you the house."

There was no sense questioning her. She was clearly

going to take her own sweet time. Not that I trusted myself to keep a civil tongue.

The door opened directly into a moderately sized room that apparently served as a mudroom, coat closet, and sitting room, based on the furnishings. To my left I could see a living room, with comfy-looking slipcovered furniture situated around a 1990s-era television set in a heavy wooden entertainment center. She apparently liked ducks because there were a lot of them in various forms scattered about the room—decoys, photos, china figurines.

"This is the front room," Melanie said, indicating the all-purpose space we stood in. "That's the living room, obviously. There's a bathroom here"—she swept her hand to another door to our left—"and Doreen's bedroom is beyond that. Here's the kitchen."

We walked into a kitchen that spanned the whole back of the house. A Formica-topped table with chrome trim and legs took up one side, along with an antique painted Hoosier cabinet. The other end of the room held the appliances and white beadboard cabinets. The decorating theme was continued here, with a cheerful if outdated border of light blue ducks adjacent to the ceiling. There were a couple of coffee cups in the sink, and the counters were cluttered with small appliances—two coffeemakers, a tabletop electric grill, a new candy apple red stand mixer that I kind of coveted, a can opener. She'd liked her gadgets, apparently.

"What's upstairs?" I asked.

"More bedrooms. I imagine Doreen didn't need the extra space so she closed it off to conserve fuel oil."

"The place is yours again. What are you planning to do

with it?" I expected her to say, "Sell it immediately." But she surprised me.

"I don't know, quite honestly. My first instinct was to sell it, of course, not that I could probably get much for it. But now I'm not so sure. Do you want it? Now that you're getting divorced, you're going to need a place to live."

This was so far from what I'd been thinking, it threw me for a loop. Spiro was the one who moved out of the Bonaparte House, not me. Sophie had told me I could live there as long as I wanted. But did I want that? Sophie had said before that she eventually wanted to move back to Greece more or less permanently. And much as it pained me to say it, she wasn't getting any younger. But she had scads of money both in the United States and in Europe. If she'd wanted to move back, she could have done so long before now, and in style. Spiro didn't want the Bonaparte House. I looked around. Could I see myself living here? I'd never lived out in the country so I didn't know. Certainly not with the blue ducks.

"I don't want to talk about that now. We came here to talk about you, remember?"

She pursed her lips. "See if she's got any coffee or tea, will you? I'm going to go powder my nose. Then I'll tell you what I can."

Well, fine. What was another few minutes to wait for answers? At least she'd look good when she came back, which was all that mattered. I opened the fridge and found a container of half-and-half. A sniff told me it was still drinkable. The metal canister of coffee—an uninspiring supermarket brand—was located in the cupboard over the coffeemaker next to a box of paper filters. While the machine worked, I washed up the two coffee cups in the sink. From what I'd seen of the general clutter, the house was going to take weeks to clean out. Was Melanie planning to have a yard sale? Order a Dumpster? Take it all back to California with her?

I reached under the sink and pulled out some spray cleaner so I could wipe down the counters and the kitchen table. Under the sink I found a box made of plastic canvas on which someone had needlepointed a design. A duck, of course, and the word BINGO. I smiled and opened the box. Inside were some teabags, a Bingo card, and some pens with a tip about the size of a half dollar and marked "Dauber Delite." There was a silver bell, as well as a small duck figurine—a good luck charm perhaps? I set the box on the counter. Paloma might want it as a memento.

Melanie finally came back and sat down. I set a mug in front of her, along with the container of cream and a spoon. There was an unopened package of Oreos in the cupboard, so I set those out too.

"All right, Melanie. Spill."

She looked out the window to the overgrown field beyond. "This wasn't such a bad place to grow up, you know? I had a dog, a couple of cats, even a horse. There were plenty of kids at Rainbow Acres, so I'd ride my horse or my bike down there after school and we'd hang out."

I twisted an Oreo apart and popped one of the chocolate discs into my mouth.

"But I came along late in my parents' lives. My mother was forty-two when I was born, my father forty-five. They thought they were infertile until I finally arrived. It was tough for them. This farm is a hundred acres or so, but most of it isn't tillable. So we had dairy cows, which are a lot of work, especially when you suddenly have another mouth to feed and no money to hire help. My parents were exhausted all the time."

Animal husbandry and North Country economics notwithstanding, this just felt like a stall tactic. Filler. I wished she'd get to the point.

"But my parents weren't just tired," she continued. "They were angry. Bitter—"

A knock sounded at the front door and we both jumped. Melanie stuck her hand into her purse.

"Who could that be? I'll go see."

Melanie got up, throwing the strap of her bag over her shoulder. She followed me to the front door. "Can I help you?"

"Hello, what is it you call yourself now? Melanie? I like it."

The man was tall and rangy, with a green and yellow John Deere cap set over iron gray hair. He was handsome in a rough way. And I knew him. Hank, from the Rainbow Acres Farm.

I glanced at Melanie. Her mouth hung open, and for once she seemed speechless.

Hank locked eyes with Melanie. "I'm no vampire. Invite me in."

I stood aside. "Of course. We're just having coffee. Come on out to the kitchen."

We trooped in and sat down. Hank continued to stare at Melanie. "You two know each other," I said. It was a statement, not a question.

Melanie recollected herself. "We grew up together," she finally said. "What are you doing here, Hank?"

"I have a sick cow and didn't make it to the calling hours or the funeral." He helped himself to a cookie. "But I saw the car here and thought I'd stop in. You're better looking now than you were forty years ago."

Melanie smiled. "And you're a silver-tongued devil, same as you ever were."

"Doreen was a good neighbor. I was sorry to hear about her death. They haven't caught the perp yet, have they?" His voice was casual, but his eyes were wary.

Interesting. From my last adventure, I knew Hank was not above bending or breaking the law if it suited him. Was he fishing for information? Could he somehow be involved?

"No," Melanie said. "They arrested someone, but the evidence is circumstantial. And there's been another murder in town—Spencer Kane from the newspaper."

His eyebrows rose. "A serial killer in the Bay? Doesn't seem likely."

"Hank, was Doreen involved in anything . . . that might have made someone want to hurt her?" I wondered if the police had interviewed anyone at Rainbow Acres.

"You mean, like an organized Bingo ring or something? Or a school kid who thought the sloppy joes weren't up to par?" He snorted at his own stupid joke. "But seriously, no. I mean, it was easy to get her riled up, and she never hesitated to let you know exactly what she thought of you, in between cuss words. In the last few weeks she seemed happier than usual when she came in to buy her eggs."

This jibed with what Inky and Paloma had told me. "Did she say why?"

Hank stroked his chin. "She was coming into some money. She didn't say from where."

This conversation had netted me exactly nothing. It was all I could do not to throw up my hands in exasperation.

Hank turned to Melanie. "Would you like to come over and see Rainbow Acres? We've expanded quite a bit since last time you were there."

She shook her head. "No thanks. Communes aren't really my thing."

He stiffened. "We're not a commune. We're a cooperative educational farm. Big difference."

"You say tomato, I say tomahto." Melanie gave her coffee a little stir.

"You say Melanie, I say Shirley," he said. And he gave her a smile and leaned back in his chair. "So who owns this place now?"

"Doreen left it to me," Melanie said.

"That's fitting. Your parents were wrong to cut you off."

"I don't know," she said. "Sure, it was tough. But I never would have gotten where I am if they'd . . . loved me." A tear glistened in the corner of one heavily made-up eye. She cleared her throat.

My gut clenched. She'd done essentially the same thing to me—she hadn't thrown me out, but she'd left me to fend for myself when I was only eighteen. The end result was the same.

Like any card-carrying member of the Man Club, Hank retreated in the face of female emotion. "I'd like to buy this place," he stated matter-of-factly.

"What?" Melanie shook her head as if to clear it.

"We've been wanting to expand the apple orchards—we want to get into the hard cider business—and open a yoga retreat center. You've got what? Six bedrooms here? And the barn would be perfect for yoga with some renovations. I've got plenty of free labor from the college kids who come stay here over the summer instead of getting paying jobs."

"I'll think about it," Melanie said.

"You do that. We had a good year last year. I'll pay you market value—though I'd appreciate a small friend discount." He rose. "Don't get up. I'll see myself out."

When the door shut behind him, Melanie seemed to deflate. "Well, that was awkward," she finally said.

"What was he—an old boyfriend?"

"Something like that."

And then a thought popped into my head. She'd never told me who my father was. Had he just walked out the door? I filed away the question for another time. There was plenty here to deal with, without adding a pinch of paternity to the stewpot right now.

Melanie went to the front window and pulled aside the curtain just enough to watch Hank drive away. She looked around. "We've got a lot to do," she said. "I don't even know where to start."

"I do. We need to go through this pile of mail and see if any bills need to be paid and cancel her credit cards. Then we can start going through her things, room by room, to decide what to keep, donate, or throw away. And while we're doing that, you can tell me what brought you back to Bonaparte Bay."

She picked up the stack of envelopes and shoved it into

her purse, which was the size, shape, and weight of a fully loaded bowling bag by now. "I'll look at this stuff later. Caitlyn can make herself useful."

Caitlyn. I wondered what our sneaky assistant was up to. "Where'd you find her? Do you trust her?"

She looked at me sharply. "She came to me from an agency, with impeccable references. She used to work for Susan Lucci. And of course I trust her. Don't be ridiculous."

"Just asking, Mel."

"Don't call me Mel. I hate that."

One more name to add to the list of things I couldn't call her. Shirley. Mel. Mom.

"We've got a couple of hours before I have to go back into town, so let's use the time efficiently." I headed back to the kitchen and pulled out a couple of trash bags, which I placed one inside the other. I opened the refrigerator door and began to bag up the contents.

Melanie just stared at me. "What are you doing? We have a whole house to deal with here and you go for the fridge?"

"Just being practical. We can't leave food to spoil. Why make a bigger mess? Why don't you go outside and see if you can find a trash barrel? We should have asked Hank what people do about trash removal here—probably they take their stuff to the transfer station, but there's not too much here, so if there's no barrel, I'll just double bag it and put it in the Bonaparte House Dumpster."

She looked like she was going to be sick, as if trash were something that didn't exist. Well, for her, perhaps it didn't. But she went outside anyway and came right back in. "Nothing."

I frowned. Well, whatever. I made quick work of the fridge

and freezer. Doreen apparently hadn't shopped in a while, or she ate most of her meals at the school, because I filled only one bag. I gave the top a twist and a knot. Next I bagged up the unopened food items in her cupboard. Opened or expired things went into the trash bag. Anything unopened and still good went into a bag for donation to the Bay Food Pantry at the Methodist Church. An unoccupied house out in the country was bound to have hungry mice waiting to descend on it. No sense giving them anything to eat.

I sprayed down the inside of the fridge and wiped it, then repeated the process with the freezer. I unplugged the unit and propped the door open with a kitchen chair. Task one, accomplished.

"Come on, Melanie. Show me the bedroom."

Doreen's bedroom was papered in a pattern of pink and blue flowers—not a duck anywhere, thank goodness. The bed was neatly made, surrounded by stacks of paperback novels. I opened the closet door and was greeted with a rod full of sweatshirts, most embellished with some kind of sparkly design. She also seemed to favor stretchy knit pants—let's face it, who didn't favor comfort like that?—of which she seemed to have an endless supply. I pulled out a big armful of clothes and piled them on the bed. I decided to take the clothes to Watertown to the Salvation Army. Dolly would help me wash everything—in fact, maybe I'd just pay her to take care of it all for me. I couldn't see Melanie or Caitlyn knowing laundry detergent from Blue Curaçao, so there'd be no help there. And Dolly would want extra money for her trip to Branson.

"Come on, Melanie. Help me." We carried the trash and

donatable food out to my car. Melanie teetered on her high heels under the load. The food went behind the passenger side seat and the trash went into the trunk.

Melanie's collagen-plumped upper lip curled in distaste. "You don't expect me to ride back to town in that overstuffed car, do you? We'll look like the Beverly Hillbillies."

"Just be glad I don't strap a rocking chair to the top and make you ride up there. Are you going to sell to Hank?" Her face was impassive. Did she really feel nothing for the place where she'd grown up? I couldn't see myself living here, now that I thought about it. But on the other hand, I'd hate to see it go to a stranger.

"Hank's offer is tempting," she finally said.

"It would make things neat and easy," I agreed. I scanned the countryside. The property, at least what I could see of it, consisted of overgrown hayfields and several outbuildings, including a large barn that had once presumably housed cows. Who knew what was stored in there now? But exploring the outbuildings would have to wait for another day.

My eyes fell on the barn again. There must be some use for it—maybe winter boat storage? I wondered how many boats could fit inside. I frowned. There was a door on the side and it appeared to have blown open.

As I made my way toward it to close it, a shot cracked through the air, then another. I instinctively hit the ground, grabbed Melanie and pulled her down with me, and rolled up to the car. A bullet pinged off the Honda. "Get in the car!" I shrieked. Melanie seemed to be in shock, so I grabbed her and shoved her into the passenger seat, keeping as low as I could. "Get down!" She slumped over. "Damn it, Melanie!"

I dove into the driver's seat as another bullet pinged off the car, then I threw it into gear and peeled out. "Melanie! For God's sakes don't go catatonic on me now." She remained slumped over as I sped down the country road, my tires spitting up bits of gravel as I fishtailed out of there.

When we reached the main road, I relaxed a bit. Until I looked over at Melanie and realized that a dark stain had appeared on the left side of her jacket. She'd been hit.

◆ SEVENTEEN ◆

Oh, hell. What should I do? I was only five miles from the Bayview Hospital. If I wasn't being followed, I could drive her there faster than an ambulance could mobilize and get out here. And I couldn't just pull off to the side and wait. I had to do something. I drove on and hoped I'd made the right decision.

"Stay with me, Melanie," I said. "It's gonna be okay." My words sounded unconvincing, even to myself. But adrenaline took over and I handled the car like an Indy driver. I glanced in my rearview mirror. A truck with tinted windows was following me. Impossible to tell if it contained our assailant. Melanie's breathing came in ragged gasps and she began to shiver. Keeping one hand on the wheel and my eyes on the road, I reached blindly into the backseat and grabbed the first garment I found. I placed Doreen's sweatshirt over

Melanie as best I could while maintaining control of the car. It would have to do.

I pulled up at the Emergency Room doors at Bayview Hospital, then exited the car and raced inside. "Gunshot victim in my car," I said breathlessly. "Hurry!"

Gloria Campbell, the nurse on duty, mobilized immediately. Within seconds a gurney was being wheeled outside, and a moment later Melanie was in the hospital. Her face was pale and her eyes unseeing as she rolled past me. I looked around stupidly. The nurse came out from behind the counter and placed a warm blanket around my shoulders.

"We have to call the police," I said. "Somebody shot at us. They might have followed us here."

"Already done, and I've got the hospital on lockdown. Standard procedure when a gunshot comes in—of course, we see a lot more of that during hunting season." Gloria put her arm around me as I started to shiver. "Is there someone you'd like me to call?"

"What's happening?"

"They'll stabilize and evaluate her, then decide if she should be moved to the House of the Good Samaritan in Watertown. But they may just call the trauma surgeon in here if it's not too serious."

"How can a gunshot not be serious?" I demanded. "She was bleeding like crazy! She can't die. She's . . . my mother."

"Have a seat, Georgie. We'll know more soon." She patted my back and sat me down in a visitor's chair. "Who do you want me to call for you? Sophie? Spiro?"

Even in my semihysterical state, they would not be my

first choices. I was the one who handled things in our unconventional family unit, not them. I shook my head to clear it, then took a deep breath. "Uh, could I have some water? I'll make my own calls."

"Of course. I'll be right back." Her scrub top was cute, I noticed, kittens on a pale green background. It looked comfortable too. It felt good to fixate on something normal.

I reached into my pocket and pulled out my cell. I punched in Caitlyn's number, but the phone went straight to voice mail. Where the hell was she anyway? "It's Georgie. Call me. It's an emergency." I hung up. And then I thought about how she always seemed to disappear just about the time people got hurt. Or worse. No. What possible reason would Caitlyn have to shoot at us? Melanie was no doubt a complete pain to work for, but Caitlyn had a good job—as long as Melanie was paying her. If Caitlyn had a reason to want Melanie dead, I had no idea what it might be.

Jack picked up on the first ring. "I'll be right there," he said. A warm feeling spread throughout me, dissipating the adrenaline-induced chill that had permeated my body. I felt absurdly grateful to have someone I could actually count on. I was getting ahead of myself, but a picture of a future that included Jack had parked itself in my brain along with an endless supply of quarters to feed the meter.

The nurse came back with a bottle of water. She unscrewed the cap and poured some into a paper cup, then handed it to me. I took a sip.

"You look better than you did a few minutes ago," she said, her voice kind but matter-of-fact. "Keep that blanket around you for a while longer, okay?"

"Is there any news? About Melanie?"

She patted my hand. "We're in luck. Dr. Dinsmore is on duty today, not Dr. Fletcher, who's old as dirt and has shaky hands. She's stable, but they've decided not to move her. The surgeon should be here anytime now."

Relief washed over me, perhaps prematurely. If they weren't racing Melanie in an ambulance to the better-equipped Watertown hospital—or worse yet bringing in the Lifestar helicopter to take her to Syracuse—the medical personnel here must have thought she was not in terrible shape.

"Now," the nurse said, her voice crisp and efficient. "Did you say you were a relative?" Her eyebrows rose just a titch. "Because we need to fill out some paperwork."

How much help could I be? "Right," I said.

"Do you feel up to it now?"

"It will give me something to do. Oh. I need to go and get her purse for the insurance information. Do you think it's okay for me to go outside?"

She consulted her computer. "Tim Arquette is outside on duty. By the way, you'll need to move your car out of the ambulance loading zone."

"Then I'll do that now." She buzzed me outside, where I blinked in the bright sun. My eyes darted around until they landed on Tim. I was glad it wasn't Chief Moriarty, who had been out of the Academy long enough that his cop skills other than diner patrol seemed a bit . . . rusty. Tim nodded and I walked over to him.

"Hey, Georgie," he said. "Got yourself into some trouble again?"

"Yeah, something like that. Can't seem to help it these days."

He smiled, but kept his hand on the butt of his service weapon.

"I've got to move my car. I'm a little nervous."

Tom looked around. "We've got another officer patrolling the grounds. I'd say you're as safe as you can be. Go ahead."

I had my doubts about that, but made a beeline for the car. In all the excitement of getting Melanie to safety, I'd neglected to lock it, so I was glad to see that both my purse and Melanie's were still on the floor of the passenger side. There were also wet, dark splotches staining the gray upholstery. Bile rose in my throat. How much blood had she lost? Would she live?

I pulled the car away from the curb and steered it into the visitor's parking lot. With both purses in hand, I locked the car and made my way back to the ER. The nurse buzzed me back in, and I sat down and opened Melanie's purse.

The bag was full with Doreen's mail and Melanie's other essentials, including the pepper spray. I replaced that gently into a zippered compartment. Was it time for me to learn about guns? Bonaparte Bay wasn't safe anymore. Dolly sometimes hunted in the fall. I could have her give me some lessons. I'd be starting from scratch, since I didn't know the safety from a souvlaki.

Suddenly the bag shifted in my lap and the contents spilled out on the hospital floor. Damn. Who knew what kind of cooties were breeding down there? I righted the bag and set it on a chair next to me, then bent over to pick up the mail.

I fanned through the envelopes. Electric bill. Cell phone bill. Bank statement. Flyer from the Akwesasne Mohawk Reservation in Hogansburg inviting Doreen to play in a Bingo tournament with twenty-thousand-dollar stakes. I shot my eyes upward. I hoped Doreen was winning in heaven.

The next envelope felt familiar—the paper was thick and expensive. The return address confirmed that this letter was from MacNamara and MacNamara, the same law firm that was handling my divorce. Well, there were only two law firms in the Bay, so it was hardly surprising we had the same lawyers. What had Lydia, the secretary, told me when I was in a few days ago? Doreen had redone her will recently. Perhaps this had something to do with that. The envelope was open, so Doreen had read it. I started to pull out the page within when the nurse called me. I shoved everything back into the bag and carried the whole kit and caboodle over to the registration desk.

"Find what you need?"

I fished around until I came up with Melanie's wallet. I felt a little uncomfortable opening it up, even under these circumstances. A person's wallet contained such personal information.

I found Melanie's driver's license and insurance card and handed them to the nurse, who was not someone I recognized. Her name tag read, "Reva Wallace, R.N." She typed the information into her computer, then made photocopies of the cards and handed them back to me. "Emergency contact? Next of kin?"

I debated. Maybe Melanie would prefer that I list Caitlyn as the contact. "Me," I said. "I'm the emergency contact and the next of kin."

She was used to dealing with private information and was too professional to say anything, but this information clearly interested her. Things could get pretty dull around these parts, especially once all the tourists went home in the fall.

"That's that, then." She made a few more swift keystrokes and finished up with a flourish.

A voice came over the intercom. "Reva? It's Tom. Somebody's here for Georgie. You can let him in."

We both turned as the electronic doors glided open. A familiar figure strode through them. Jack.

My shoulders sagged with relief. He'd dropped whatever he was doing and come. For me. Strong arms wrapped around me in a hug I wished would never end. I burst into tears.

◆ EIGHTEEN ◆

Jack kept one arm around me and pulled back. He wiped away the droplets from my cheeks. "Are you okay? How's Melanie?"

I sniffled and reached for a tissue from the end table next to the visitors' chairs. "I'm okay. Better now that you're here. We're waiting for the surgeon to arrive from Watertown."

"What happened?"

My stomach knotted up again. "We were out at Doreen's and somebody shot at us from the barn. One of the bullets hit Melanie. And I can't find Caitlyn."

My cell rang. The display read *Liza*. "Hi," I said.

"My God, Georgie! You've been shot at?"

Liza had a preternatural knowledge of Bay news, almost before it happened. She'd never shared where she got her information.

"I'm okay. Melanie's in surgery, or will be as soon as the doctor gets here."

"Do I need to come over there?"

"No, Jack is here with me." I smiled at him and he squeezed my hand. "Have you seen Caitlyn? She's not answering her cell, and I need to tell her about Melanie."

Silence. "I didn't want to tell you about this now. You've got enough on your plate. She and Melanie stayed with you last night, right? Well, she's been back over here today, and I caught her snooping around, trying to get into my office again. I'm keeping my eye on her. I'm positive she's up to something."

"I think you're right. If you see her again, tell her to call me."

"I will. Take care of yourself, Georgie." She clicked off.

Jack kept his arm around me, and we sat there in a comfortable silence for a while, until my agitation level began to creep up again.

"What's taking so long? The surgeon should be here by now."

At that moment Dr. Dinsmore came into the waiting room. In his early forties, with close-cropped hair and a dark tan, he clearly spent some time out in the sun, probably on one of those expensive cigarette boats that raced up and down the river. He and his wife were regulars at the Bonaparte House. She usually ordered the Greek salad and grilled chicken. He usually ordered the gyro, extra onions, extra sauce.

He wore a pale blue dress shirt with a matching tie, which he was adjusting as he came toward us. I wondered if he'd just changed his clothes—removed his bloodstained scrubs perhaps. A lump the size of a lemon and just as acidic formed in my throat.

"Hi, Georgie," he said. "I'm sorry about your . . . mother, isn't it?"

"Yes. What can you tell me?" I tried to swallow the lemon, but it just stuck there.

Dr. Dinsmore patted my arm. "The surgeon is scrubbing up now. There are no guarantees, but I'm cautiously optimistic. It appears she was struck by only one bullet. My guess is that she'll lose her spleen."

"Spleen? You can live without that, right?" Jack squeezed my hand.

The doctor nodded. "If there's no additional damage, she'll live a perfectly normal life and be back at work on that television show of hers in a few months."

It was too early to feel relieved—I'd seen enough medical dramas on television to know that things could go horribly wrong in the blink of an eye—but I did feel marginally better.

Dr. Dinsmore looked down at his pager, which was beeping. "They're ready to get started on the surgery. It's going to be a couple of hours, then she'll be in recovery for an hour until we move her to a room." He turned to Jack. "Why don't you two go take a walk or grab a bite to eat somewhere, then come back? We have Georgie's number and we'll call if, for some reason, she needs to get here quickly."

Jack nodded. "That's a good idea."

I shook my head vehemently. "That's *not* a good idea. I'm not leaving her." *The way she left you all those years ago*, a little voice piped in. True. But that was who she was. It wasn't who I was. I'd be at the Bayview Hospital until my mother was out of danger.

"Okay," he said. "When did you last eat?"

Who knew? Right, cookies and coffee at Doreen's—no, my mother's house now. "A while ago," I admitted.

"How's the food in the hospital cafeteria? Never mind. Let's not risk it. Why don't I go get you a bowl of chowder from the Sports Page? Maybe Midge or Dolly could come and sit with you while I'm gone?"

I wasn't especially hungry, but we were going to be here for hours. Soup sounded as good as anything, and it would keep me full for a long time. "Chowder, yes. But I'll be fine by myself. You go ahead."

His blue eyes searched mine. "I'll be back as soon as I can." He dropped a kiss on the top of my head and left.

The room around me was long and narrow. Last time I'd been in here was a few years ago when Cal broke her arm playing soccer. The décor hadn't been updated. I gathered up the two purses and slung both over one shoulder.

Nurse Reva was at her post behind the sliding glass window. She looked up from the novel she'd been reading and opened the window. "Need something, Georgie?"

"No, Jack's gone to get me something to eat. Listen, is there someplace I can wait other than out here in the ER lobby? I'd feel safer if I weren't so exposed."

"Sure. There's a family waiting room just down the hall. Want a book to read?" She opened a drawer and peered down into it. "I've got plenty—romance, mystery? The night nurse likes science fiction, so there might be some of that here too. Not crazy about the tentacles personally."

I shook my head. "That's okay. Maybe later. I've got some paperwork to sort through so I'll just take care of that."

"Let me know if you change your mind. We've got a

decent library. It's pretty dull here most of the time. And I like it that way." She pointed to the hallway. "Family lounge is down that hall on the left. I'll send Captain Hottie in when he gets back."

I smiled and headed for the lounge.

The room was bright, with a full wall of windows overlooking the river. If I recalled my history correctly, the hospital was built on the site of one of the Bay's grand old nineteenth-century hotels, all of which were now gone. Today this piece of prime real estate would never be approved for a hospital, but less rigid zoning laws in the mid-twentieth century gave today's sick and injured a lucky break. A big white boat with a giant paddlewheel spinning at the back motored past. Either the *Lady Liberty* or the *Lady Liberty II*. I was a little surprised to see tours going out mid-week until I remembered that it was Thursday afternoon, and the tourists would have already started trickling in for the weekend. I wondered if I'd be able to get the Bonaparte House open for tomorrow's dinner seating. What if something happened to Melanie?

Well, something *had* happened to Melanie. I took out my cell phone then reached inside her purse and pulled out Doreen's stack of mail. Might as well sort through the paperwork and start notifying the companies she'd done business with.

As I sorted the mail into piles—bills, bank statement, magazines, miscellaneous—my mind refused to focus on anything except two questions that had been playing in a more or less continuous loop. Who had shot at us? And why?

I couldn't even be sure the bullets had been intended for Melanie. What if someone wanted *me* dead? Goose bumps rose on my arms and I rubbed them down. I'd gotten unintentionally involved in some shady business a little while ago. Maybe that wasn't truly resolved, even though the authorities seemed to think it was.

One thing was for certain. Even Melanie was not a good enough actress to fake getting shot. No one would go to such lengths to try to cover up killing her own cousin or a newspaper reporter. It was simply too dangerous. But she was involved somehow, I knew it. And someone wanted her dead.

I pulled the last envelope out of the bag. The MacNamara and MacNamara envelope. The seal had already been broken, and the flap was tucked back inside. The letter was written on the same heavy bond paper as the envelope. It felt both luxurious and wasteful in my hand.

The date was one month ago.

Dear Ms. Webber:

This office represents the Elihu Bloodworth Trust. In accordance with the terms set forth by Mr. Bloodworth, the trust will expire next year and all proceeds are to be distributed to certain of his beneficiaries. We have identified you as a potential heir. Please make an appointment to discuss this matter with me at your earliest opportunity. Bring an original or a certified copy of your birth certificate and a photo identification with you to the meeting.

Cordially,
James MacNamara, Esq.

Whoa. I leaned back in the chair and blew out a breath. It was true. Doreen really was expecting money. Of course, who knew how much money was in the trust or what her share would be. Doreen probably would have been ecstatic with a few hundred or a few thousand dollars. But surely it must be a substantial amount if someone were willing to kill her for it—if that's why she died. So far there'd been no formal announcement of the police's theories regarding motive.

It didn't take a rocket scientist to figure out the simplest motive of all: One less heir to the Bloodworth Trust meant a bigger share for the remaining heirs.

I didn't know whether Melanie was related to Doreen through her mother or her father. Had she said their mothers were sisters? But it didn't matter—or maybe it did. Doreen had written a will naming Melanie as her sole executrix and beneficiary. So it might be that no matter where in the family the trust money came from, Melanie was going to inherit at least one share. Two shares, if Melanie was an heir to the trust herself. And that might very well be enough to kill for.

Except Melanie was lying on an operating table right now, fighting for her life.

Which could mean that there were one or more heirs out there who wanted the whole, undivided trust.

Which could also mean that I, and my daughter, who were Melanie's beneficiaries upon her death, were in danger.

Bloodworth. The name seemed familiar, like I'd heard it a long time ago, but I couldn't place it.

I gathered up all the envelopes and put them back into

Melanie's purse, then zipped it closed. Jack would be back any minute and I needed time to digest all this.

And I needed to find Caitlyn.

I punched in her number just as Jack walked in. He set a brown paper bag down on the table and I inhaled the aroma of hot fish chowder. Caitlyn's voice mail picked up. Again. "Caitlyn, this is Georgie. Call. Me. Immediately." I rang off.

"Remind me never to make you angry," Jack said, giving me his movie star grin, the one that made a deep dimple appear in his sculpted cheek.

"Then don't ever lie to me. Or take off without telling me where you are." My words were harsher than I'd intended, but it had been a tough couple of days.

Jack's face froze, just for a moment.

"I'm sorry. I'm just keyed up, and my blood sugar's probably low. That soup smells delicious."

He relaxed. "Not sure if it's perch, pike, or walleye in here, but you're right. It does smell good." He pulled out two white cylindrical containers, two plastic spoons, and two packages of saltines, and set one of each in front of me.

"Doesn't matter," I said. "As long as it's one or more of the above and fresh from the St. Lawrence, it's fine with me." I dipped my spoon into the chowder and took my first taste. It was thick, creamy, and had a lovely pool of yellow butter floating on the chunky surface. Oh, yeah.

Jack crumbled his crackers on top of the soup, gave a stir, and dug in. After a couple of bites, he looked up. "I should have gotten us something to drink. I'll run out to the vending machine. What would you like?" He stood.

"Since they probably don't sell chardonnay here at the hospital, I'll just have a bottle of water."

"One water, coming up. And I'll see if there's any news on Melanie while I'm out there."

I watched Jack's fine behind and long legs walk out the door of the family lounge. Where we would end up, I didn't know. But for right now I was pretty happy with where we were.

The door suddenly flew open. My heart flew into my throat. Caitlyn. The wandering assistant had finally returned.

◈ NINETEEN ◈

My blood pressure skyrocketed. "Where the hell have you been?" I demanded. She didn't work for me, and she was almost young enough to be my daughter, but I didn't care whether I had the right to yell at her or not.

The girl was visibly upset and she sat down hard in a chair. Her head dropped into her hands. A moment later she looked up, the tears in her big brown eyes magnified by her enormous glasses. If I wasn't angry with her, not to mention suspicious, I would have felt some sympathy. As it was, I just wanted answers. But before I could question her, she asked one of her own.

"She's been shot? Shot?" She was almost hysterical.

Jack came back in at that moment and looked from one of us to the other. He set one bottle of cold water in front of Caitlyn. "Drink," he ordered. "Georgie and I will share this one."

I felt an absurd little rush of joy. Sharing a bottle of water with no cups in sight? That had to be significant for our relationship. My joy didn't last long as anger came rushing back in.

Caitlyn gave what would have been an adorable little hiccup under other circumstances and took a long drink of the water. It seemed to restore her, because she looked up at me. "She sent me out to do some research. I had to go to Watertown, the county seat, to do it. If I'd been with her, this might not have happened."

I resisted the urge to snort. This petite little hipster with her skinny jeans and black-and-white saddle shoes thought she could have prevented this? What would she have done? Immobilized the killer with her exceptional cool?

"I think it's time you told me what's going on. The truth." My maternal truth phaser was set to stun.

She looked from me to Jack, then back. She stalled by taking another long sip of the water, then wiping the condensation on her pants. "I can't. She'll kill me. I promised not to tell. Besides, I'm not done with my research anyway."

"Georgie, can I talk to you for a minute?" Jack motioned me over to a corner.

"Don't say I'm being too hard on her. She and Melanie are in some kind of mess and they've dragged me into it. They owe me answers, and right now she's the only one who can give them." Caitlyn could probably hear every word I was saying.

Jack rubbed a hand down my arm, leaving a trail of tingles in its wake. "She might not want to talk in front of me, which I understand. If you're sure you're okay, why don't I leave you two alone for a little while. Maybe she'll open up to you. Then if you don't mind my bachelor's quarters, once we know Melanie's resting comfortably, you can come over and I'll make you dinner."

If I was in some kind of danger, I didn't want to be alone tonight. Oh, let's face it. I didn't want to be alone ever. Over the last couple of months Jack had given me a glimpse of what life could be like with a real partner. And I liked what I saw.

"That sounds good. I'm dying to find out the extent of your cooking skills. And we still need to put Monty's files back together."

"Don't worry about that," he said. "Although I do have to get these boxes to Trish in Albany before she leaves for her field work. She'll just have to live with the mess."

I didn't want to get off on a bad foot with the sister I'd yet to meet. "No, I want to help. It'll keep my mind off things."

His hand was still on my arm as he pulled me in for a hug. "I'm so glad I met you," he said simply.

"Me too," I whispered. "Call me later."

He nodded to Caitlyn and left.

I sat myself back down at the table. My Jack-induced warm-fuzzy feeling chilled to the temperature of my luke-warm fish chowder. I put the lids back on the containers and deposited all the trash in the receptacle by the windows. Hopefully this trash got emptied every night because it would be quite fragrant by morning.

"You two are cute," Caitlyn said.

"Don't try to change the subject. In case you haven't noticed, trouble came to Bonaparte Bay the minute you and Melanie arrived. When was that exactly?"

She chewed her lower lip. "The day before Doreen died. We stayed in Watertown that night. That day, we went to see her."

Why was I not surprised? My mother had gone to see her cousin before she came to see her own daughter. "And?"

"And what?" The girl was infuriating.

"And why did you go to see her?"

She fiddled with the cap on her water bottle before she answered. "Melanie had some . . . business to discuss with Doreen."

"Let's cut the crap, Caitlyn. I know about the trust." Well, not everything. But enough.

She started. "What *do* you know? She'll fire me if I tell you any more."

"If she dies, you'll be out of a job anyway."

We both turned as the door to the family lounge opened. Dr. Dinsmore came in, smiling. "She's in recovery and doing fine."

Both Caitlyn and I nodded, relieved. Although Caitlyn's relief may have been more a result of us having been interrupted than the update on Melanie's condition. Uncharitable of me, I knew.

"It was the spleen, as we'd thought," the doctor continued. "We removed it along with the bullet and repaired the rest of the damage. She'll go home in a few days, and then she'll need a couple of months to recuperate."

"Will she have any lasting limitations?" Caitlyn had pulled out her phone and begun typing into it. "The producers of the show will have to be notified and I need to know what to tell them."

"Probably not. People can live quite normal lives without the spleen."

"Can we go and see her?" I wasn't going to get any more information out of Caitlyn now anyway.

"She'll be in her room shortly. Second floor. I made sure she had a private room with a view of the river."

"That was thoughtful of you, thanks."

Melanie lay in her hospital bed. Her face was as pale as fine marble. She was hooked up to an IV bag on a pole as well as to various monitors that emitted a beep every now and then. I was glad she didn't have a mirror because her normally perfectly coiffed hair was a big blond hay bale, with pieces sticking out in all directions.

My heart squeezed. No matter what she'd done to me, or what she still had up her sleeve to torture me with once she recovered, she was my mother. We'd never have the kind of relationship I had with Callista, but we might be okay someday.

Her eyes, which were nested in deep purpley shadows, began to flutter. Caitlyn came and stood next to me. The lids opened and closed again in slow motion, as though her eyelashes were an immense weight. Finally, she looked at me, then at Caitlyn.

"They said I'd been shot," she rasped.

"That's right. But you're going to be good as new in a few weeks. Do you want a sip of water or anything?" My hand reached automatically for the plastic pitcher on the bedside table.

She shook her head. "Caitlyn."

The girl bent closer.

"A few weeks?"

Caitlyn nodded. "That's what the doctor said."

"Fix my hair a little. Lipstick. Take my picture." She lay back and closed her eyes again, exhausted from the effort of the conversation.

I frowned. "Melanie, are you sure about that? Why don't you wait until you're feeling more like yourself?"

But Caitlyn was already reaching for Melanie's purse, which I'd set on a visitor's chair when we came in. She pulled out a zippered bag and proceeded to give Melanie a touch-up.

While she was playing Max Factor, Melanie's enormous purse tipped over once again and some of the contents spilled out. As I shoved them back in, a business card fell out of one of the pockets. It was bright white with a stark black border. *Sheldon Todd*, it read. In small black letters under the phone number and e-mail address was a single word: *Genealogist*.

I shoved the card into my pocket.

The floor nurse came in. "What's this?" she said crisply. "Time for me to check Ms. Ashley's vitals, then she needs to get some sleep." She leveled her steely gaze at Caitlyn, then me. "Go home and get some rest of your own. She'll be much more alert tomorrow during visiting hours."

Caitlyn snapped a couple of photos with her phone.

"Come on, Caitlyn. Time for us to go."

"Tweet it," Melanie rasped. "My fans."

Oh, for heaven's sake.

❖ TWENTY ❖

Caitlyn drove off in the black rental. She said she was headed to the Camelot to stay overnight rather than going back to the Spa. I was fairly sure she wasn't going to leave town, not with Melanie in the hospital. My grilling could wait until tomorrow.

It felt like it had been days since I'd been back at the Bonaparte House, even though it had only been hours. Tomorrow was Friday, and we were scheduled to be open for dinner, with lunch and dinner services on Saturday and Sunday. Dolly and I had done the advance work while we prepped the funeral luncheon, so the rest of the evening stretched out in front of me.

The card from the genealogist was burning a hole in my pocket. I pulled it out. *Sheldon Todd*. The phone number had a local area code. My watch read seven fifteen—it would probably be rude to call him now, if I even dared. Would he tell me anything? I wasn't his client.

But it wasn't too late to do some other research.

I walked the two blocks to the Bonaparte Bay Free Library. Marina's Diner was closed and dark, and Aunt Jennie, the smiling neon figure who graced the roof, was unlit. I hoped Marina and Sophie were winning money on their trip to the casino.

The nineteenth-century library, made of gray, rough-cut blocks of Gouverneur marble quarried twenty-five miles away, had a Gothic-style façade. The broad stone steps dipped a bit in the middle from generations of feet ascending them. When I got to the top, I sent Jack a text message, asking him to pick me up there when the library closed.

The temperature dropped as I entered the library. I was glad I'd put on a sweatshirt. I had virtually no time to read for pleasure during the tourist season, but I patronized the library during the winter and early spring. Fiction was the only section I was familiar with, so I approached the front desk.

The library had exactly one full-time employee, JoJo Linton, who was chewing gum and typing something into the keyboard in front of her. The library relied on volunteers for their other staffing needs. "Hi, Georgie," she said, snapping her gum. "I didn't expect to see you for another month or so. We just got in a couple of yummy new mysteries, if you're interested."

"Tempting. But I'm here to do some research. Where's the local history section?"

"Haven't you already figured out all the secrets of the Bonaparte House?" She giggled.

It was probably best not to tell her too much at this point. "I don't know if I can take any more surprises, honestly. No, I was interested more in the general history of Bonaparte Bay and the surrounding area. Uh, you know, people who might have lived around here, that sort of thing."

She looked thoughtful. "Well, I guess the first place to start would be *Hanson's Illustrated History of Bonaparte Bay*. That will cover the nineteenth century. If you're looking for something specific, we can do a database search and see what we've got. The historical society's been working on digitizing all the old newspapers and our fragile history books, but the project isn't complete yet."

"Let me take a look at that book," I said quickly. JoJo seemed discreet and trustworthy, but you never knew.

"Sure." She led me to a section in the back of the tiny library. Her fingers ran nimbly over the spines of the books on one shelf, stopping when they reached a leather-bound book with gilt trim. "Here it is." She pulled it out and set it on the table. "You can just thumb through the pictures—lots of the big island houses are in there—or there's an index in the back."

"Thanks," I said, taking a seat and opening the book.

"Let me know if you need anything else." She started toward her desk, then turned back. "It's funny."

"What's funny?" I resisted the urge to look at the old pictures and turned directly to the index.

"There seems to be a run on requests for Bonaparte Bay history the last few days."

My spine stiffened. "Oh?" Did I sound casual?

"Some girl was in here yesterday. I'd never seen her before, which is why I remembered her."

I felt like the Grinch, thinking up a lie and thinking it up quick. "You know, there was a girl at the Bonaparte House the other day looking for a job for next summer. What did she look like?"

JoJo didn't hesitate. "Petite, dark hair, big glasses. Dressed a little weird."

Caitlyn.

"Hmmm, no, my girl was a blonde."

"You know who else was in?"

But wait, there's more? "No . . . who?"

"Spencer Kane. He was here the day before he died."

I sat back in the chair. Spencer had said he had something he wanted to talk to me about. Something I was never going to know now. What had he found? And could I find it here?

"Oh, wow," I said. "Did you tell the police?"

"Yeah, some cop came and asked me about him. You know, how often did he come in, was he behaving normally that day? Spencer was in here a lot for various things, so I didn't think much of it at the time. As for behaving normally, well, he was naturally a little weird. Not that I would want to see him dead," she added hastily.

"No, of course not."

"Well, I have to get back and process some interlibrary loan requests. We're closing in a half hour, but you can always come back tomorrow." She gave her gum a snap and went back to her desk.

My index finger traced the entries in the index until I came to the B's. *Bloodworth.*

Hands shaking, I turned to the page.

A photo of a man took up a quarter page. He was dressed in severe black with a white shirt and funny little tie, sitting in a big carved chair that framed his white hair. His light-colored eyes pierced through the years and seemed to stare right into my soul. The man's face was gaunt, with sunken cheeks only partially camouflaged by chin whiskers and bushy sideburns. His lips were set in a hard, thin line. Yikes.

Elihu Bloodworth, 1832–1901.

So this was the guy who'd established the trust. I read on.

Elihu Bloodworth was the son of Eleazer Bloodworth and Mary Jenkins Bloodworth, who were among the first settlers of the Town of Alexandria in the early part of the last century.

I skipped the parts about where Elihu went to school and what church he attended.

Elihu Bloodworth when a young man removed to Watertown, where he established on the banks of the Black River a lumbering mill that became the most successful such operation in the North Country. In 1864, upon returning to his native home after service in the War Between the States, Bloodworth married Zerilla Mason. Three sons and two daughters were born of the union.

The rest of the write-up was so flowery and complimentary, I wondered if Elihu had paid the author to write something nice. Because he certainly didn't look like a very pleasant guy despite the fact that he was quite wealthy.

So Doreen was most likely descended from this man if she was a beneficiary of his trust. Possibly Melanie and I were too. I tried on the name "Bloodworth" and found it a bit creepy.

I flipped back to the index. There was another entry for Bloodworth. *See Montgomery.*

Montgomery. Gladys. Now I remembered where I'd heard the name "Bloodworth." What had Gladys said? Her husband's mother was wealthy. A Bloodworth. So what did that mean? Was Gladys also a beneficiary of the trust? And if so, was she in danger?

The page took me to another photo, this one of a large Victorian house.

The residence of Mr. and Mrs. Gerald Montgomery at Bonaparte Bay. Mrs. Montgomery is the former Melvina Bloodworth, daughter of Elihu Bloodworth.

I studied the photo. Yup. Gladys's house.

The lights dimmed then came back up. JoJo's voice sounded from the loudspeaker. "The library is closing in twenty minutes. Please bring all materials to be checked out to the front desk."

I closed up the book and left it on the table. Best to let the professionals reshelve it in the correct spot, since my Dewey Decimal System skills were rusty.

"Thanks, JoJo," I said as I walked past the circulation desk.

"Hope you found what you needed."

I'd found something, but what it meant remained to be seen.

Jack's Jeep pulled up just as I walked out onto the covered front porch. It was a high step up into the boxy vehicle. I grabbed the handle and pulled myself into the seat, not quite as gracefully as I'd been intending. Jack gave me his movie star smile. "Ready for a romantic night of . . . paperwork?"

I laughed. "Shall I stop at the restaurant and pick up a bottle of wine? Or maybe a six-pack of beer?"

"Way ahead of you," he said, indicating a brown paper bag on the floor of the backseat. "I stopped at the liquor store and picked up both. And a pizza from Mama's."

Mmmm, pizza sounded so good. I rarely had it. It wasn't on the menu at the Bonaparte House.

We pulled up at the Suds-a-Rama and parked in the back. The Laundromat was open for another hour, but the place was empty except for Earl Welch, the owner, who was out back having a smoke. He raised an eyebrow when he saw me in the Jeep, gave a nod, and blew out an enormous and rather fascinating smoke ring.

"Hey, Earl." Jack offered me a hand to get down out of the high vehicle.

"Jack." Another puff. Another curl of smoke from his nostrils.

"Any news about the break-in in Jack's apartment? Did they take anything from you?" A big, lean, but healthy-looking cat with fur the color of a Creamsicle wandered out from behind the trash cans and began to twine itself around my ankles. "Hey, there, fella. Where'd you come from?" I reached down slowly and, when the cat didn't appear to want to bite me, gave it a stroke. In return it gave me a satisfied purr. I'd always wanted a pet—unfortunately, the party poopers at the Board of Health did not want me to have one.

Earl flicked the ashes from his cigarette, then pushed up the bill of his Yankees cap. "Naw. I was here working. Whoever it was wouldn't have gotten much. I'd just emptied the machines and gone to the bank."

Jack looked thoughtful. "I'm sure the police asked you, but did you see or hear anyone going up the back stairs that day?"

"Naw. I didn't see anything, and with the machines running, it's loud in here."

I nodded. I could hear them whirring and spinning now, even outside the building.

The cat undulated around my feet once more, then wandered off.

If the breaker-enterer didn't even try to get the easy money at the Suds, he—or she—must not have had robbery in mind. Which meant she—or he—was looking for something specific.

Jack and I went up the back stairs to his apartment. I'd been here a couple of times. I couldn't even say it was a typical bachelor pad. It was far more barren than that. Living room attached to the kitchen, small dining table with metal legs. Beyond that were a bathroom and the bedroom. Not that I'd been invited in there yet. If we ever did go all the way (I sounded like a teenager in a health class movie about

STDs), I did sort of hope it was someplace nice. Romantic, even. Although I was probably going to be so nervous when the time came I wouldn't even notice my surroundings.

The place was neat and clean. No stray clutter, dishes done, remote control on the end table by the couch where it belonged. Not surprising—Jack was a twenty-year Coast Guard officer. Orderliness was ingrained in him.

He set the pizza and the drinks on the counter. "I hope you don't mind paper plates and plastic cups and silverware. Most of my stuff is still in storage in Oswego." That explained the lack of dirty dishes in the sink and the clean countertops.

"No, that's fine. Let's eat. I'm starving."

He pulled out a drawer and found a corkscrew, which he used to open the wine. He popped the top on a Riverbrew Beer for himself.

We dug into some excellent pizza. After a few bites, and a few sips of wine, some of the stress I'd been under for the last few days began to slip away. When Jack stood up and began to massage my shoulders, his skillful fingers kneading out the knots, I thought I'd died and gone to heaven.

"Mmmmm." My eyes closed. Not that I'd ever had a professional massage so I didn't really have anything to compare it to, but I wondered if it could be any better than this. Jack bent down, moved my hair aside, and brushed his lips against the nape of my neck. I gave a delicious shiver.

"As much as I'd like to continue this, we should probably get to work."

Work? What work? Oh, right. The artifacts. Duty called. "Let's get it done," I said.

Once the leftover pizza was stored in the fridge and the plates and utensils were thrown away, I wiped down the table with a spritz of cleaner and a paper towel, then ran the towel over the counters as well. Jack poured me another glass of wine and set the box of paperwork on a spare chair.

"So this was the only thing the intruder disturbed? It doesn't make sense. Why would somebody go to the risk of breaking in for this?" I took a sip of my wine and set the cup on the table, as far from the paperwork Jack was pulling out of the box as possible. I could just see myself spilling liquid all over and ruining everything.

"I know," Jack said, stacking loose papers in a pile. "I can't imagine what could be in here that anyone would want. Arrowheads turn up all over the North Country, all the time."

"So what's the system here?" The papers all seemed to have a numbered label affixed to the back. The file folders had similar labels. There were photos too.

"I'm pretty sure all we have to do is check the numbers and refile everything into the corresponding folder. It shouldn't be more complicated than that."

"Sounds easy, and mindless enough after a long day." I rolled my head around my neck, luxuriating in the feel of the loose, warm, pain-free muscles.

"I'm sorry. If you want to just go lie down, I'll do this."

Tempting as that was, I shook my head. "No, I want to help." I grabbed a handful of loose papers and began to stack them into number order. They seemed to be detailed notes about what Monty had found, where he'd found it, and when. And there were several photographs associated with each file. In each case the artifact had been photographed, as had been the hole or surface where the item was found, as well as the surrounding countryside. The number labels that had accompanied each of the actual artifacts we'd boxed up would presumably match these file numbers. The work was not difficult, and it didn't take long to put everything back into its proper file.

I reached for another stack. "So when does your sister expect these?"

"I need to drive them to her in Albany tomorrow." He hesitated. "We haven't seen each other in a while and she's leaving for Arizona on Sunday. I was thinking about taking her out to dinner and staying over, then driving her to the airport and coming back Sunday morning. But I don't want to leave you alone."

My Jack-induced warm-fuzzy feeling intensified. As much as I wanted to beg him to stay, I wasn't ready to put myself out there and ask for what I needed. I'd been a caretaker, the fixer, the smoother-overer, for too long. Maybe, just maybe, an ability to depend on someone else would come in time.

"No, no. I'll be fine." Sort. File. Sort.

He raised an eyebrow at me.

"No, really. I won't be alone at all tomorrow. I'll go visit Melanie at the hospital, then there'll be lots of people in and out of the Bonaparte House all day till we open for dinner." I smiled. "And Melanie's got a police guard, and Chief Moriarty and his wife have a dinner reservation. I'll be fine. Really, I want you to go."

A shadow passed over his face, and I reached for his hand. "That's not what I meant, silly. Go have fun with your sister."

He relaxed. "Okay, then. If you promise me you won't try to investigate anything by yourself."

Me? Investigate? I wouldn't call what I did investigating. More like stumbling onto the truth. "Okay."

I hoped that was a promise I'd be able to keep.

It didn't take long to get through the pile. I put the folders back into numerical order, then began to reinsert them into the file box.

"That's odd. There's a file missing." Folders were marked 55 and 57. No 56.

Jack frowned. "We didn't misfile it, did we? Monty was so meticulous." He fanned his thumb slowly through the files from front to back.

"Did it fall down to the bottom of the box under the rest of the files?"

He pushed the files against the back wall and slid a hand underneath. "Nothing."

"Is that what your intruder came for? Maybe he got it."

Jack nodded. "The last folder is labeled *Index*." He withdrew it and spread the pages on the table in front of us. "Here it is: fifty-six. Bartlett Farm, September 1966."

The blood drained from my face. "My maiden name was Bartlett," I whispered. "And it's Melanie's birth name and it would have been her parents' name as well."

Jack's lips were set in a thin line.

"Doreen's farm," I said simply. "Jack, where are the artifacts? Did you check those?"

He rose. "I looked at them quickly, but I didn't open the boxes. Come on. They're in the bedroom."

Under other circumstances I would have been delighted to follow Jack to the bedroom, any bedroom. But right now my brain was working overtime and it had nothing to do with love. How did a Native American artifact figure into this increasingly complicated scenario?

Jack dropped to his knees and lifted the simple beige bed skirt. "Reach in that night table drawer, will you? There's a flashlight."

I found it and handed it to him. He switched it on. "I'm going to have to ask the cleaning lady to do a better job. There's dust."

I leaned down for a look. "Those boxes have been moved," I said. "See the trail that was left amid the dust bunnies?"

"You're right." He pulled the six boxes out and began to open them until he found the one containing the artifacts numbered in the fifties. The lid flew off with a flourish and landed on the floor.

"Damn!" he said. "Fifty-six is gone."

❖ TWENTY-ONE ❖

Jack replaced the boxes under the bed and stood up. He offered me a hand and pulled me to my feet.

"Let's go look at that index again," I said. "Did it say what the item was?"

Jack stood behind me and read over my shoulder. "Arrowhead. Onondaga chert. Early Woodland Meadowood Phase circa 1,000 B.C.," he said.

"That doesn't tell us much." I frowned. "A three-thousand-year-old arrowhead?"

"No idea. What would somebody want with it?"

"Clearly it was specifically targeted. It couldn't be random." I tapped my finger on the paper. "I don't suppose Monty kept photocopies anywhere?"

Jack laughed. "Pretty sure he didn't, but we could ask Gladys when she gets back. This paperwork goes back to the days of mimeographs and ditto machines. And Monty's been dead for twenty years."

"I'm not sure it would tell us anything anyway. If you look at the contents of the rest of these files, it's pretty simple. Photographs and a write-up of the procedure used to uncover the item." A yawn escaped my lips. I was suddenly dead tired.

"Come on," Jack said. "Let's get you to bed." He rose.

I looked at him quizzically, not sure where this was going. In theory I would have loved to sleep with Jack. Had thought about it often. In reality, I was a bit reticent to take our relationship to the next level. And it probably had something to do with the fact that historically I had *Titanic*-like taste in men. Disasters. It was difficult to trust myself to know how I really felt, let alone trust someone else.

He brushed his lips across mine. "Don't worry. I'll behave like a gentleman and sleep on the couch."

I leaned in closer. "I'm more worried about myself not acting like a lady."

He laughed and took my chin in his hands, lifting it up so I could see his forget-me-not-colored eyes. "When the time comes, it's going to be spectacular. I promise."

"Do you always keep your promises?"

"I do my best. If I ever don't, you'll know there's a very good reason."

That was all I could ask for.

I woke the next morning in Jack's arms, wearing one of his T-shirts, with my head nestled on his shoulder. *I could get used to this.* He pulled me in closer and I caught a faint whiff of yesterday's aftershave. Nothing had happened. And yet something had. My defense shields had dropped a little.

"Mmmm," he said. "This is nice."

"Yes, it is." I took a deep breath and blew it out. The clock said six thirty—later than I usually slept until the restaurant closed for the season. I sat up and a shiver went through me.

"Come on, get dressed. Let's go out for breakfast at the Family Diner. I feel like pancakes with real maple syrup and some of those homemade sausages they make. We've both got busy days lined up."

I grabbed my clothes and went into the bathroom to change. I ran a finger through my hair and inspected my teeth. After pizza last night, my breath could not be fresh.

"There's an extra toothbrush in the medicine cabinet," Jack called.

A couple of decades of living with Spiro Nikolopatos had made me suspicious. Why would Jack keep an extra toothbrush? Did he have a girlfriend? Did he do one-night stands with women he picked up at Fat Max's? I reviewed what I'd seen in his nightstand when I looked for the flashlight last night. Nope, there'd been no condoms. Not that that meant anything. He could have kept them somewhere else. I brushed my teeth.

"Uh, should I just throw away this toothbrush?" My voice was tentative and I hated the wussy sound of it.

"Why? I bought it for you. Just put it in the holder. It'll be fine right there next to mine until the next time you need it."

I relaxed. Right. Next time. He'd bought it for me.

When I reentered the bedroom, Jack was dressed in a

navy polo shirt and khaki shorts that showed off his long, tanned legs. He threw on a fleece jacket. "Ready to go?"

My jacket was where I'd left it on the hook by the front door. "Do you think we should take Monty's collection with us? What if someone tries to break in again?"

"We could, but it wouldn't be safer in my soft-top Jeep. There's no point even locking it, you know. Anybody who wants to get in will just slit the fabric top. No, I think whoever our intruder was, he got what he came for." He held the door open for me and I brushed past him out onto the stairs.

"You're probably right."

The ten-minute drive to the Family Diner, a little greasy spoon in the next village over, was uneventful. The Jeep was loud and it made conversation difficult without yelling. I reviewed what I knew, but I couldn't make sense of any of it. When I got back to the Bonaparte House, I would try again.

We sat down in the same booth we'd sat in the first time we'd been here. Jack's idea. I was glad I was wearing jeans because the vinyl seats here were always sticky with duct tape repairs. But the table was clean. Patty came out from behind the counter, her pink and white uniform hugging her voluptuous curves. Her face broke into a broad smile as she set a plastic-coated menu in front of Jack and dropped one in front of me without acknowledging my lowly existence.

"Hello, handsome," she said. "Did you come back to take me away from all this?" She waved her long metallic burgundy nails around the diner.

"You can do better than me," Jack said with a laugh.

"I haven't yet. Coffee?" She filled our cups, then left and

came back with glasses of ice water. "Do you know what you want?"

We gave our orders: pancakes and sausage for Jack, Mexican omelet for me. Neither one of us was a sparkling conversationalist this morning, and though we hadn't come right out and said it, we each knew it wouldn't be a good idea to talk about anything that was going on. As it was, I heard people at the counter discussing the murders. Not that you could blame them. Other than arrests for public drunkenness and bar fights, we didn't get a lot of excitement in Bonaparte Bay or out here in this little village either.

The omelet should have been delicious—three fluffy eggs, fresh salsa, a fat gooey layer of local cheddar cheese, and the best part, I didn't have to cook it or clean up after it. But the thoughts running round and round my head overrode my taste buds.

"Don't worry, Georgie." Jack forked up a pile of pancake soaked in maple syrup. "I'll stay. Trish will just have to wait for this stuff."

I shook my head. "No, go do what you have to do. Nothing's likely to change between now and tomorrow when you get back."

"Promise me you won't be alone." His eyes held mine.

Truth was, I had a plan. And it involved me going somewhere . . . by myself. "I'll be fine."

"Promise me," he repeated.

I squirmed, then relented. "Okay, I promise."

"Good. Now eat something. I'd like to get on the road as soon as I drop you off."

Within a few minutes, Jack had cleared his plate and even

tried some of my mostly uneaten breakfast, which made me feel a little less guilty about leaving so much food on the plate. He paid the bill and walked me out to the Jeep.

He dropped me at the kitchen door of the Bonaparte House. Dolly's enormous Crown Vic was in the lot, taking up its usual space and a half next to Sophie's white Lincoln and my little blue Honda. Sophie and Marina were due back from their trip tomorrow, so it was just Dolly and me in the kitchen today and that suited me fine.

"I'll be back tomorrow by early afternoon," Jack said. "If you can get away, we'll go talk to Gladys and see if she's got any idea what's so important about that arrowhead."

I nodded. "I'm going to call to check on Melanie. If she's awake, I'll go see her. Otherwise I've got plenty of work to do here, and Dolly's around to keep me company."

Jack pulled me close and gave me a soft kiss. "Be careful."

"Keep kissing me like that, and I'll forget what 'careful' means."

He grinned. "See you tomorrow."

"Bye."

Country music was turned up loud in the kitchen, a song about pickup trucks and freedom sung by a guy with an overdone twang and a gravelly baritone. Dolly was at her usual station, behind the prep counter.

"Mornin', boss," she said, her face lighting up with a smile. Her hair was teased up higher than usual today, so I wondered if she'd just had it done. "I got started early. I see you did too." She waggled a sharply plucked eyebrow at me.

Let her think what she wanted. As soon as Sophie came

back, I was going to tell her about Jack and get our relationship out in the open. Chances were she already knew, but I'd feel better if she heard it directly from me.

"I'll be right back," I said, heading for my office.

Dolly waved me off with her chef's knife. "Go on. Things are under control."

I sat down behind my big desk, the one that had once belonged to Sophie's husband, Spiro's father, Basil. I dialed the hospital. The nurse on duty said that Melanie had had a good night and was doing well. She was heavily sedated and probably wouldn't wake up until this afternoon. A little stab of guilt pricked my gut. I was relieved I wouldn't have to go see her until later. Was that wrong of me? Probably.

Thoughts continued to swirl. There was some kind of connection between all the events going on here. Something I was missing. And it must have to do with that arrowhead. But what?

Gladys was out of town until tomorrow, on the same seniors' bus trip to Niagara Falls and the casino as Sophie and Marina it turned out. So she'd be no help.

Melanie was hospitalized and unconscious.

Caitlyn knew something, but she wasn't telling.

My fingers drummed on the surface of the desk. There was one place where answers might be found. I knew what I had to do.

Back in the kitchen, I grabbed a clean apron from the stack on the shelves back near the walk-in cooler, put it on, and tied the ends around my waist. After washing my hands, I snapped on disposable gloves and got to work.

Dolly had already started on the salad. We could probably

expect to sell a hundred dinners or so this late in the season, so the prep didn't take long.

We worked together companionably for a few minutes, each of us knowing the rhythm without the need for chitchat after so many years. Finally, I wiped my hands on my apron.

"Dolly, what do you have planned for the afternoon?"

She paused. "Well, I was going to go home, maybe turn on the wrestling match and clean the fish tank. Why?"

"How'd you like to make some extra money for your trip to Branson?"

"You're playing my song, boss."

An hour later we had passed Rainbow Acres and pulled into the driveway of Doreen's house. Before we got out of the car, I scanned the house and countryside. This place was so far out in the sticks someone would have to have a vehicle to get here, and there was none visible. Unless someone walked down the dirt road or across the fields from the Acres. Hank had seemed pretty keen on buying this farm for his yoga retreat. He'd been involved in some shady business before. But would he kill just to annex this property? Didn't seem likely, yet the possibility was there.

"So this is where you got shot at, huh?"

She didn't have to remind me. I felt bad about possibly putting Dolly into harm's way. But I'd promised Jack I wouldn't go anywhere alone. And Dolly, well, she was as savvy as they came. She could take care of herself. She could probably take care of me too. And I had to get into this house.

"Ready? Let's go."

We exited the car and made it to the front porch. I put the key, the one I'd taken from Melanie's purse before we left the

Bonaparte House, into the lock and gave it a twist. The door swung open. The house was silent as I cautiously stepped inside the door. We went to the kitchen. The back door was still locked. So it seemed probable that we were alone. An intruder—or killer—would hardly lock himself inside a house.

I debated how much to tell Dolly and decided the less she knew, the better. "I thought you could go through and sort the rest of Doreen's clothes for me, then wash them and take them out to the Salvation Army in Watertown. Also the bedding, dishes, and pots and pans. Of course, keep anything you want, or if you know someone who needs this stuff, go ahead and take it for them. Leave the red stand mixer," I added.

I directed her toward the bedroom, and she got right to work. "I'll be upstairs."

The upstairs was full. Four bedrooms' worth of full. And dusty. It was clear Doreen, and probably my grandparents before her, had never lived up here, just continued to add to the piles with items they might someday need.

Problem was, I didn't know what I was looking for. My gut feeling told me it would be paper of some kind. Perhaps a copy of the Bloodworth Trust documents? That would explain so much, but it seemed unlikely.

There were a number of boxes lined up along the wall in the hallway. That seemed as good a place to start as any. As I pawed systematically through them, I was gratified to see that most of them were empty. The box for the coffeemaker. A ceramic hair-straightening device. The box and instructions for the expensive stand mixer. How had she afforded it? Those things cost several hundred dollars. Well, perhaps she had won it at Bingo or bought it on installments at QVC.

I decided to kill two birds with one stone and opened the two-foot-by-two-foot window that looked out on the driveway, the road, and the overgrown field beyond. The window stuck as though it hadn't been opened in years, which was almost certainly the case, but after giving it a little muscle, I raised it. I tossed the empty boxes out into the yard. Doreen had a fifty-five-gallon oil drum out back that she probably used for burning. Not very environmentally conscious, but this was a big job.

Other boxes contained clothes of varying sizes. Doreen had been a Rubenesque woman. I wondered if these were her skinny clothes. Or her fat clothes. Or some combination thereof. They seemed to be of fairly recent vintage, so I assumed they had not belonged to my grandmother, who'd been gone for decades. I gave the boxes a quick going-through then set them aside to add to Dolly's hoard.

A cool breeze fluttered in through the small window, blowing dust around. I sneezed, three times in rapid succession, then headed for the first bedroom. The room was small, containing two twin beds with brown metal frames and a small dresser in between them. The old-fashioned floral wallpaper had peeled away in a couple of spots, revealing another layer underneath. This room seemed to be full of old linens. Musty sheets and pillowcases, a couple of old quilts made from charming feed sack fabrics, probably dating to the nineteen thirties. They appeared to be intact, though I saw some rusty-looking stains. Perhaps they could be cleaned. I set them aside.

The dresser drawers revealed nothing. There did not appear to be a closet, which I guess was normal in an old farmhouse like this. I checked under the mattresses and under the beds. Nope.

When I opened the second bedroom door, my spirits soared, then sank even lower. The room was full of paper. Books, boxes, and loose papers covered the double bed and the small table in between them. And yet paper was what I thought I was looking for. I fanned quickly through old farm records. Receipts for milk pickup. Records of gallons produced by each cow. Breeding documentation.

My eyes fell on an old-fashioned scrapbook, the kind with two hard covers held together by a string tied with a bow. I didn't really have time for a trip down non–memory lane, but I was curious. Were there photos of my bitter, angry grandparents in here? I wondered why they were so bitter. Farming was a difficult life, no question, and their only daughter had disappointed them. But according to Melanie, they'd been disagreeable even when she was a child.

I flipped through the pages. Melanie's report cards from elementary school. She'd done well in reading and social studies, not so well in math. So we had that much in common. Her school pictures were placed inside glued-on corner tabs. She looked happy enough in her pigtails and Peter Pan–collared blouse. And I could see the resemblance to my own daughter. Teeny, tiny twinge of nostalgia. I missed Cal so much.

The next few pages were newspaper clippings, yellowed and brittle. Wedding and anniversary notices from the *Bay Blurb* for people I'd never heard of were pasted onto the pages. Each clipping had a date, presumably the date the announcement had appeared in the paper, written in fading ink in a flowery hand. My grandmother's?

My hand stilled. The next clipping was an obituary with an accompanying photo. I stared. *Herman "Monty" Montgomery, age sixty-seven, dies at home.* Underneath the caption was a photo of Monty, one I recognized from the photos hanging on the wall in the artifact room at Gladys's house. He looked young and handsome with his shirtsleeves rolled up and a pre-Indiana-Jones-style fedora pushed back on his head.

> *Herman Montgomery, age sixty-seven, long-time resident of Bonaparte Bay, died at home with his wife at his side on February 23rd. Montgomery owned and operated several marinas along the St. Lawrence, and was a silent partner in many local businesses.*

Once she sold the businesses, Gladys would have been quite well off, which explained her ability to maintain both the river house and a condo in Florida.

> *He was the son of Gerald and Melvina (Bloodworth) Montgomery, both of this town, who died many years ago. Montgomery was the last surviving grandchild of Elihu Bloodworth, who was at one time the richest man in the North Country. Arrangements are with the Miller Funeral Home.*

I sat back on the bed, causing a small cloud of dust particles to rise into the air. Monty had been a self-made man, Gladys had said. Why had none of the Bloodworth wealth trickled down to him, though? Or through my grandmother, for that matter? It appeared she'd never had it easy. There could be any number of reasons, all of them speculation at this point.

My eyes returned to the clipping. The written-in date was February 25. Twenty years ago, the date the notice had appeared in the paper. And written underneath was a second date: February 23 . . . of next year.

This date was in the future, just a few months from now.

I did a quick calculation, my math skills being adequate for the job. Twenty-one years from the date of Monty's death.

What was it Doreen had been telling people? *The time is almost up.* I wished I could have seen the Bloodworth Trust documents, which would probably have confirmed my thoughts. From the attorney's letter, I knew the trust was about to expire and I would bet that date was February 23 of next year. "Just how much money are we talking about?" I mused out loud.

But this just confirmed what I already knew. The unanswered question was what, if anything, that arrowhead had to do with this puzzle. After an hour's worth of work, I was no closer to solving it.

I jumped at the sound of a sharp whistle. "Georgie," Dolly called from the bottom of the stairs. "Come take a break. There's no cream for coffee, so I made tea. She had orange spice in a box on the table."

I must have missed that when I cleaned out the food, when? Was it just yesterday?

"Be right down."

I squirted some dish soap on my hands and gave them a good scrub before sitting at the table. Dolly was dunking her tea bag up and down in the china mug.

"This ain't too bad," she said, slipping into the sometimes sloppy speech patterns of the North Country. "If you want, Tuesday I'll borrow Harold's truck and we can start loading up the big stuff." She slurped up some tea. "Unless you want to have a garage sale or something with the furniture?"

"Can Harold get along without the truck for the day?" Dolly's second husband worked a civilian job at Fort Drum. I wasn't quite sure what he did, come to think of it.

"Yeah, he can take my Ford. I can round up some muscle for us too."

Muscle. I thought of Channing, naughty girl that I was. "Oh. I should get somebody to winterize the house. Melanie has to decide what she's going to do with this place, but we could get a hard freeze anytime. Don't want to be dealing with burst pipes."

"Harold's putting in overtime at the base until we leave for Branson, or I'd have him come out and do it." Dolly did some more dunking, then placed her soggy tea bag on a small saucer.

"That's okay. I'll hire a handyman." Might as well give Liza's boyfriend some work. "Have you ever heard the name 'Bloodworth'?" Dolly had lived in Bonaparte Bay her entire life. Couldn't hurt to ask.

She pursed up her bright pink lips and shook her head. "No, can't say that I have. How come?"

"Oh, no reason. I just came across it recently and thought it was an unusual name." Back at my office, I'd run a quick search and hadn't come up with anyone in the Jefferson County area who still bore the name. And poor Elihu. Apparently famous—or at least very, very rich—in his time, today he didn't even have a Wikipedia page about him.

I changed the subject. "Where'd you find the tea? I thought I'd cleaned out all the food. Did I miss a cupboard?"

"Doreen must have liked her tea at Bingo. She kept some in her Bingo box." Dolly indicated the needlepoint plastic canvas box on the table. I'd meant to take that with me yesterday and see if Paloma or any of Doreen's other buddies wanted it.

I pulled the box toward me. "We may as well keep the bags here at the house, along with the kettle. It's going to be a lot of work cleaning this place out and we may want it."

The lid lifted off easily since there was no latch. Inside were half a dozen orange spice tea bags, which I retrieved and stacked on the table. "I guess these will be all right. The mice won't bother them with the house being unoccupied, will they?" Even though the bags were wrapped in a coated paper, a strong scent of orange rind and clove wafted up. It reminded me of Christmas.

"Nah, they won't like the smell."

I dumped the contents of the box onto the table. Two tokens for free drinks at the Legion, which I passed to Dolly. She and Harold could use them, whereas I—or Melanie—never would. Two fat Bingo daubers. I shook each one and was rewarded with the sound of sloshing ink. Paloma would want these. A single Bingo card lay on the bottom of the box. The B and the I were scribbled out. The number 68 was circled with a purple gel pen, not daubed, in the O column. I picked up the box to replace the items and felt something shift inside it. Huh?

The box was empty. And yet something was definitely inside it.

My cell phone rang. The charge nurse was calling. Melanie was awake and asking for me.

I stowed the box under my arm. There had to be an explanation but figuring it out would have to wait till later. "Let's head home, Dolly. You want to take the clothes now or come back for them?"

"I still haven't checked all the pockets for stray cash. Why don't we come back next week? It'll give you and your mom a chance to decide what you're going to do with this place. We should be able to sort through everything in a few days. There's no rush, right?"

Dolly was right. There was no rush.

We drove back to the Bay with the music turned up loud. Fine with me because I didn't really want to talk. Dolly offered to empty my trunk and deliver the food to the Methodist Church Food Pantry on her way to work tomorrow. I took her up on it.

I went into my office and pulled out a pad of paper and an "I Heart 1000 Islands" pen that some customer had left on a table.

Melanie had made me wait a long time for her. She could wait a little longer for me.

I started doodling, letting my thoughts wander. *Doreen*. I drew a circle around the name. *Spencer*. Another circle. *Bloodworth Trust. Arrowhead*. I continued till I had pretty much covered the paper with my bubbles.

Melanie and Caitlyn had come back into town and visited Doreen the day before she was killed.

According to the tabloids, Melanie was in financial trouble. That might or might not be true, but what was certain was that she stood to inherit not only the farm she'd grown up on, but Doreen's share of the Bloodworth Trust, which was about to be distributed. That gave her a pretty good motive for murdering Doreen. Except she herself had been shot by an unknown assailant. What if Melanie killed Doreen, then somebody else who'd gotten a letter from Mac-Namara and MacNamara, attorneys at law, had tried to kill her to increase his or her share?

Caitlyn was sneaking and snooping around and doing some kind of research. Melanie had apparently sworn her to secrecy and she was getting paid to be loyal. Yet it wasn't outside the realm of possibility that Melanie had provided for Caitlyn in the event of her death. Melanie had told me that she'd recently written a will with my daughter Cal as the beneficiary. That didn't mean she hadn't left something to Caitlyn. But would it have been enough to kill for?

And what about Spencer Kane? He'd said he had something important to talk to me about, and he'd been doing some research of his own. But before he could tell me, he was bludgeoned to death in the yard behind the funeral home. Could I get a look at his notes, see what he'd been working on? My guess was no. The police would almost certainly be examining the notes as evidence in their search to find the killer. One thing I did know: Spencer had been looking into the history of the Bay.

And I was willing to bet he was researching the Bloodworths. Everything seemed to revolve around the trust. Not for the first time I wondered just how much it was worth.

Inky had been framed, and rather clumsily so. As far as I knew, he had no connection to Melanie or Spencer or Gladys and her husband or the Bloodworths. My guess was that someone had taken advantage of the fact that Spinky's was undergoing renovations and had used that opportunity to pick a convenient target. It could just as easily have been Spiro who was arrested.

I drew a second circle around *Arrowhead* and tapped the pen against it. That was the piece that didn't fit, and I kept coming back to it. The artifact had been found at my grandparents' farm in the sixties, according to Monty's index. It seemed to be unremarkable—there were several similar artifacts and entries on the index, and Jack had said that arrowheads turned up all the time. So what was special about this one? Someone had stolen both the arrowhead and the associated folder. It meant something. It had to. But what?

The small clock-radio I kept on the corner of the desk read eleven thirty. Time to go see Melanie, then come back here and get ready to open at three o'clock.

Dolly had finished unloading my tiny trunk into her own more spacious one. "I'll go drop this stuff off at the church, run a couple of errands, and be back by two."

"Thanks." I honestly, truly did not know how we would manage without Dolly.

Nuts. I still had to find Spiro and Inky a cook or they'd try to steal her away again. And that was a headache I did not need. Of course I wanted Spinky's to succeed. Just not at the expense of the Bonaparte House.

I pulled into the front parking lot of the hospital and went in through the main doors, which slid open noiselessly in front of me. I nodded to the nurse at the main desk, someone I didn't recognize, and took the stairs to the second floor rather than waiting for the elevator.

A Jefferson County sheriff's deputy sat in a molded plastic chair outside Melanie's room. He rose when I approached.

"Name?"

"Georgie Nikolopatos."

He consulted a clipboard and checked something off, presumably my name. "You're on the approved visiting list. Let's see your ID, then you can go in."

I pulled out my license, which he examined. He nodded his head toward the door.

Melanie lay in the hospital bed with her upper body at a slight incline. She was hooked up to various intravenous drips and the same beeping monitors I'd seen yesterday. Her eyes fluttered open as I came toward her and sat in the chair by the bed.

"Hey, Mel. How're you feeling?"

"Water," she said, her voice raspy. "Don't call me Mel."

"Right. Sorry. Has the doctor been in yet this morning?"

"How long could rounds take in a place this size? Yes." She wrapped her lips around the straw and sucked. Even without makeup, she didn't look too bad. Plastic surgery, insanely expensive skin care products, and a dermatologist on call could probably do that for you.

"And?" I reached over and took the plastic cup from her, placing it on the tray table.

"And I'm going to be here at least three more days. He doesn't want me traveling for a few weeks. So I'll be staying at the Spa during my recovery."

Wow. That was going to cost a mint. Not that I wasn't glad for Liza. Castles weren't cheap to run. I just hoped Melanie wouldn't try to stiff her on the bill.

"Where's Caitlyn?"

"Running errands for me. She'll be back soon."

"What kind of errands, Melanie? If you needed something from the drugstore, Kinney's is just down the street from the restaurant." But I had a feeling she wasn't out buying deodorant or a hairbrush. How much longer was my mother going to hold out on me?

"Oh, I had her working on a research project for me."

Research. There was that word again.

"What's she researching?"

She shifted in the bed and let out a groan, her face contorting with the effort. "Not now." One of the machines attached to her IV drip made a little chirp, perhaps dispensing medication.

I leaned in closer and dropped my voice to a harsh whisper. "Do you not realize you were almost killed? And that two other people are dead? I found Doreen's letter. I know about the Bloodworth Trust. Did you get a letter about it?"

It was probably unfair of me to grill her when she was in an obviously weakened state. But I didn't want any more deaths and she and Caitlyn were the only ones who might have answers.

"Yes. Letter. Trust. Rumors." Her eyelids fluttered, then closed. "Rumors," she whispered, and fell asleep.

That had gone well. *Rumors.* It could mean anything.

The deputy checked me off his list as I headed toward the elevators. I punched Caitlyn's number into my phone. She didn't answer.

Damn. I'd promised Jack I wouldn't be alone today. Although I was pretty well convinced at this point that I wasn't a target. Melanie and Doreen were heirs to the Blood-worth Trust. I, however, had received no such letter from the attorneys. Which must mean that I wasn't eligible to receive the proceeds, for whatever reason, and therefore I stood in no one's way of getting the money.

I could go and confront MacNamara Junior or Senior, but I counted my chances of getting any information out of them at slim to bupkus. That pesky attorney-client privilege would prevent them from telling me anything about the trust. I could go in and say I was handling Melanie's affairs while she was incapacitated, but without a properly executed power of attorney, they'd never buy it.

Which left me with Caitlyn as my only source of information. I went into the family lounge and closed the door. I pulled Melanie's cell phone out of my purse. My intent had been to leave it on the table for her, but I'd forgotten while I was upstairs. Caitlyn might not answer calls from me, but she would from Melanie. I fired off a quick text.

Call me with update.

It was a matter of seconds before a response came back.

Georgie? Is that you?

Curses. Foiled again. How had she known?

The phone rang and I answered it.

"Melanie doesn't text," Caitlyn informed me. "She says it ruins her manicure. What do you want?"

My eyes darted around the room, making absolutely sure

I was alone. "I want to know what's going on. What are you researching?" My tone was harsher, more demanding than I'd intended.

"I've already told you I can't talk about this until Melanie gives me the okay. Which she hasn't done."

"Caitlyn, people are dying. An innocent man is accused of murder. And I think you've got information that will explain everything." I was just getting warmed up when she cut in.

"You'd be surprised what I *don't* know."

"What's that supposed to mean?" My blood pressure rose.

"It means that I don't have all the answers. And when I do, I'll go straight to the police with them."

"What do you know about an arrowhead?"

"Huh? Like a Native American thing?" She sounded genuinely surprised by my question, but it was hard to know for sure without being able to see her face.

"Never mind. I've got to go to work. But this isn't over. As soon as Melanie wakes up again, I want you over here getting permission to tell me what you know."

"Uh, sure." What she really meant was probably something like, *No way in hell. You're not paying me.*

I rang off and threw the phone into the depths of my purse.

When I got back to the restaurant, Dolly had also returned. "Be out in a few minutes," I called, closing myself up in my office. I reached into my secret drawer and pulled out a half-eaten bar of dark chocolate. The square melted in my mouth as I closed my eyes, leaning back in the chair. When I opened them again, they fell on Doreen's Bingo container. I dumped the contents onto the surface of the desk and gave the box a shake. There was something in there, and yet the box was empty. How could that be?

What would Nancy Drew do? She'd check for a false bottom, that's what. I grabbed a ruler and stuck it inside the box, jotting the number on a piece of scrap paper. Then I measured the height of the box from the desk. Sure enough, there was a discrepancy. It was only a quarter inch, but it was there.

The sides of the box had been needlepointed in a pattern of raised stitches. And one row of stitches, a quarter inch from the bottom, was done in white yarn that was a couple of shades off from the rest of the box.

I grabbed the scissors from their usual spot in the mug containing my pens and pencils and gave a snip. The stitch popped open and the yarn, which had been under a bit of tension, relaxed. I straightened one loop of a paper clip and used it to pull out the stitches one by one. When I made it all the way around, the false bottom broke free and I took it out.

I half expected to see an arrowhead. But on the real bottom of the box lay a key.

I blew out a breath, then picked up the key for a closer look.

It was small and flat with an uncomplicated profile. Definitely not a door key. It might go to a desk or dresser drawer, a cabinet, a padlock, maybe a small lockbox. My thoughts flung back to the farmhouse and I groaned. It would be like looking for a needle in a haystack. This key could go to anything.

And yet, Doreen had gone to a lot of trouble to hide it. She would have had to create the false bottom and sew it in, and this was about as obscure a place as she could find. My eyes landed on the daubers. They seemed ordinary enough. The Bingo card, though, wasn't.

She clearly hadn't played this in any Bingo game at the Legion or the Reservation. The crossed-out letters at the top, the circled number 68. They meant something. I just didn't know what.

I shoved the box and its contents into my bottom drawer with the almost-gone chocolate bar and my private bottle of wine. The key went into my pocket. Perhaps proximity to my body might allow it to communicate with me. *What do you open, little key? And what's inside the thing you open?*

My musings were cut short by the sounds of footsteps and voices in the hallway outside my door. The wait staff had arrived.

I took a moment to call the hospital. Melanie was still in and out of consciousness, but seemed to be improving, so there was no cause for concern there. The nurse predicted she'd be more alert tomorrow when the effects of the anesthesia and pain medication would have lessened. She was still under police guard, and would be until the person who shot at her was caught.

The second call I placed was to Liza.

"Hey, girl," she said. "I haven't seen Caitlyn, if that's what you're going to ask. She doesn't seem to have been back in at least a day."

"I think she's been staying at the Camelot. Maybe the boat rides were cramping her style."

"Any idea yet what she's up to?"

"No, but I'm working on it."

"I took it upon myself to help your investigation. Since she's felt free to wander around my castle pretending to be lost, I felt free to freshen her and Melanie's room personally."

"Did you find anything?" I leaned forward with interest.

"I would never invade my guests' privacy." Damn. I might. "But in my general straightening up, nothing seemed out of place."

"How about any paperwork? Notebooks, folders, anything like that?"

"I put fresh sachets in each of the drawers in both rooms. Nothing but clothes and some toiletries. Same with the closets. And nothing under the mattresses or the beds."

I was willing to bet that Caitlyn kept everything electronically on her phone. It would be simple enough to snap pictures of whatever she was working on, then organize everything into folders she could access anywhere. Simple enough for a young woman of her generation anyway.

"The reason I called was to ask for Channing's number."

Slight hesitation. "Channing? I'd thought I might keep him . . . engaged for a while this afternoon."

I laughed. "Tempting as the divine handyman is, Georgie doesn't poach, you know that. I want to hire him to winterize Doreen's house before it freezes. You know, drain all the water pipes so they don't burst, that kind of thing. I was hoping to meet him tomorrow morning, say nine o'clock. It has to be early because we're open for lunch tomorrow."

"I had him scheduled to work around here tomorrow morning, but that can wait. Unless one of us calls you back, expect him at nine."

"Thanks. And, uh, have a nice afternoon."

Her laugh was mischievous. "Oh, we will." She rang off.

The Bonaparte House did a bustling business that night. A hundred and forty dinners—significantly more than I'd expected—and we managed not to run out of anything. I put aside several of the cash transactions for Sophie. That always made her happy. She didn't know—or maybe just didn't care— that the computerized ordering system kept track of it anyway and we still paid taxes on the income. It was a sport for her.

By the time eleven o'clock rolled around and I called eighty-six, I had a roster of happy servers with pockets full of tips. I offered them each a complimentary dinner for a job well done, but they'd all made plans to go to Fat Max's after work. "Have a good time," I called out after them. "Don't drink and drive." All I got was laughter.

Well aware that I was breaking my promise to Jack, but unwilling to ask Dolly to stay with me, I set all the alarms and went to bed.

❖ TWENTY-TWO ❖

Almost before I knew it, the birds that hadn't flown south for the winter were chirping outside my window. The sun was just coming up over the river, painting the sky in shades of butter and salmon.

I made the bed and tossed a load of laundry into the washer before I got into the shower. Fifteen minutes later I was toweling off and had even managed to wipe the sink and counter. It felt good to do something as mundane and mindless as housework, and yet I still couldn't get the puzzle pieces to stop rattling around in my brain.

When I got back out to the farm this morning, I'd focus my attention on figuring out what Doreen's little key went to, not that I'd have a whole lot of time before I had to get back to the restaurant. There didn't seem to be any alternative other than trying it in every drawer and cabinet until I found what it fit. The prospect was daunting. It might not even be in the house. It could be out in the barn, a place that was probably full of furry wild critters I had no interest in getting to know better. I could ask Channing to go in with me if necessary. He looked like the type that could fight off slavering beasts for a lady.

It was a lovely morning for a drive into the countryside. I stopped at Rainbow Acres for a load of hothouse lettuce and tomatoes, which I packed into the coolers I'd stowed in my trunk. We'd sold a lot last night, so I was glad to have a chance to restock. The weather was good, which meant a lot of day-trippers coming into town for the leaf-peeper cruise on the *Lady Liberty* tour boat. And that usually translated into a good night at the Bonaparte House.

I drove slowly as I approached Doreen's farm. I supposed I should start thinking of it as Melanie's farm, since it had only been Doreen's temporarily. I'd stayed alone last night in my own home with no problems, but shots hadn't been fired at me there. Still, if Channing didn't get there soon, I was going to have to go in. There wasn't much time this morning to dillydally.

I pulled over next to a field dotted with huge round wheels of hay. My teeth caught my lower lip and I pulled the key and Doreen's Bingo card out of my purse.

Card. Key. Arrowhead. Card.

I examined it again. The B and the I were scribbled out. That left N, G, O.

N, G, O. I tried rearranging the letters. G-O-N. Gone? N-O-G. Nog? Maybe if it were New Year's Eve.

G-O. Go. Go . . . north?

My heart rate sped up. The number 68 was circled. Go

north 68 . . . degrees? I'd need a compass for that and even
then I might not be able to work it. What about 68 . . . feet?
Yards? Paces?

After the initial burst of excitement, my spirits sank. Even
if I was right about what the card meant, it did me no good.
If this was some kind of X-marks-the-spot map, there was
one crucial piece of information missing. There was no starting point.

Back to square one.

Or was I? Assuming what I was looking for was at the
farm, which direction was north? No clue. And I was fresh
out of compasses.

I heard a car coming up behind me on the gravel road. I
glanced in my rearview mirror. A car was approaching a
little too fast, sending up a fine spray of dirt and tiny stones.
Channing had a red pickup, but this clearly wasn't him
because it passed the driveway to the house. My eyes again
went to the rearview mirror and the lighted E in the lower-
right-hand corner. The Honda was pointed east. Apparently,
I did have a compass.

I turned the key in the ignition and moved the car until
the display read *N*. North was a big meadow behind the
house. My eyes fell on a tableau of rusty metal. Atop a
gentle knoll was some kind of ancient-looking farm machin-
ery, the kind that was probably drawn behind oxen or draft
horses back in the old days. My estimating skills were not
well developed, but it could be sixty yards or so from the
back door of the house. Something certainly could have
been hidden in that old machine.

What if it were buried, though? Digging was hard work

and I'd never find it without a metal detector. Did Dolly and Harold have one? Possibly, but it did me no good right now.

I debated. Should I wait for Channing? It was already nine fifteen and he was late. If he didn't show, I wouldn't be able to test my theory until tomorrow, and even then I'd have to interrupt someone else's day to come with me.

The heck with it. No way was this waiting until tomorrow. Melanie was the target, not me. I pulled the car into the driveway, parked, and made my way out back.

Despite telling myself that I wasn't in danger, I'd never felt so exposed in my life as I did walking across that open field. My heart beat wildly and the pulse pounded in my ears. Ridiculous. Mine was the only car here. Still, I glanced over my shoulder more than once as I made my way through the damp knee-high grass.

The knoll was gently sloped up only two or three feet above the surrounding earth. It was circular, with a pronounced depression in the middle, like a bowl made out of dirt and grass. Inside the bowl was an assortment of metal detritus. In addition to the large horse-drawn implement— a hay rake perhaps—there were a number of other items I couldn't identify. All were in various states of rust and decay, clearly having been left out over many, many harsh winters. A metal milk can was the only intact object, its lid off to one side. I peered into it. Empty.

This had been a waste of time. There was nothing here that required a key, unless it was buried, and I wasn't about to go digging when I had to go back to work so soon.

I started back across the field, my legs and feet wet from the dewy grass. A woodshed was built onto the back of the house, like most old farmhouses in this area. Above the woodshed were two windows that overlooked the field, half covered by old curtains. Had I been in one of those rooms yesterday? I tried to orient myself but it was no use. I had no sense of direction and probably never would.

A curtain moved. I started, then shook my head. The house was a hundred and fifty years old and had likely never been insulated. It would be full of drafts. And it occurred to me I had left a window open upstairs yesterday.

A dark red pickup truck sat in the driveway. I hadn't heard it pull in. This must be Channing. I was never so glad to see someone else's boyfriend in my life.

Only, I didn't actually see him. The cab of the truck was empty, unless he was lying on the front seat. He wasn't on the front porch, nor was he in the yard. There'd be no reason for him to be in the barn. I hadn't been inside the house yet so the doors were still locked. Or were they?

The front door stood slightly ajar.

"Channing?" Maybe I'd neglected to make sure the lock was engaged yesterday. He must be inside evaluating what needed to be done.

Nonetheless, I put my hand on the canister of pepper spray I'd lifted from Melanie's purse before I left.

I approached the door and gave it a gentle kick. It swung open on creaky hinges. "Channing? It's Georgie."

A grunting sound came from the back of the house.

"In the kitchen. I'm looking at the pipes under the sink."

I relaxed. As I suspected, the front door must not have latched properly. Mr. Handyman Hottie could take a look at it before he left.

At the kitchen door, I froze.

Channing wasn't under the sink.

He was holding a knife to Caitlyn's neck.

I took a deep breath, determined to stay calm even though panic was rising like spring snowmelt through my chest and head.

"Channing. What are you doing?" Did my voice quiver? For Caitlyn's sake I would not show fear if I could help it. How had she gotten here? Had he brought her in his truck?

He snorted. "You're not really in a position to be asking questions." His dark eyes flashed. "But why don't you ask your little friend here?"

It wouldn't do much good. She had a gag in her mouth and wouldn't be able to answer. Her pale skin shone with perspiration.

"She's not my friend." *Forgive me, Caitlyn.* "What's she done?"

"Don't lie to me. You're in on this with her and Mommy." He had a handful of Caitlyn's hair and he pulled back, exposing her throat. She winced. "She's been following me around for days, trying to pretend she's crushing on me. It's ridiculous. I'm way out of her league."

Conceited ass. "Why's she following you? I honestly don't know." If he was talking, he wasn't cutting—or killing.

"She almost ruined everything with her snooping." Caitlyn squirmed and emitted a muffled cry through the gag. "Sit still! I'm not through with you yet."

I decided to press the issue. Gently. "What did she almost ruin? Because I can tell you she's been a serious pain in my ass too." I wished Caitlyn could see my face, so she'd know

I was doing everything I could for her, but her head was pulled back at too sharp an angle. Apologies would have to come later—if there was a later.

"The trust, idiot."

Understanding dawned as I fought the urge to lash out at him for calling me a name. "You're an heir to the Blood-worth fortune. A descendant."

Understanding faded with his next word.

"No."

"Then why do this? It doesn't make sense. You don't have a pony in the race."

"There's only one rightful heir to those millions. And it wasn't Doreen and it isn't your mother." He pulled the tip of the knife away from Caitlyn's throat and pointed it at me. "But I'm going to finish the job I started on her just as soon as I take care of you two. No loose ends, no one to stand in the way when the truth comes out."

What the hell was he talking about? He was keyed up, but he didn't seem crazy. Although how sane could someone be who killed over and over for a fortune that wasn't even his?

Three sharp knocks sounded at the front door. All three of us froze.

"Georgie? Channing? Can one of you stop by the Acres on your way back to town? I've got a yogurt delivery and my truck broke down." Hank stepped into the kitchen doorway.

I saw my chance. I pulled out the canister of pepper spray and gave Channing a blast full in the face. He dropped the knife and threw his hands up to his eyes as he broke into a full-out sweat. Hank kicked the knife out of Channing's reach and grabbed him in a bear hug from behind. Channing writhed in his arms, in pain that was almost palpable. This stuff really did work.

I ran to Caitlyn and untied her. She was panting, and her light sheen of sweat had turned into a full drenching. She coughed. "My glasses," she wheezed. "The spray hit them. Take them off me," she begged.

"What should I do with him?" Hank grunted. He was sixty if he was a day, not to mention a smoker.

Before I could answer—and not that I knew the answer anyway—the younger, more agile Channing twisted out of Hank's sinewy arms and ran for the front door. I grabbed Caitlyn's arm and pulled her along behind me.

Channing jumped into the front seat of his truck and started the motor. Hank raced after him, but had to jump back when Channing peeled out of the driveway. He fell to the ground.

"Take the Beemer," Caitlyn said. "It's faster than your car."

"Where is it?" I demanded. I was not going to let him get away, and the Beemer was nowhere in sight.

"In. The. Barn." Caitlyn continued to wheeze. Was she asthmatic or had she gotten more exposure to the spray than I'd thought?

I glanced back at Hank, who had gotten to his feet and had a cell phone to his ear, presumably dialing for help. I threw open the barn doors and we raced into the car. She tossed me the keys and I backed out after Channing, who was approximately a quarter mile down the road by now.

My foot jammed the pedal to the floor. "Call the State Police or the Sheriff's Office," I said, oversteering a bit and having to correct my course. "For God's sake, don't call 911." Cindy in dispatch couldn't be trusted to get the message right.

"I can't look up the number without my glasses!" she wailed.

Well, nuts. Channing crested a hill ahead of me. There was an intersection just beyond that. I sped up so I'd be able to see which direction he turned.

"Call 911, then. The numbers are big enough for you to see, right?" Maybe we'd get lucky and Cindy was off today.

I didn't dare take my eyes off the road to see if she was managing. Channing made a left turn, back toward the Bay, wobbling all over the road, probably because he couldn't see through his physical reaction to the spray. I followed as fast as I dared drive.

"Hello? This is Caitlyn Black. I'm Melanie Ashley's assistant. Yes, that Melanie Ashley. I know who killed Doreen Webber and Spencer Kane. It's Channing Young and he's headed—"

Out of the corner of my eye I could see her turn toward me. "Route 12 south toward Bonaparte Bay."

She repeated my directions. "Red pickup truck. I don't know the license plate but he's got one of those big silver toolboxes in the truck bed. And he's driving erratically."

Caitlyn turned her head in my direction. "They're sending out cars now."

"I hope they hurry. There's no telling where he's headed. If he makes it back to the Bay, he could find a place to hide the truck." I oversteered again and the car fishtailed slightly.

When we were back on course, I said, "You want to tell me what happened back there?"

Channing surprised me by not turning right into the village of Bonaparte Bay under the neon "Welcome" arch. He bypassed the village and continued south on Route 12. Where was he headed? If he made it as far as Watertown, his chances of hiding out for a while were even better.

"Uh, not really," Caitlyn said.

"Yes, really. This has to end. So let's start with what you were doing at the farm. Why did you hide the car?"

"There's some . . . documentation I've been looking for. The same documentation Channing was looking for, but for different reasons. When I overheard Liza telling Channing that you wanted to meet him at the farm today, I was sure he'd take the opportunity to look for it. So I got there early, hid the Beemer in the barn, and went into the house with the extra key I had made."

My lips pursed. Channing was still headed south. We were lucky he couldn't go at maximum speed. It seemed to be all he could do to stay on the road.

"And this documentation is what? From where I sit, neither Channing nor you for that matter stands to benefit from the trust. So why are you two involved up to your necks?"

At that moment Channing slammed on his brakes and took a sharp right onto the exit for the Can-Am Bridge. He left skid marks and the smell of burnt rubber in his wake. I braked more gently and pulled off. Sirens wailed in the distance.

He couldn't possibly be trying to cross into Canada, could he? Would he have had the foresight to bring his passport?

But there was no way he was getting past the border patrol in his current condition anyway.

The sirens drew nearer. Channing passed the duty-free shop and entered the base of the bridge. I pulled up behind him, honking my horn to try to attract the attention of the guards. It apparently worked, because all of a sudden there were border patrol agents everywhere, some with guns drawn.

I found myself on the bridge behind Channing. There was nowhere to pull over, so I kept going. As we approached the highest point of the bridge, Channing pulled off sharply with his truck at an angle. I slammed on the brakes to avoid hitting the truck. A line of cars with top lights whirling had formed from both the Canadian and the American sides. Channing was trapped.

He got out of the truck. Caitlyn and I followed. We shouldn't have, what with all those firearms aimed in our direction. But I had to see this through.

Channing climbed up onto the framework of the bridge. What was he doing? It was a hundred or more foot drop into the St. Lawrence. I looked through the lattice of steel girders. A laker honked its horn as its bow passed under the bridge.

He stood up straight on the outside of the bridge, holding on with both hands as though he'd just conquered the world's largest set of monkey bars.

"Don't move," came a voice magnified through a bullhorn. "Or we'll shoot."

Channing spun his head in one direction, then the other, until his dripping eyes landed on me.

"Tell her I'm sorry. Tell her I tried."

And with that he let go, threw his arms out perpendicular to his body, and sailed through the September air.

I squeezed my eyes closed. But of course that couldn't mask the sickening thud as Channing's body hit the deck of the giant oceangoing freighter. I reached for Caitlyn and wrapped her in a hug.

✦ TWENTY-THREE ✦

"What?" Liza's voice was weak and thready, as though she'd lost her composure—for the first time ever.

"I'm so sorry. I wanted you to hear it from me rather than the police." Or wherever it was she got her information about happenings around the Bay, which she always seemed to know about before anyone else.

"I—I don't understand."

"He tried to make a run for the border, then committed suicide when the authorities had him surrounded. He"—I cleared my throat—"he killed Doreen and Spencer."

"This can't be real," she said after a pause. "I thought I knew him. It wasn't as though I loved him, of course. But he was . . . special to me."

A shadow passed over the sun. Eclipse? No. It was the burly form of Lieutenant Hawthorne of the New York State Police. He towered over me, not quite touching but close enough to be intimidating. Well, I'd been through enough today. He wasn't going to scare me.

I held up my index finger in a *wait a minute* gesture.

"Liza, Channing's last words were, *Tell her I'm sorry. Tell her I tried.*"

There was silence on the other end of the line.

Lieutenant Hawthorne must have popped one of his ever-present sticks of gum into his mouth because I could hear it snapping as he chewed and the crinkly sound of a piece of paper being rolled up. I was pretty sure if I looked up, I'd find a not-amused expression on his nicely chiseled face.

"Sorry?" she said. "He tried? Tried what?"

"I was hoping you might know what he meant."

"I wish I did. Now I suppose I'll never know. Look, Georgie, it means so much to me that you called to tell me, that it didn't come from a stranger. But I . . . need to be alone for a while. To try to make sense of this."

"Of course. I'll check in on you later. And I'm always here for you. You know that, right?"

"I do. Bye."

"Bye." And she was gone.

Caitlyn was leaning up against a cop car. She appeared to be giving a statement to a good-looking young officer. He handed her a box of tissues, and she wiped her nose and dabbed at the tears that still dripped from her eyes. I wondered if it would do any good for her to go to the ER and get her mucus membranes flushed or treated somehow to get rid of the burning pepper oil. Or maybe it just had to wear off. At least she'd gotten a very low dose. Despite her ordeal, she seemed talkative, almost flirty. Well, as I said, the officer was cute.

"Georgie."

"Yes? Let me guess. You want to take my statement."

His expression was stony. "We have to stop meeting like this."

Truer words were never spoken.

Caitlyn and I sat in Melanie's hospital room, one on either side of the bed. She was finally awake, and had agreed to try some orange gelatin, which she was now slurping daintily from a plastic spoon.

"How do you feel, Melanie?" It wasn't just a polite question. I'd done some soul-searching in the last few hours and come to the realization that holding on to resentment and anger did no one any good, least of all me who had so much to be thankful for. Not that Melanie was going to win any mother-of-the-year awards. But a truce was the beginning of, perhaps, an understanding. And if she truly did want to be part of Cal's life, I would not be the one to stand in the way of that relationship.

"Plenty of drugs. Plenty of bland, soft foods. A moderately cute doctor. What more could anyone ask for?"

"How about some information?"

She sighed. "I suppose you want to know about the trust. I wish my great-great-grandfather had just given the money away to charity. So many lives would have been saved."

Caitlyn nodded. "Elihu Bloodworth made a fortune in the

lumber business, basically cutting down, processing, and selling every tree he could get his hands on. Of course, sustainable growth and the biological necessity of having trees weren't known then. In those days it was just take, take, take."

"Not so different now, though I think things are changing," I said.

Melanie continued. "Elihu had three sons and two daughters. By all accounts he was a crotchety old coot and by the time his children were married, he decided he didn't care for them or any of the spouses. And he seems to have felt that since he himself had made his own fortune, his children should not have their fortunes handed to them."

Caitlyn said, "So he sat down with his lawyers and created a generation-skipping trust. Upon his death, his entire estate was to be liquidated and the assets placed into an interest-bearing account, to be managed by his loyal friend and attorney, Jonas MacNamara."

"As in MacNamara and MacNamara?" I said.

"Yes," Caitlyn said. "The law firm has been run by MacNamaras for more than a hundred years. Back to the trust, legally the money could not be tied up forever. There had to be an end date."

"Let me guess." I thought back to the newspaper clipping I'd seen in the scrapbook at the farmhouse. "February twenty-third of next year—twenty-one years after Monty died."

"Twenty-one years after Elihu's last grandchild died," Melanie corrected.

"I know Gladys and Monty never had children of their own. So the MacNamaras identified you and Doreen as the only heirs?"

"That's right. Our grandmother was the daughter of one of Elihu's daughters. Monty was descended from Elihu's other daughter."

"And now, with Doreen's death, everything comes down to you, Melanie. How much money are we talking about?" I sat forward on the edge of my seat.

She paused. "It might be as much as a few hundred . . . million."

Wow. No wonder Melanie was selling her Bel Air home. She was probably planning to buy something bigger. Like property on the moon.

"When the time comes," Melanie continued, "you and Callista and I will sit down and figure out what to do with the money. For sure we'll plant some trees, to make up for the forests Elihu destroyed."

I rose. It was time for me to head back to the restaurant.

"You don't have to include us, you know. The money's yours, fair and square."

She looked at me. "It's ours. Fair and square."

Back at the Bonaparte House, Dolly had already arrived. "I heard what happened," she said sympathetically. "I can handle the kitchen tonight if you want."

I was grateful, but the busier I stayed, the less likely I was to hear, over and over in a loop in my head, the thud of Channing's body as he hit the deck of the ship.

I tied on an apron and washed up.

Channing. Why had he killed Doreen and Spencer? He'd admitted that he wasn't an heir, so he had no personal stake. I assembled the ingredients for the salads, methodically lining up the components. *There's only one true heir to the*

Bloodworth fortune, and it wasn't Doreen and it's not your mother.

But the attorneys said otherwise. And since they'd been involved since the inception of the trust, they must have been keeping track of every birth and every death in the family.

Tell her I'm sorry. Channing's last words bounced around my mind. Sorry about what? Murdering two innocent people, one a cousin I never knew I had, and one a newspaper reporter who had, perhaps, gotten too close to the truth? But what was that truth? Or was he sorry for something else?

Lettuce, shredded carrots, and chopped celery went into the big stainless steel bowl. The wetter ingredients, tomatoes and cucumbers, went into separate bowls to be added later.

"Dolly, you've lived in the Bay your whole life, right?"

She looked up from the lemons she'd been slicing to go into the water glasses.

"Yup, born and raised ten miles away, never lived anywhere else. Never wanted to."

I knew what she meant. The North Country had its issues, for example, lack of good-paying jobs for young people just starting out. Oh, and the fact that there was sometimes snow on the ground and frigid temperatures from November to May. But I loved it here too.

"Did you know Doreen? Did she ever mention any relatives?"

Dolly smiled, her pearly dentures on full display. "I didn't know her too well, would see her over at the Legion playing Bingo once in a while. Just recently she mentioned being related to a television actress. Of course, nobody believed her. But it turned out to be true, didn't it? Who'da thunk that you'd all turn out to be related?"

Yeah. Who'da thunk it? "Did she ever mention anyone else?"

Dolly pursed up her fuchsia lips. "Her parents, that would be Lorne and Bea Webber, her mom was a Smythe, you know. They died years and years ago. Her father had a heart attack and I think she got pneumonia and didn't think she was sick enough to go to the hospital. Dead in a couple of days. Then there was Helene and Joe." My grandparents. The bitter ones. "I don't remember what they died of, but it was within a year or two of each other. Can't think of anyone else."

As I continued to work, my mind wandered. Melanie had said the Bloodworth Trust was worth millions. Possibly hundreds of millions. I thought about my grandparents. No wonder they were bitter. They must have resented having to eke out a living on a farm when the only way anyone was going to see any money was when they were dead. And maybe they resented Melanie, the daughter who would inherit twenty-one years after Elihu Bloodworth's last grandchild died. Her getting pregnant with me had been just the excuse they needed to send her on her way—maybe every look at her was a reminder of what they didn't have, and could never have, all because of the whims of one spiteful lumber baron a hundred years ago.

"Georgie?"

My head snapped up. "Huh?"

"That's more salad than we need," Dolly said, waving her chef's knife at the enormous pile of lettuce I'd chopped as I'd been musing.

"Oh. I wasn't paying attention. Well, let's put the extra in the walk-in and whatever we don't use you can take home. I'm going to go check my e-mail." I untied my apron and peeled off the gloves.

"Go on," she said. "I've got it from here."

And she did. Dolly could easily run the kitchen if I or Sophie weren't here.

A whiff of stale air hit me as I entered my office. It had been closed up for a few hours and it had been a warm day. I crossed the wide pine floors and opened the window overlooking the employee parking lot and frowned. My car wasn't there, of course. I'd completely forgotten that it was still out at Doreen's farm. I checked my watch. Not enough time to go out there this afternoon before we opened for dinner, unless I wanted to stick Dolly with the cooking and supervising the wait staff and running the credit cards. Impossible. *Oh well*, I thought. It's not like I'm going anywhere tonight. I'll have somebody drive me out there in the morning. And I knew just the woman for the job. Caitlyn.

Back at my desk, I booted up my laptop. It had been a couple of days since I'd heard from Cal. While I waited for the Internet to connect and the programs to load, I glanced around my desk. I'd been trying to keep my desk neater. Feng shui, or the Law of Attraction, whatever you wanted to call it, I figured it couldn't hurt. A piece of foil lay on top of the server schedule. I picked it up and rolled it into a ball. Chocolate wrapper, of course. I flicked it into the wastebasket. Two points, though it didn't feel like much of a victory.

The computer clicked and whirred. Whoa, Nellie. I sat up straighter. My eyes scanned the top of the desk. Where was it? I opened drawers until I remembered it was still in the pocket of my jeans. The card from the genealogical investigator. I stared at it for a moment. Would I be able to pull it off? Only one way to find out.

I punched the numbers on the card into my phone, holding my breath when it rang. On the fourth ring a man's voice came on the line.

"Sheldon Todd."

"Hello, Mr. Todd. My name is Georgie Nikolopatos. I'm Melanie Ashley's daughter."

There was a pause. "Yes, Georgie. What can I do for you?" The voice was low and a bit gurgly, as if he needed to clear his throat.

I was a terrible liar. "Uh, I don't know if you've heard, but Melanie has had . . . an accident. She's in the hospital here in the Bay. She mentioned that she had you working on a project for her. Could you give me a status update so I can report back to her?" Mentally I crossed my fingers, then did it for real just for good measure.

"Why didn't that assistant of hers call? She's the one I've been dealing with."

"She's taking care of other things for Melanie. They're very busy, you know." I hoped I sounded just a little bit frosty—enough that he'd know I meant business but not so much that he'd get annoyed with me.

Another pause. "Well, you can tell her that I've hit a dead end. There's no marriage license, no birth records, and no church records anywhere to be found. I'll keep working on the newspapers. Did Caitlyn find anything yet? We split up some of the research."

Pieces were starting to fall into place, but there were still so many missing. Why would Melanie be looking into genealogy? And whose genealogy was she looking into? There was only one answer. There was another heir out there, possibly more. The lawyers apparently didn't know about whoever it was, because they would have notified all the potential heirs.

"Caitlyn? No, I don't think she's found anything yet. Say, have you been paid? You know, with Melanie's illness I want to make sure you don't fall through the cracks."

"She gave me a big retainer a couple of months ago. I'm still using it. Believe me, I'll let somebody know if it runs out. It takes a lot of hours to go through the newspapers looking for documentation, you know."

"Newspapers?" I blurted. *Don't blow it now, Georgie.* "Uh, Melanie didn't tell me what research methods you were using to . . . complete the project." Ugh. Even though genealogical investigators were apparently not bound by the same vow of confidentiality as attorneys, he could shut me down at any moment.

"A hundred years ago newspapers had community correspondents. The local writers would send in their village's gossip—who was sick, who attended the church social, who opened a new business."

"Sounds nosy." Keep him talking.

"Eh, it's like those celebrity news shows today. People love to know about other people's business." A deep wet cough sounded on the other end of the line. "I've gotta go. I have a lot of papers to go through today. Tell that assistant I'll send her an e-mail regarding my progress." He hung up.

That hadn't gone especially well. I'd been able to confirm

that Sheldon Todd was working for Melanie, but not much else. I considered my options. No way did I have enough time to go to the library and hunt through years of microfiche. With so little to go on, I might not recognize the crucial piece of information anyway. Presumably it was about the Bloodworth family, but even that wasn't a sure thing. No, best leave this to the professional, who could work far more efficiently than I could.

I glanced at my watch. Still an hour before we officially opened tonight. Time enough to go check on Melanie. But I still had no car. I could take Sophie's White Whale, the enormous Lincoln, but the thing was so hard to park. And by the time I maneuvered the beast through the narrow streets of the Bay and found a place to park it where there was no chance of someone with a more sensible vehicle dinging the doors, it would be just as quick to walk. "Be back in a few," I said as I waved to Dolly and exited the kitchen door.

Bonaparte Bay was bustling. Late-season tourists milled about, stopping to window-shop. Midge had placed a rack of clearance items outside the T-Shirt Emporium, and I was happy to see customers taking sweatshirts inside to pay for them. Like a bear puts on fat to prepare for hibernation, the shops and restaurants of the Bay depended on this last infusion of cash to get them through the long, no-income winter. Things were looking good.

Spinky's was on my left. If I didn't stay to chat too long, I could check on Inky. And get a look inside the restaurant.

The front door was open, so I went in. "Hello?" The newly upholstered red vinyl booths had been installed, as had chrome-edged tables and a new black-and-white-tile floor done in a checkerboard pattern. Framed records and vintage album covers hung on the walls—Elvis. The Rolling Stones. Tom Jones. Zorba the Greek. The effect was kitschy but fun. I predicted they'd do well selling burgers, fries, and onion rings.

Inky came through the kitchen door, a broad smile splitting his face and making the snake tattoo on his neck twitch. Spiro came out behind him, looking spiffy in dark-wash jeans and an emerald green polo shirt that brought out the green in his eyes and complemented his olive skin beautifully. I always felt a bit . . . dowdy next to these two.

"Georgie sandwich!" Inky wrapped his muscular arms around me, then Spiro followed. By the time they released me, we were all laughing. It had been a long time since I'd laughed with Spiro. It felt good.

"I just came in to check on you, to make sure Inky has been cleared of all the charges."

Inky waved his long slender artist's fingers. "The lawyer's taking care of the final issues, but yes, I'm off the hook." He grinned again. "And while I was in the lockup overnight, I convinced some of the guys in the cells to make appointments for new tats when they get out. So it's all working out."

Spiro spoke up. "That bastard Channing was here working, you know. We hired him to do some of the carpentry— I mean, if you have to hire a handyman, you might as well get a good-looking one, right?"

I nodded. I'd been ready to hire him to winterize the farm too. And Liza had also been taken in by his tool belt and pretty face.

Inky continued. "So he had access to the kitchen, the plastic wrap he used to strangle poor Doreen, and the perfect opportunity to frame one of us for the murder. And he might have gotten away with it"—he gave me a gentle buss on the cheek—"if it weren't for you, you meddling kid."

I laughed again. "Glad everything is working out here. I'm headed over to the hospital to check on Melanie. Come for dinner in a couple of weeks, will you? Sophie's leaving for Greece and I want to give her a bon voyage party."

"That's nice of you, Georgie," Spiro said. "Mana will be pleased."

Wow. If I'd ever had any doubts that Inky was good for Spiro, they were erased now. The change in him was wonderful to see.

We gave each other quick hugs and I was out the door.

◆ TWENTY-FOUR ◆

The hospital had a slightly stuffy, antiseptic smell as I made my way to Melanie's room. The guard was gone, now that the danger was passed. Melanie was propped up on pillows with the head of the bed elevated. Her lips were pursed as she held a small mirror with one hand and applied a pale pink lipstick with another. Her blond tresses were artfully disheveled, and she wore a luxurious satin bed jacket. Caitlyn stood in one corner of the room, deep in conversation with a bearded man holding a clipboard and wearing a wireless headset. On a small folding table sat a huge video camera.

"Hey, Melanie. How are you feeling? What's going on?" But I had a feeling I knew.

Melanie smiled. "Georgie, meet Louis. He's the assistant director of *The Desperate and the Defiant*."

I nodded in Louis's direction.

"Nice to meet you," he said.

"Let me guess. The show is writing in a hospital storyline for you."

The satisfied expression on her face confirmed my guess. "Not just a hospital storyline—a gunshot. I've gotten myself mixed up with the mob trying to protect one of my daughters, and I was shot and left for dead. Until a very handsome doctor came along and rescued me, taking me to his mountain cabin and nursing me back to health until he could get me to a proper hospital. After an avalanche closed off all the roads, of course. But we'll film all that later."

She was clearly in her element. Spleenless and stitched up, she was still an actress. I had to admit that, even though it was one of the things that had kept her away from me for so many years, she still had her passion for her work. A thing I could understand, given my love for the Bonaparte House. Although it wouldn't have hurt her to pick up the phone once every decade or so. Passion and family were not mutually exclusive.

"Has the doctor been in today? When are you getting out?"

She shifted in bed, wincing only slightly. "Tomorrow, as long as I don't have to travel. And as long as we're done filming, of course. The show is making a nice donation to the Hospital Auxiliary Fund in exchange for letting us use this as a set."

I was glad to hear it. Our tiny hospital needed all the help it could get. "You could come home with me. I don't have any formal nurse's training but I can change the sheets and keep you comfortable and well fed." As soon as I said it, I knew it would never work. There was no bedroom on the first floor, and she'd never be able to handle the stairs. Still I was glad I made the offer.

Melanie stared. "You'd do that for me? After . . . everything?" Her voice was soft and pitched up in a question, as if she couldn't quite believe her ears.

I patted her hand, the one without the IV attached. "You're not completely forgiven." I smiled. "But of course you can stay with me if you want." The restaurant was closed this week. It wouldn't be hard to move tables and set up a bed in one of the dining rooms. Well, it would be a pain in the behind. But it was doable.

Her eyes misted over. "Thank you," she whispered. "But Caitlyn has already made arrangements for us to stay on at the Spa. And once the producer here sees the place, I feel pretty confident he'll want to film there. Win-win for everybody. I get to recover in luxury, the show gets some spectacular castle footage, and your friend Liza gets paid."

I felt a swell of relief pierced by a teeny-tiny pang of disappointment. As angry as I still was, it would have been nice to spend some time with her.

"Why don't you come and spend a few days at the Spa with me?"

"I'd like that, Melanie." And it was true.

Caitlyn, who'd been busy with the producer, approached us. She didn't seem to be any worse for having been tied up, gagged, and having a knife held to her throat. "Louis says we're almost ready. There's a local actor coming in this afternoon to play the staff doctor, and a couple of the nurses here are going to play themselves."

Melanie nodded, her self-satisfied smile returned to its rightful place on her lips. "Georgie, are you free tomorrow morning?"

I nodded.

"Then would you go out to the farm with Caitlyn? I've decided not to sell to Rainbow Acres just yet. But I've agreed to lease it to them for the yoga retreat and I'd like you and Caitlyn to work out the details with Hank before we take it to that law firm in town to draw up the agreement. You can have the rent," she offered, her voice tentative.

Tempting. It would be nice to fatten up my nest egg, getting me that much closer to my dream of buying out Sophie from the Bonaparte House when she was ready to sell. But it didn't seem right. I wanted to own that dream and earn the money myself, not just have it handed to me.

I shook my head. "I have a better idea. Why don't we donate the rent to various groups and charities in the Bay and the surrounding area? There are plenty of places where that money could do some real good, like the volunteer fire department and the school PTO."

Melanie drummed the fingers of her free hand on the bed rail. "Brilliant," she finally said. "Another win-win. I'm sure we can get some nice publicity out of it."

I turned to Caitlyn. "Pick me up at nine o'clock tomorrow morning, and I assume you'll call Hank to meet us there?"

"Yes," she said, punching something into her ever-present phone.

"You're not afraid to go back to the farm, are you?"

She looked up. "What? No. Not with Channing . . . gone." Her expression was unreadable. I wondered if she really had liked him and that's why she'd been following him around. Or was it just her mysterious "research"?

Which reminded me. "Melanie, I realize we can't discuss

this here." I cut my eyes to Louis, who was talking into his cell phone and paying no attention to us. "But I want you to give permission for Caitlyn to tell me tomorrow all about why you're really here and what she's been working on. You owe me that much."

Melanie looked thoughtful. "Yes, I suppose you're right. I didn't want to talk about this until we had it all settled. If it can be settled." Melanie turned to Caitlyn. "Tomorrow you can tell Georgie everything."

Caitlyn nodded. "Okay."

I looked at my watch. Five minutes till the Bonaparte House opened for the dinner service. There was just enough time to hustle back there. Not enough time to even try to guess what Caitlyn was going to tell me tomorrow.

Fortunately, the customers came in steadily all night, so there was no opportunity to dwell on the upcoming revelation. Sophie had returned just after we opened, dragging her enormous hard-sided suitcase through the kitchen. She called eighty-six at nine o'clock, earlier than usual, but the streets were empty. We had two more weekends to go, then we'd be done for the season. It was always bittersweet closing up on the last day. But this winter I was looking forward to having the Bonaparte House to myself. And to spending some time with Jack. And I had a project to keep me busy— sorting through Gladys's recipes. Somehow I thought I might not miss going to Greece after all.

I followed Sophie up the stairs. She had a pocket full of cash receipts tonight, and had won a thousand dollars at the casino, so she was in a good mood.

"How's the tramp?"

Snort. "You mean Melanie? She's getting out of the hospital tomorrow, then she's going to stay with Liza at the castle." Just wait till the episodes with Melanie and the mysterious doctor aired. Sophie would have the screaming meemies.

Sophie opened the door to her room and turned to face me. Her hazel eyes narrowed. "You okay about her here?"

I was pretty sure Sophie could find a way to get rid of Melanie if I'd asked. "It's all right. We're . . . getting to know each other again. I still don't quite trust her, honestly."

Sophie bobbed her head up and down, her lacquered burgundy helmet moving not a fraction of an inch. "That's good. You gonna be careful."

I wondered. Did Sophie feel threatened by my new relationship with Melanie? After all, she'd taken me in and treated me like a daughter. "Sophie," I said.

She looked up at me.

"I love you." And I wrapped her in a hug.

Her body stiffened, then relaxed and she returned the hug. "I love you too. Now go to bed."

A grin played at my lips. There was nobody like Sophie.

I threw on an oversized T-shirt and crawled under the covers. Normally I would have taken a quick shower before bed to eliminate the food smell from my hair, but tonight I didn't feel like bothering. The television remote was where it belonged, for once, on the night table, so I flipped through the channels until I settled on a ridiculous pseudo-documentary about UFOs.

As the interviewee replayed the details of her abduction, my mind wandered over the revelations of the last few days. Two murders. A trust worth millions—maybe hundreds of millions. A family that had died out, all but for my mother, me, and my daughter.

Or had it? Channing apparently thought there was another heir and was willing to kill—twice—in order to see that person get his or her share of the inheritance. Which meant he had some connection to this person. Maybe whoever it was had paid Channing to look for proof. As a handyman, he had worked for dozens, maybe hundreds, of people and businesses around the Bay. So he had access to a lot of homes and shops—which was how he'd managed to frame Inky.

My thoughts turned to Sheldon Todd, the genealogical investigator. He'd said he was looking for documentation. What if Channing had not been trying to find evidence for his enigmatic employer so that person could prove a claim? What if Channing had been paid to destroy it?

Then there was the arrowhead and the associated file that had been stolen from Jack's apartment. Channing had worked for Gladys, so he could have taken those objects anytime. Why wait until Jack, a trained Coast Guard officer, had taken possession of them before the theft? It would have been far simpler—and safer—to take the items from a little old lady.

And what the heck did that arrowhead have to do with any of this?

I certainly wished I'd brought a glass of wine upstairs. But it was warm under the covers and it was a long way down the spiral staircase, across the dining rooms, and into my office and my locked desk drawer.

I sat up in bed. The quilt fell off my shoulders, but I barely registered the change in temperature. Something other than my semisecret bottle of wine was in that drawer:

Doreen's Bingo box. And the key I'd removed from the false bottom.

And the Bingo card with the odd markings. It *was* a treasure map. I was almost sure of it now.

Suddenly I understood. It wasn't the interesting but not valuable arrowhead itself that was the final clue, which was why the pieces wouldn't fit. It was the location where the arrowhead had been *found*, dug up by Herman Montgomery and my grandfather fifty or so years ago.

And I was pretty sure I knew where that was. On that little mound covered with the rusted farm implements out back of the farmhouse. Jack had said there were mounds built by indigenous people several thousand years ago all over the North Country, so it seemed likely that that was where this particular artifact had come from. Tomorrow, I'd have another look at the pile of junk. And bring a shovel from the toolshed, just in case there wasn't one in the barn.

The television droned as I put all the pieces together one more time. And this time, they all fit. There were two remaining questions. What would Doreen's carefully hidden little key open? And what would I find inside?

It was somewhere around two in the morning when I finally fell asleep. I woke, bleary eyed, five hours later to find the television still on and an infomercial for an expensive exercise program playing. I shut it off, lest I get any ideas. Long walks and an occasional evening yoga class in the high school gym were more my speed during the winter months.

After a quick shower, I headed downstairs. Sophie was already up, sitting with Dolly at the kitchen counter and drinking coffee. A box of donuts from the local bakery sat on the counter. I filled the third cup with coffee and cream, then sat down and selected a glazed jelly.

"You're here early, Dolly," I said.

"Sophie wants to go to Olive Garden for lunch, so we're going to go pick up Marina and head for Watertown. We might see that new George Clooney movie while we're there." She wiped her fingers on a napkin. "What about you?"

It wouldn't hurt to have two more people know where I was supposed to be, even though Hank would be meeting us there. "Melanie's assistant and I will be out at the farm today." I took a bite of the donut. Delicious.

Sophie frowned. "You want Marina's gun?"

"What? No, no, I'll be fine. It's safe, and I won't be alone." Marina had given me her miniature antique gun once before. Not that I'd had the chance to use it, which was probably for the best.

The frown deepened. "You be careful."

I patted the sleeve of her cardigan. "I will."

An hour later they had left and I'd cleaned up the breakfast dishes. I retrieved Doreen's Bingo box and its contents from my desk, then went outside to wait for Caitlyn. It was a beautiful morning, the sky a clear, pale blue and the leaves on the oak tree at the edge of the parking lot a bright golden yellow. I thought about sitting at the picnic table, but the benches were still wet with dew so I stood.

Anticipation bubbled through me. If Caitlyn followed Melanie's instructions, today everything would be laid out on the table. And I'd get to test my theory about the Bingo card and the key.

Something brushed against my legs, then did it again in

the opposite direction. I jumped involuntarily and looked down. An orange-and-cream-colored cat sat at my feet, its long tail swinging sinuously.

"Well, hello there." I reached down slowly so as not to scare the creature away. When it didn't run, I gave the cat a scratch on the top of its head. "Where'd you come from?" But I thought I knew. This was the same cat that I'd seen near the Suds-a-Rama and Jack's apartment a few days ago.

"You're a wanderer, aren't you?" The animal meowed and twined itself around my legs. "Are you hungry, boy? Girl?" My experience with pets was extremely limited. I unlocked the kitchen door and retrieved a can of tuna.

I had to shove the cat aside gently with my foot when I stepped outside again. "Sorry, fella, but you can't come inside a restaurant kitchen. You'll have to dine al fresco."

The cat purred and began eating the tuna from the paper plate I'd put it on. The animal looked well fed, but I suppose it was a lot more efficient being fed by a human than having to catch a rodent dinner.

A familiar sleek black BMW pulled into the parking lot. I left the cat to its meal and approached the car. The passenger window rolled down. "Get in," Caitlyn said.

"Hi, Caitlyn. Nice to see you too."

She looked sheepish. "Sorry. Melanie's got me running ragged what with the show coming to film here and then all this extra work with Doreen's estate and leasing the farm to those old hippies."

"Did she give you some terms we can present to Hank before we take it to the lawyer?" I could only imagine what she'd want.

"Only a couple of things, really. She wants Hank to reno-vate the barn, at his own cost, and use the hayloft for the yoga studio. She's got an idea she wants to add a floor, seats, and a stage to the ground level."

"A stage?"

"She's talking about putting together some summer stock shows."

Hmmm. A professional theater in the North Country? It might just work. Boutique wineries were popping up all over Jefferson County. If somebody could organize bus tours from New York City or even Montreal or Toronto, that could be good news for all of us business owners.

Caitlyn drove out of the parking lot, and we made the main road out of town in record time. "So," I said.

She held up a hand, fingers splayed into a half star. "Georgie, I promise I'll explain everything when we get there, okay?"

Oh, fine. What was a few more minutes when I'd been dying of curiosity all night? So I leaned back on the seat and watched the countryside go by. Out here in the sticks the sugar maples were ablaze with scarlet leaves. In five months those trees would produce a fine-quality syrup with a little help from some wood-fired evaporators.

I wondered what my life would look like in a few months. My divorce would be final. Sophie would be in Greece for the winter. Cal would be there with her. Melanie would be back in California. Inky and Spiro? They hadn't shared their plans with me, but it seemed likely they'd be around if they were going to get Spinky's up and running for the spring. I'd have Liza, of course, and things seemed to be progressing with Jack. At least they were on my end. What he thought remained to be seen.

Almost before I knew it, we were pulling into the driveway of the farmhouse. "What time are we meeting Hank?"

Caitlyn shut off the ignition and whipped out her phone. "I told him to meet us here at ten. That'll give us time to go over everything."

I nodded. Finally I would get some answers. The front door swung open when the key was applied, and I stepped in cautiously. There was an umbrella in a stand by the coatrack and I grabbed it. It wouldn't be any good against a gun or a knife, but if I had the element of surprise, I might be able to buy us enough time to get away.

But somehow I didn't think we were in danger. If there was someone else out there pulling the strings, he didn't seem to want to get his own hands dirty.

Caitlyn sat down at the kitchen table. She opened the flap of her enormous messenger bag, but didn't take anything out of it, and set the bag on a chair. I parked myself opposite her and gave her an intent stare.

She took a deep breath and began. "You already know about the Bloodworth Trust. Elihu Bloodworth, your great-great-great-grandfather, was an extremely wealthy man. After he cut down most of the trees in Jefferson County and had made his fortune processing and selling them, he turned his attention to making the lives of his grown children and their spouses miserable. His wife had already gone to an early grave. Out of spite, he willed all his assets into a trust, giving his children a set amount of money with instructions to make their own way in the world, as he himself had done."

"Okay, I knew all this. But go on." I tapped my fingers impatiently on the Formica table.

"But the law does not allow a trust to exist permanently. There is something called the Rule Against Perpetuities. Elihu set up the trust to vest, or become the property of his heirs, twenty-one years after the death of his last grandchild born before the trust was established. Any grandchildren born after the trust was established—and we haven't been able to find any—would not be entitled to inherit, nor would their heirs."

Whew. That was a lot of legalese, but it corroborated what I'd figured out from the newspaper clipping I'd seen upstairs, the one with my grandmother's handwriting on it and the date of next February.

"So who are the heirs? We know about Doreen and Melanie. But before he died, Channing said, 'There's only one true heir to the Bloodworth Trust.' So who did he mean? Are Doreen and Melanie somehow disqualified?"

Caitlyn pushed her glasses up on her nose and looked at me. "We don't know."

"I don't understand. The lawyers must know who the grandchildren were, and it's only been a hundred years. The descendants should be easy to trace."

"Oh, they are. But they're not the problem."

I blew out a breath. "Okay, I'll bite. Who is the problem?"

Caitlyn turned toward the window, then back to me. "Again, we just don't know."

She was talking in circles, and it made me a little bit crazy. "Caitlyn, spit it out. We don't have all morning before our company arrives."

"There are still gray areas. And I'm just the messenger,

by the way. Elihu's granddaughter, your great-grandmother, was, by all accounts, pretty angry about being effectively cut out of the will. She started digging into Elihu's background, probably in an effort to come up with something she could blackmail him with. And what she found shocked her."

I leaned forward in the chair, wishing she'd get on with it. Hopefully, this story was about to get a lot more interesting because it had been pretty uninformative up to this point.

"It seems that Elihu came to Bonaparte Bay from downstate. He married your great-great-great-grandmother. But he neglected to tell her that he already had a wife."

❖ TWENTY-FIVE ❖

My jaw dropped. "You mean he was a bigamist?"

Caitlyn nodded. "Elihu apparently traveled quite a bit, on business. But in fact he was splitting his time between the wives."

"And only the first marriage was valid." I was beginning to understand. "The second marriage, to my however-many-great-grandmother, was illegal. Which means her four children were illegitimate, even if she didn't know it. So does that mean their descendants are not eligible to receive the proceeds of the trust?"

"The lawyers interpret the trust documents, at least as far as they've told Melanie, to include *all* his children. There doesn't appear to be any language restricting the inheritance to legitimate heirs."

I asked the obvious question. "Did Wife Number One have any children?" Because that would explain a lot.

Caitlyn frowned. "That's what I've been working on for months now, and what we hired the genealogical investigator for. So far, we've come up empty."

"Then how do we know there even was a Wife Number One? Surely there must be some kind of documentation—church records, birth certificates, mentions in the newspapers?" The same things Sheldon Todd had told me he was looking for.

"Rumors," Caitlyn said, echoing Melanie's words to me after she'd been shot. "Melanie's mother told her about it when Melanie was a kid. And Doreen knew about it too. The story goes that Elihu's granddaughter was so angry that she broke into her grandfather's office one day while he was away and stole the marriage certificate from a locked desk drawer."

"And did what with it?"

"Hid it. We think she didn't want to embarrass her mother by making it public, but planned to blackmail Elihu privately. Maybe she did."

She pulled a folder out of her oversized messenger bag, followed by a zip-top plastic bag filled with what appeared to be fluffy white cotton, and set both items on the kitchen table.

I glanced at the tab on the slightly yellowed manila folder. My heart stuttered. Monty's missing file. And the plastic bag must contain the arrowhead. I stared at Caitlyn.

"Why do you have this?" I demanded. "How did you get it?"

She was nonplussed. "When I couldn't get it that day at Gladys Montgomery's house, I, uh, broke into Jack's apartment and took it."

Wow. This girl had some skills. "How did you know you needed it?"

"After they got the letters from MacNamara and Mac-

Namara, Melanie got in touch with Doreen. Doreen scoured the house and grounds—and found the marriage certificate. She hid it again, and when we got here, we decided to leave it where it was for now since she assured us it was in a safe place. But before we could see it or figure out what to do, Doreen was dead."

"And you still don't know the hiding place." She nodded. My mind raced. I pulled Doreen's Bingo box out of my oversized shoulder bag, then opened the lid and looked at the Bingo card. N-G-O and the number 68. North, Go 68. "Come on, Caitlyn. Let's go see if we can find that piece of paper that's worth millions to somebody."

I headed out the back door and for the mound crowned with junk, not bothering to count my steps or estimate the yards. If I needed the shovel, I'd go back for it.

Caitlyn and I searched through the rusty ghosts of farm tools past, looking for anything that Doreen's tiny key might fit. If there had ever been a depression or any other sign that an arrowhead had been dug up here, it had long ago blended into the ground and been covered over with grass. There were no signs of recent digging either. We examined each of the farm implements, looking for places that a small box might be concealed. Skunked.

I brushed up against an old-fashioned milk can and looked down at the smear of oxidation that appeared on my jeans. Nuts. I stared down at the offending can, its top lying off to one side. The screw threads at the top were shiny, in contrast to the dull surface of the rest of the can, as though they'd been recently scraped. I turned the top over with my toe. Yup. Similar scrape marks. This can had been opened recently. "Caitlyn! Over here."

We bent over the can together.

Still empty.

My heart dropped like an amusement park ride. If this had been where the document or documents had been stored, someone had beaten us to it.

Caitlyn looked up at me.

"This doesn't mean anything, you know. Doreen could have found it and hidden it somewhere else." She looked doubtful.

"I suppose. But have you seen that house? It's full of clutter. What are we going to do? Lift every floorboard? Break up every plaster wall looking for something hidden inside? Not to mention the barn. Damn it!"

The truth was, why did we care? Even if there was another heir out there, it seemed there was plenty of money in that trust to go around. Hundreds of millions split two ways was still a boatload of bucks.

Except that the Mystery Man might not feel like sharing. And he might have paid Channing to murder Doreen and Spencer. Would I ever know what Spencer had wanted to tell me? It must have been about the Bloodworth Trust. Had he found one or more additional heirs? Or evidence that Channing had killed Doreen? Speculation was useless. If Spencer had notes or other documentation, the police would find it. He'd been a real pain in the behind at times, but he'd tried to warn me. For that I was grateful. And sorry that innocent people had lost their lives, all because of greed.

"Let's go back to the house." Defeat. "Hank will be here soon."

Buzz. Buzz. My cell phone vibrated in my pocket. I pulled it out and looked at the display. My spirits lifted. It was Jack.

"I'll take this outside and watch for Hank," I said to Caitlyn. She nodded.

"Hi," I said into the phone. "Did you have a nice time with your sister?" I plunked myself onto one of the old metal chairs on the front porch.

"Hi, yourself," he said. "And yes, it was great catching up with Trish. She sends her love."

"She doesn't even know me."

"She will soon." A warm fuzzy spread throughout my body. I filled him in on everything that had happed in Bonaparte Bay since he'd been away.

"Good God, Georgie. Are you all right? Melanie? Sophie? I knew I shouldn't have left."

"We're all fine. Please don't worry. When are you coming back?"

There was a silence on the other end of the line. "Georgie, something's come up and they need me at the Oswego Station. I'm not sure how long it will take. A few days anyway. I don't think I can get out of it."

The warm fuzzy grew wings and flapped away in a cloud of disappointment. "Oh, okay." Wow. That was pathetic. My eyes focused on the flowerbed near the front steps. The mums and asters still looked good, but there were some brown stems from some summer flowers that needed to be cut down. The gnome wearing the Giants football jersey stared back at me. *Get it together, Georgie,* he seemed to say. *Maybe it will work out with Jack. Maybe it won't. But you owe it to yourself to give it a try.*

"I'll call you as soon as I can." It was clear from his voice that he was conflicted. "I'll be back soon and then we can spend some time together. I've got Gladys's big house to take care of, remember?"

I smiled. Gladys's back parlor would be a nice place to spend a winter evening, curled up on the couch with a bowl of popcorn and a movie. And a hot Coast Guard officer, who I wasn't about to ask to make a choice between me and his career. "I'm safe. And I'll miss you. See you when you get back."

"I miss you already." He rang off.

My eyes roamed back over the yard and landed again on that silly gnome. Now it seemed to be mocking me from atop its pedestal. A number was painted in flaking white paint on his round belly. Number 68.

N-G-O 68.

Not Go North 68.

Rearrange the letters and you got G-N-O. Gnome.

I raced over to the garden. The gnome was ceramic, about a foot and a half high. One hand on his pointed hat and one hand on his butt, I tipped him up. As I suspected, he was hollow inside. I peered into the inner cavity and was rewarded with . . . nothing.

Damn! I could not catch a break. I went to set him back on his pedestal. A door with a small ring handle lay flush on the surface. My finger inserted itself into the ring, seemingly without any conscious effort from me. I pulled up, just as Caitlyn came out the front door. "What are you doing?" she called, walking over to me. I probably looked odd to her, bent over in a flower bed.

I restrained myself from peeking until she got there. Her face lit up. "Did you find it?"

"Let's find out." I plunged my hand into the opening, thinking too late that there could have been bugs—or worse, small furry rodents—inside. My fingers grasped a plastic bag and I pulled it out. Inside the sealed bag was another sealed container, dull orange 1970s-vintage Tupperware like we'd had when I was growing up.

"We should open it inside," Caitlyn said, ever efficient and practical. "Whatever's in there, we don't want to drop it or have it blow away."

Impatient as I was, of course she was right. I closed the door and replaced the gnome on his throne. We trooped inside and I set my find on the kitchen table.

"Ready?" My hands shook slightly as I unzipped the bag.

"As we'll ever be," she responded, leaning forward.

The lid of the Tupperware container proved difficult to remove. I wondered if some kind of glue had been used to stick it down. One broken fingernail and some inventive cursing later, the lid lay on the table.

I reached in and pulled out a small metal box, the inexpensive kind someone might use to keep cash in at a yard sale. The little key fit perfectly. I gave it a twist and we heard the metal-on-metal snick of the lock opening.

Inside lay a sheet of yellowed paper, folded into a neat square. Next to that lay another folded page, this one a lighter color.

"Which one shall we read first?"

Caitlyn blinked behind her big glasses. "It doesn't matter. Pick one."

Arbitrarily, I went for the one on the left.

Unfolded, the page was about half the size of a sheet of letterhead. The creases were deep and the paper had worn through in a few spots. It was covered in faded old-fashioned flowery handwriting. My voice trembled.

My Dear Helene.

That was my grandmother's name. And this was as close as I'd ever get to her.

If you are reading this, it means I am gone. Enclosed with this letter you will find a certificate of marriage. The contents will no doubt shock you. Please do not feel shamed or embarrassed. We cannot choose the family into which we are born.

Wasn't that the truth. I continued.

You may wonder why I never destroyed this document, which brought my mother such pain. It is because, after she retrieved it from her father's study, she asked me not to. When the time came, many years into the future, she believed that God would make the situation right. If the fortune exists at the time the trust is disbursed, our heirs should be the ones to decide whether to reveal—or conceal—the secret.

I looked up. "So Doreen had read this letter and seen the first marriage certificate?"

"She was the one who told us about it, said, 'an arrow marked the spot.' Not 'an arrow *pointed* to the spot.' So I put two and two together and figured out that it must have been located on the site of the archaeological dig, which was reported in some of the newspapers at the time. But since I didn't know the exact location of the dig, I needed Monty's file."

By all accounts, Doreen had had a prickly personality. She might have gotten a perverse pleasure out of making Melanie wait to find out about her potential long-lost cousin. Or cousins. Who was to say there weren't a whole passel of descendants out there from Elihu Bloodworth's first, legal marriage?

"It was only a couple of days before we arrived that she'd located it. She never did say where, but now I have to guess your grandmother hid it in the milk can on the site where the arrowhead was found."

"And then Doreen re-hid the document inside the gnome. But why would she leave the Bingo card, a makeshift map? Was she afraid she'd forget?"

Caitlyn frowned and her tiny nose wrinkled up. She looked me square in the eye. "Georgie, there's something else. Something Melanie wanted to tell you when we'd put all the pieces together."

Caitlyn and Melanie had been hiding plenty from me all along. Why couldn't I have a sweet, banana-bread-baking mother like Gladys? Gladys. Something Gladys had said in passing niggled at me.

Suddenly, the pieces shifted into a new pattern. Big Dom

diTomasso, the restaurant owner whose murder I'd solved, sort of, a few months ago, was a distant relative of Gladys's husband, Monty. What if Dom hadn't been killed for the reasons we all thought? What if Dom had been killed because he was an heir to the Bloodworth fortune?

Doreen must have known her life was in danger, which was why she hid the documents and left a clue for Melanie in the form of the Bingo card. In case something happened to her. Which it had.

I reached for the second piece of paper, unfolded it, and uncreased it gently with my hand.

Certificate of Marriage.

The groom's name, as expected, was Elihu Bloodworth. The bride?

Mary Elizabeth Grant.

Caitlyn's thumbs moved furiously over the surface of her phone. After a moment, she stared at the screen, then up at me. "I just plugged that name and birthdate into the biggest online genealogy site."

She didn't have to tell me. Mary Elizabeth Grant. My friend Liza, at the Valentine Island Spa, was also named Elizabeth. Elizabeth Grant. Unless this was the biggest coincidence on earth, my friend was also my distant cousin.

"According to the notes attached to the family files, Mary Elizabeth and Elihu had a son. He apparently changed his name legally to his mother's maiden name. We can only guess that he found out about the bigamous second marriage and wanted to distance himself from it."

I sat back in my chair, gobsmacked. But thrilled at the same time. I'd longed for family all these years, and a cousin had been right under my nose, being my friend, the whole time. Tears welled up in my eyes.

Caitlyn snapped pictures of both documents with her phone. "Of course, Liza's name isn't on these charts. And we'll have to have the attorneys verify the line of descent, but that should be easy now that we have a name to go on."

The attorneys. "Let's reschedule with Hank. We should get this stuff to the MacNamaras and let them get to work. And then we'll go see Liza."

❖ TWENTY-SIX ❖

We dropped off the papers at the lawyers' office, then took the water taxi to Valentine Island.

Liza looked from me to Caitlyn and back again, her eyes questioning, but she was too phlegmatic to come out and ask anything. I was bubbling with excitement.

We made ourselves comfortable in her private sitting room.

"Mineral water? Glass of wine? It may be well before noon, but we don't stand on ceremony here."

"Maybe later. This can't wait."

We explained what we'd found out and showed her the marriage certificate. If the news had hit me like a ton of bricks, Liza looked as though she'd been hit by the whole brickyard. And the kiln. I'd never seen her calm, competent demeanor ruffled. Ever. I was grinning ear to ear. Caitlyn? Well, there was no telling what she was thinking.

Liza rose. "I think I'll have that wine." She sent off a text and a few minutes later an employee came to the door bearing a bottle of Chardonnay in an ice bucket and a tray of cheese, crackers, and sliced green apples.

When we had drinks poured all around and had each taken a few restorative sips, Liza spoke.

"This explains so much." She nibbled on a cracker, thoughtful. "My father always said the family had changed their name a hundred years ago, but he never said why. He may or may not have known. Or maybe not enough time had gone by and he was still embarrassed by the bigamy."

"Or the fact that Elihu was such a jerk," I added helpfully. Artisan cheese on homemade crackers, and fresh local apples. Heavenly.

"A rich jerk," Caitlyn said.

We nodded in unison.

There was a question that needed to be answered, and I struggled with how to bring it up. Liza saved me by broaching the subject herself.

"Channing." She inclined her head toward one of the windows, but she didn't seem to be seeing anything. I wondered what thoughts were going through her head.

"He must have known about my relationship to this Elihu Bloodworth and he romanced me—or tried to anyway—to try to get his hands on my share. He asked me to marry him, you know."

"I take it you didn't accept?" I was the teeniest, tiniest bit hurt she hadn't told me.

"Of course not. He was beautiful, of course, and the sex was quite lovely. But that was all the relationship was based on. For me anyway."

"How could he have known when you didn't yourself?" I asked. "Channing wasn't stupid by any means, but he was no Rhodes scholar."

"I might be able to explain that," Caitlyn said. "When Melanie and I got here, I saw him coming out of your office, Liza, when you weren't there. It seemed odd, so I decided to follow him. When I found him at Gladys Montgomery's and he caught me, I suspected he might be trying to use his handyman business to gain access to people's homes for whatever reason. Theft or blackmail maybe. But I didn't have any real proof that I could take to the police, just a gut feeling. And when I found out he'd been at Spinky's, it was too late anyway."

Liza nodded. "I have the estate paperwork for my parents and grandparents locked in a filing cabinet in my office, not that I've looked at that stuff in years. There might very well be something in there proving the connection to Elihu. Channing was . . . good with his hands. I'm sure he was capable of opening a locked filing cabinet without damaging it."

"Remember Spinky's used to be the Sailor's Rest, Big Dom's restaurant. So Channing could have been looking for something there too. For what it's worth," I said, "at the end he seemed genuinely sad. As though he'd failed you."

Liza's lips twisted up into a half smile. "Or failed himself, once he figured out he was never going to get his hands on that fortune."

I raised my glass to her. "Welcome to the family, my friend."

She clinked her glass on mine. "I can't think of anyone else I'd rather be related to."

EPILOGUE

"Opa!" I threw back my shot of ouzo in unison with the other people gathered around the table in the Bonaparte House. I smiled, warm with the glow of the anise-flavored drink and the company of the people I loved. Jack was seated next to me and he took my hand. Gladys was on the other side of him.

Small plates lined the table, filled with fat Kalamata olives, slices of the last ripe tomatoes of the season, chunks of briny feta, and grape leaves stuffed with rice and lamb. The Greeks call these nibbles *mezedes*. I called them delicious.

Inky had hitched up his smartphone to a speaker, which was currently broadcasting bouzouki music. It was impossible not to feel happy listening to the notes wafting through the air. Later, after dinner, even though there were only two native Greeks in the room, the tables would be pushed back for dancing.

A gold bracelet—eighteen carat—shone on my wrist. I glanced over at Melanie. She wore an identical one. Unbeknownst to me, she'd commissioned Roger at the jewelry shop to make three. One for herself, one for me, and one for Cal, the granddaughter she hoped to get to know soon. I thought about having one made for Liza.

Dolly sat a few seats away from me, talking intently to Paloma, who'd been hired as the new cook at Spinky's. With training from Dolly, I knew she would do well. And she could keep her job at the school, with benefits. As Melanie would say, win-win.

Sophie presided at the head of the table, our guest of honor, with Marina next to her. Their bags were packed and loaded into the cavernous trunk of the White Whale. In the morning Spiro would drive them both to the airport in Syracuse for the first leg of their journey back to Greece for the winter. She'd taken it surprisingly well when I told her I was staying here for the winter. But when I delivered the news that I was seeing Jack, she set her lips in a hard line and gave me a gentle swat with the gossip magazine she'd been holding. "You dum-dum," she said, not unkindly. "You think I don't know? He's very good-looking. Does he have a father?" I'd answered that his parents were both still alive and married to each other. She took it in stride. "How about an uncle?"

My heart beat in time with the music and swelled as I heard the laughter of the people I loved best. Almost all of them anyway. I understood, in a way I never had before, that being part of a family doesn't necessarily mean being related by blood.

My phone buzzed in my pocket. I pulled it out and looked

at the screen, then got up and went to the hallway to take the call.

"Callista? Is that you? We're just having a farewell party for Yia-Yia."

"Mom, I miss you and Daddy. I'm coming home."

Gratitude and joy bubbled up inside me. "My love, you can't get here soon enough for me."

AUTHOR'S NOTE

The Thousand Islands consist of 1,864 islands located from the juncture of Lake Ontario and the St. Lawrence and stretching about fifty miles to the northeast. And yes, there is a very specific definition of what an island is! To make the count, a piece of land must be above water all year long, have a minimum area of one square foot, and support at least one tree.

For more than a century, people have vacationed in the islands and the small villages along both the Canadian and the American sides of the St. Lawrence.

But long before the area became a tourist destination, the Native Americans called this area the Garden of the Great Spirit. Artifacts such as arrowheads, spear points, and pottery shards are frequently found. Numerous mounds these ancient First Peoples constructed are still visible today—although their purpose remains a mystery.

RECIPES

❖

Gladys's Banana Bread

Makes 1 large loaf or 3 mini loaves

¼ lb. (1 stick) unsalted butter, at room temperature
1 c. sugar
2 eggs
1½ c. all purpose flour
1 t. salt
1 t. baking soda
1 individual-size container banana-flavored
Greek yogurt, approximately 5.3 oz.
1 c. very ripe banana, mashed (about 2)*
1 t. vanilla extract
½ c. chopped walnuts, optional

Preheat oven to 350 degrees. Butter a 9-by-5-by-3-inch loaf pan or three mini loaf pans.

Cream butter and sugar. Add eggs and combine well. Add dry ingredients and mix.

Add yogurt, banana, and vanilla. Mix well. Stir in nuts if desired.

Pour batter into pan(s). Bake approximately 1 hour for large loaf, or 35 minutes for smaller loaves, or until a toothpick comes out clean.

Cool completely before slicing. Banana bread is even better the next day (try it with softened cream cheese) and, if tightly wrapped, freezes extremely well.

Note: If you have very ripe to slightly overripe bananas but don't want to make your bread right now, place the whole unpeeled bananas into a zip-top freezer bag and freeze. When you're ready to use them, just let them thaw on the counter or in the refrigerator.

◈

Keftedes (Greek Meatballs)

Serves 4

2 slices bread
½ c. milk
1 lb. meatloaf mix
(any combination of ground beef, veal, lamb, or pork)
1 small onion, chopped fine

1 clove garlic, pressed or chopped fine,
more if you're a garlic fan
1 t. dried oregano
1 t. dried mint
splash of white wine or cider vinegar
1 egg, beaten
pinch of freshly grated nutmeg
olive oil for frying
about 1 c. of flour, mixed with salt and
freshly ground pepper and placed in a shallow dish

Soak bread in milk for several minutes, then gently squeeze out milk. Place remaining ingredients in large bowl, add bread, and mix gently until all items are combined. Roll mixture into meatballs, roll in flour (shake off excess) and fry in olive oil until browned on all sides and cooked through. Drain on paper towels. Serve with warm pita bread or Greek Lemon Rice and Tzatziki Sauce.

❖

Tzatziki Sauce

Serves 4

1 c. plain (unflavored) Greek yogurt
1 medium cucumber, peeled, seeded,
and grated, excess juice drained

2 T. finely grated onion, excess juice drained
squeeze of lemon juice
pinch of salt

Combine all ingredients in serving bowl. Keep refrigerated.

◈

Greek Lemon Rice

Serves 4

½ c. finely chopped onion
2 T. butter
1 c. long grain white rice
2 c. chicken broth
¼ c. lemon juice
freshly chopped parsley

Sauté onion in butter until softened. Add uncooked rice and sauté for 2 minutes. Add chicken broth and lemon juice, bring to a boil, then reduce heat. Cover and simmer for approximately 20 minutes, or until rice is cooked. Sprinkle with chopped parsley if desired.

For more recipes, visit the author's website at
www.susannahhardy.com.

M2G0610